A SAM CABLE MYSTERY

JUNE BUG

SCOTT BELL

June Bug
A Sam Cable Mystery™
Red Adept Publishing, LLC
104 Bugenfield Court
Garner, NC 27529
http://RedAdeptPublishing.com/

---

1.   http://StreetlightGraphics.com

Chapter 1

"I MAY BE OLD-FASHIONED, but I thought murder was against the law." Farley Granger as Guy Haines, Strangers on a Train, *1951*

SAM

Rusk County Sheriff Donnie Keith Monahan slid the murder book across his cluttered desk like an icebreaker clearing a path. "Taniqua Johnson. Last seen arguing with her baby daddy, Mr. Rashad Phillips, outside the Longview Cineplex."

Jowly and ponderous, Sheriff Monahan tipped the scale at Type II diabetes, verging on heart attack. He wore a starched white shirt held together with heroic buttons. His cream Stetson hung on a rack by the door, as clean and unsullied by sweat as a storybook princess. He wore two rings besides his wedding band, one of them a diamond pinkie ring.

I flipped through the pages as Monahan drawled out the story. While hunting copper in an illegal dump next to a rural highway, two scrappers had found the sixteen-year-old wedged between a rusty washing machine and a soggy mattress. Her killer had choked her and bashed her head in with a brick, which was found next to her body, before covering her with moldy gypsum board. Cause of death: blunt-force tragedy.

Small animals had fed on her soft tissue. The crime scene photographs included a close-up of ants marching in and out of her open mouth. The fetus she carried—a girl—had died with her.

"And Mr. Phillips is...?"

"Hell-if-I-know." He offered up a one-shoulder shrug. "It's why I called you, Ranger Cable. I'm down two detectives and gotta park empty cars on the flippin' highway to make people think the po-po are still around."

"Budget cuts?"

"Budget decapitations is more like. I got no time to go lookin' for *anothah brothah* killed his baby momma."

Monahan's office phone rang, and he picked it up. An old-fashioned swivel fan atop a metal filing cabinet stirred the leaden air. Propped against the cabinet was a stack of campaign signs still in the plastic wrapper. *A Vote for Donnie Monahan is a Vote for LAW & ORDER!* Applying everything I'd learned from my extensive law enforcement training, I deduced Monahan was up for reelection in the fall.

Taniqua's mother had given a statement. It suggested Mr. Phillips sometimes worked at All State Tire and Battery off US 259 in Kilgore, which was about fifteen miles northwest of where Taniqua had been dumped.

"Thankee kindly," Monahan said into the phone and hung up. He stood and collected his hat and keys from the desk. He hitched his chin at me. "I gotta run. Think you can help me out here?"

"You got a hot date?"

"A damn Kiwanis lunch."

"No rest for the politician, huh?"

"Not for a second."

"I assume Taniqua was not a constituent."

Monahan's eyes narrowed to snakelike slits. He came around the desk to stand over me and glare. I steeled myself to avoid shaking. "The hell is that supposed to mean?"

I unfolded from the chair, causing Monahan to look up... and up. I tucked the murder book under my arm, clamped my hat on my head, and matched looks with Monahan until he stepped back. His puffy eyes narrowed to a pair of beans in a bowlful of jelly.

"Have a nice lunch with the Kiwanis, Sheriff." I touched the brim of my hat and left.

I HEADED TO ALL STATE Tire and Battery, which was located just across the Rusk County border, southeast of Kilgore, Texas. As deep into the Piney Woods of East Texas as anyone would care to get, Kilgore was home to the Kilgore Rangerettes, the high-kicking drill team of Macy's Thanksgiving Day Parade fame. That Tuesday morning in late May, the gray sky threatened rain, and a fitful wind knocked my SUV around the highway. The pine trees lining the highway tossed their limbs, and debris swirled along the shoulder.

Gravel crunched when I pulled into the All State lot at a quarter till noon. I rolled to a stop and climbed out of the Expedition, jamming my battered hat atop my head. A gust threatened to knock it right back off, but I caught it before an embarrassing chase across the parking lot ensued.

Four guys—all young, all black—loafed in front of the open bay doors: two in metal lawn chairs, two on stacks of tires, all drinking soda from glass bottles. When they saw me coming, a skinny guy, wiry with muscle, set his Coke on the ground and stood. Fixing his eyes on my badge, he called out over his shoulder, "Yo, check it. My man here, he lost. He lookin' for Jesse James or somethin.'"

I nodded. "That's right. Any of you guys seen him around?"

A guy with a red bandana and blue coveralls pointed a waggling finger down the road. "They went thataway, Sheriff!"

"Not a sheriff. Texas Ranger, Sam Cable."

The wiry guy had peeled his coveralls down to the waist, leaving his upper body bare, and wore a flat-brimmed ball cap on sideways. He flashed a gold tooth. "You really a Texas Ranger? Like dat Walker, Texas Ranger? Be knowin' kung fu and shit?" He struck a Karate Kid pose, arms up, hands dangling, one leg raised.

"Nah, they teach us cowboy fu," I told him. "Much stronger than kung fu. What's your name?"

"Ezikyle."

"Ezekiel?"

"No, like Ezza-kyle."

"Y'all know where I can find Rashad Phillips?"

"This about Taniqua?"

"Yup."

"I try Chantina, was it me," Ezikyle told me then turned to his pals. "Y'all know Chantina?"

"Chantina Moore," said a kid atop a tire stack. "He stay wit' her sometime."

The others agreed. Chantina Moore, they said, worked at the Burger King on Fifth Street, near the college. Rashad would sometimes stay over at her place. Or if he wasn't there, maybe with his aunt. When I asked why they were all so happy to give up their buddy to the police, all four tire busters agreed that Rashad was not a likeable person.

"He a fuckmuppet" was how Ezikyle expressed it.

"That would explain it." I nodded to the mechanics, got back in the Expedition and headed for the Burger King.

CHANTINA MOORE WAS off work when I went to the Burger King on Fifth. The assistant manager gave me her address without the usual show-me-your-warrant bullshit. I found that so refreshingly kind that I bought an apple pie and a cup of coffee.

The address was for an apartment complex on Trent. Kilgore was a modestly prosperous town in East Texas. In addition, Jefferson Davis

College was a private school with a small but well-to-do enrollment. The area where Chantina Moore lived was near neither of these educational landmarks. It was in a run-down, sloppy neighborhood filled with thrift stores, taquerias, payday loan stores, and pawn shops.

I plugged the address into my GPS and rolled in that direction. When I pulled up to the apartment house on Trent, I found a two-story building, flat and featureless as a prison. Window unit air conditioners stuck out of the front of every apartment, except for one where the window was boarded over. The neighborhood reminded me of *National Geographic* pictures of Third World cities. Like Detroit.

"Well lookie here," I muttered aloud.

Some days it's better to be lucky than good. Rashad Phillips scuffed along the weedy concrete walkway, looking just like the booking photos from his last three incarcerations. Nasty, angry, and tall.

I threw the Expedition in park and stepped out. Rashad turned at the sound, a plastic bag from the Sack'N'Save swinging from his hand. Black, nineteen years old, arms like anacondas, Rashad dressed in what I called urban basketball. Loose jersey, looser shorts with the hem hanging below the knees and the waistline down to mid-ass. Oversized basketball shoes. Some kind of thing on his head—what we used to call a do-rag, but I wasn't sure it was called that anymore.

"Mr. Phillips," I said. "Got a second?"

He tried out several different expressions, from sullen to indifferent, before settling on bemused contempt. "What kind of poh-leece is you?"

"Sam Cable, Texas Ranger." The badge on my chest was plainly visible, but I held my creds up, showing my photo ID.

He made no attempt to look at it as I walked up. The humid and huffy wind rattled the plastic bag he carried.

"I want to talk to you about Taniqua Johnson."

And he bolted. Phillips went from standing still to full blazing sprint in less than a heartbeat. He never telegraphed a thing. Jetted away so fast he was at full acceleration before the grocery bag hit the ground. I made a lunge, but all I caught was his body odor.

"Damnation." In an instinctive response to a sudden move by a suspect, I touched the butt of my Kimber .45. My rational brain caught up in time to abort the pull. No way was I shooting a fleeing man in the back without better cause than he was a murder suspect. And considering the racial issues stirred up when I was involved with the April Fortney mess, killing an unarmed, fleeing black man would drop me in the lowest circle of hell without appeal, no matter the justification. Some people still thought I was responsible for Fortney's death, despite the confession of her campaign manager.

No, it was best to let Rashad go. I could find him later. Guys like Rashad never went far, having a limited circle of acquaintances and even more limited imagination.

By the time I reached my Expedition, Rashad Phillips was around the corner.

And gone.

Chapter 2

"I LOVE TO SEE A YOUNG girl go out and grab the world by the lapels. Life's a bitch. You've got to go out and kick ass." – Maya Angelou

RITA

FBI Agent Rita Goldman stepped through the exit at Dallas-Fort Worth International Airport's Terminal C, Gate 27, and wilted like steamed spinach. Soggy air settled over her with pressure-cooker intensity. A weak breeze stirred the collar points of her Michael Kors pleated blouse, but it barely touched the heat building under her double-button charcoal blazer. She wheeled her roller bag upwind of the smokers, found an open space... and waited. And wilted. And cursed the heat, Dallas, and everything to do with the state of Texas.

Special Agent Paul Fiegenbaum was, by her watch, twelve minutes late when he nosed the government-issue Ford along the line of cabs, pickup trucks, limos... and one pickup truck limo. She recognized the car by the government-issued plates and its complete lack of style. She waved to the government-issued agent behind the wheel, who pulled the car over and popped the trunk.

Rita tossed her bag in, banged the truck lid down, and had the passenger door open before the special agent had unbuckled his seat belt.

"Agent Goldman? I'm Fiegenbaum. Call me Paul."

She shook his hand. "Rita."

He waited until she was seated and buckled before moving off. "Waiting long?"

"No. Just a few minutes."

"Sorry about being late. I was at my grandson's soccer game."

"No problem." Rita fiddled with the vents until the cool rush of air blew across her cheek. "It's May, and it's already hot as hell in this frickin' place."

"From New York, aren't you?" Fiegenbaum would look more at home on the golf course—the senior PGA, maybe—than as a supervisory special agent. In his early sixties and close to retirement, he was still fit, although the skin around his cheeks and neck was just beginning to sag.

"How could you tell?"

Fiegenbaum chuckled. "You remind me of somebody... an actress." He snapped his fingers and pointed at her. "That gal, what was her name? Played the girlfriend in *My Cousin Vinny*. Marissa? Marilissa? Something like that."

"Yeah." Rita looked out the window at the passing concrete. "I know who you mean, but I can't think of her name, either." Goldman checked the polish on her nails.

"Anyway, with that accent, you could play her stunt double or something."

They rode in silence while Fiegenbaum navigated a bewildering array of signage and piloted onto the I-635 freeway entrance ramp. When the morning sunlight beamed into her eyes, Rita flinched and pulled down her visor.

"Thanks for coming," Fiegenbaum said. "It's not often we get somebody from the national CT Analysis Branch down in our patch."

Rita picked up no sullenness or sarcasm in the special agent's tone. She expected some resentment, but Fiegenbaum seemed sincere and genuinely grateful. "Well," she admitted, "when I saw your report on a Chechen terrorist cell in Texas, of all places, I says to myself, 'That's a first; I gotta know more about it,' so I saddled up my bronco and rode on down. It was either that or paint my toenails. Know what I'm sayin'? Besides, it sounds like a fascinating case."

Rita ignored the little voice in her head that admonished her with *"And the fact that a long, tall, handsome Texas Ranger lives here has not a thing to do with it." Focus on that and keep repeating it.*

Fiegenbaum drove like an old man. He locked the Ford into the left-center lane and stayed there, regardless of traffic flow and oblivious to gaps that would get him into faster-moving lanes.

She bit her lip and fanned her blouse to get some airflow around her ribcage. "Tell me about Vodka Dishrag."

"Huh? Oh. Vahka Deshiriyev." Fiegenbaum flicked a glance at her before he riveted his eyes back on the road, hands at the ten-and-two position on the wheel. "Born in Chechnya, immigrated to the US eight years ago. Made a pile of money in the cash advance business, then sold the business for an even bigger chunk of change. These days, Vahka is on a mission." The older agent paused to turn on his blinker and check his mirror and blind spot, then he moved one lane to the right.

"Vahka," he continued, "had a little sister in Chechnya named Laila. When Laila was fourteen, a group of Chechen separatists—radical Muslims—broke into Laila's home when her folks were gone. They took her back to their camp, and they, ah, repeatedly—ahh..."

"Yeah, I get it."

Traffic bogged down. Rita ground her teeth and studied the scenery. The senior agent looped around a long, curving ramp that carried them onto a northbound toll road. They passed the Dallas Galleria mall, and Rita felt a sudden urge to shop.

"Vahka tried everything to find her," Fiegenbaum said. "It took him eight months, but he finally succeeded. She was strung out, diseased. Near dead. In one of those places in Prague where men line up, pay the equivalent of a dollar, and use the girl on the bed. Like in that movie... What's it called? About the guy with the special skills?"

"I don't know. My friend Sam Cable could tell you. He's into movies and shit."

"Ever since then, Vahka has used his money and his contacts to get inside the Chechen mob and their buddies, the terrorists."

Fiegenbaum signaled, pulled off the toll road, and made a right turn onto a street whose name Rita didn't catch. An impressive neighborhood of monster-sized houses swallowed the agent's SUV.

"What's he got for us this time?" Rita asked.

"Hmm?"

"This Vahka. What's he want to give us?"

"Ah. He wouldn't say much over the phone, but apparently, he's getting some rumors of a WMD the Chechen mob has either... made or acquired, I'm not sure which. It's some real nasty stuff, he says."

"Nasty how? Like nuclear or dirty-bomb-type nasty?"

"He wouldn't say."

Fiegenbaum stopped the car in the driveway of a cathedral-sized house with an arched glass entry showcasing a glittering chandelier hanging in the foyer. Tall bushes flanked the porch, and a magnolia tree the size of a mushroom cloud dominated the front yard.

Fiegenbaum pulled the key from the ignition and tapped the metal point on the steering wheel before fixing Rita with washed-out, tired-looking green eyes. "I know it sounds melodramatic, but I'll say it anyway. He's a tough old bastard, Vahka is. He has to be utterly fearless to play the games he does with people who kill your whole family to make a point. What has me worried about this deal? Vahka sounded scared."

Vahka Deshiriyev didn't look like a Chechen ex-pat millionaire undercover informant. Standing about an inch taller than Rita's five-three, he looked more like the guy who ran the dry cleaners on Birchall Avenue, not far from the Bronx Park subway stop. Small-boned, he had mousy-brown hair going gray at the temples and almost delicate features. His body was thin, with the exception of a bowling-ball stomach. The man wore a sweater over a plaid shirt, and loose-fitting, green corduroy pants. He looked for all the world like Mr. Rogers. *Can you say Chechen terrorist? I knew you could.*

"Ms. Goldman." Deshiriyev shook her hand, holding it in both hands like a politician, except she found it sincere rather than creepy. Genuine caring and humility radiated from the man with the power of a space heater. "Welcome to my home. Please, come to sit." He swept an invitation with one hand and guided them into the room with the other.

Deshiriyev invited her to take a seat on a velvet sofa in the middle of a Romanesque living room. Ornate decor, including cherubic statuettes holding bowls, red-and-gold brocade curtains, and wall sconce lighting gave the room a *Masterpiece Theatre* feel.

Deshiriyev asked if they wanted tea or coffee. When both agents declined, he said, "Well, then, straight to business, yes? Agent Goldman—"

"Call me Rita."

"Rita, you are with FBI, yes?"

"Yes, that's correct. I'm with the Counterterrorism Division. I follow the money the bad guys use to fund their activity."

Fiegenbaum scooted to the edge of his seat and leaned forward. "So what's up, Vahka? What's got you spooked?"

"Always to business, this one." Deshiriyev looked at Rita but nodded at the older agent. "Yes, you are right, Paul. I am truly, ah, spooked, as you say. I like that word. Spooked."

"It's yours," Rita said. "On the house."

Deshiriyev aged in the space of time it took him to sink back into his chair. The man's thin shoulders slumped. He deflated with a sigh. "I cannot be involved in this any further, once I have told you this news. It is not much, but it is enough to get me killed. Without me, my sister..."

"Understood," Paul said.

The Chechen tightened his lips and sniffed a deep breath through his nose. "I have an acquaintance. A distant, distant relative. This is not uncommon in Chechnya, yes? It is how much business is done. Through... networks"—he looked at Rita and interlocked his fingers—"of relatives and friends and friends of friends."

Rita nodded.

"My distant, distant relative is in the organization—I should say the *criminal* organization—of a fellow countryman. Sergei Romanovitch Tarasov."

"Holy cow," Paul whispered. "*The* Sergei Tarasov?"

"Yes. *The* Sergei Tarasov, as you say."

"Wait," Rita said. "Who's Sergei Tarasov?"

"Mob boss," Paul told her, his voice flat and dry. "What the Russian guys would call an *avtorityet*, or authority, in command of a brigade. Only, the Chechen mafia isn't that well organized." He checked with Deshiriyev, who nodded. "Tarasov is old-school. Bitter hard. Mean as hell, and he likes getting his hands dirty. What's he doing, Vahka? It can't be good."

"Yes, Paul, you are correct. It is not good. Tarasov has... acquired a... How do you say? A weapon that makes people sick?"

"A bio-weapon?" Rita supplied.

"Yes, exactly that. A bio-weapon."

"Oh, shit." Fiegenbaum's face went slack.

Rita felt a chill climb out of her gut.

"A little of this substance"—Deshiriyev pinched his fingers together—"can make many people to die. Almost one hundred percent fatal."

"One *hundred* percent!" Rita blinked. Neither Ebola nor anthrax had a perfect mortality rate. She whistled under her breath.

"Tarasov is very excited. He is much sympathy to the radical Islamic people in my country. Much, much of his illegal profits go to these separatists killers of the innocent."

"Fact or fiction?" Rita asked. "How solid is the intel?"

"Very solid. My... distant relative is very worried. He is a crook, not a killer, this one."

"Do they plan to strike targets here in America?" Rita's knee bobbed like a runaway sewing machine. She forced her leg to stop moving. "Who has this material? How do we find it?"

"I do not know much more about it than what I have told you. Except..." Deshiriyev steepled his long, pale fingers in front of him, reminding Rita of an undertaker in a bad horror film. "Tarasov has instructed that his people test the germs. My source says these testings are being carried out by a low-level meth dealer, name of McVee. I do not know why this man has been given this task. Perhaps for to be cut-out? You know cut-out?"

Fiegenbaum nodded. "Someone easy to keep separate from the main organization. Expendable and unconnected."

"Where will they be conducting this testing?" Rita asked.

"I do not know but believe it to be not far from here. My relative say McVee lives near Longview. In East Texas. You know of Longview?"

"No, not a clue," Rita admitted. A smile twitched her lips. "But I know somebody who does."

Chapter 3

"I VOLUNTEER!" I GASP. "I volunteer as tribute!" – Jennifer Lawrence as Katniss Everdeen in Hunger Games

THE LID ON MY TAKEOUT cup ambushed me on the way to work. Escaping coffee splashed my hand and nailed my crotch with that "this is going to be a bad day" kind of accuracy. It was my second-best pair of Dockers, too.

"Ain't that a joy."

I wheeled my SUV into the parking lot of my home base, the Longview Police Department headquarters, and squeezed into a spot next to an unmarked Crown Vic. I popped the SUV's door and stepped down, rubbing my hand across the front of my pants. Like that was going to brush away the stain.

The building's glass doors flashed, and Detective Skip Meyers strolled from the building, carrying his pumpkin belly, a duffel bag, and a ring of keys. He sported a fresh-mowed flattop haircut. The Crown Vic next to me chirped when he clicked the key fob. "Hey, Cable. Your girlfriend's lookin' for you."

"My *what*?"

"Some she-fed." He held a hand up near his waist. "About so high, with a New York attitude in her Gucci bag. She invaded Conference B, and she's settin' up a war room in there. Like Patton in a skirt."

My stomach did a weird flip-flop. *Goldman? Here?*

Whiskey Tango Foxtrot?

What could Rita Goldman want in Longview, Texas? The feisty little Tasmanian devil struck me as someone who would take a bullet before willingly coming out to the Piney Woods. I hadn't seen or spoken with her since she pulled my butt out of the Gila National Forest almost a year ago. *So why is she here now?*

I didn't have to wait long to find out. Three steps from my office, an obnoxious, drag-the-bleeding-stumps-of-your-fingernails-across-a-chalkboard voice megaphoned from thirty yards away. "Hey, Cable? You got a minute?"

I cringed like I'd bitten tinfoil.

Heels clicking, a well-dressed Rita Goldman arrowed straight for me. Trim legs flashed from the mid-length skirt of her business suit. Built like a whippet, lean and muscular with thick black hair—more Brillo pad than Breck girl—she reminded me of the women cast in action movies these days. Muscular. Taut. Ready to kick the ass of any guy three times her size. She probably used 9mm silver bullets and had a katana strapped to her back, ready for werewolves, zombies, or rednecks, whichever needed killing the most.

"Hey, Goldman. What's up?"

She stabbed a hand out from three feet away and followed it in, as if cutting the air. Her head barely came to my shoulder, but part of that was hair. She leaned back to look me in the eye. "Oh. My. Gawd. I forgot how big you were. They feed you by the cattle car, or what?"

"I use the bones of Englishmen in my bread."

"What? Oh, fee-fi-fo-fum. I get it. Hah! I forgot—you think you're funny, too. Look at your pants! Did you wet yourself, or are you just happy to see me?" After a glance at my trousers, she barged past me and invaded my office. "I smell coffee. Where can I get some?" She claimed my lone visitor chair, setting her leather portfolio down beside her.

"You'll have to take your chances on the breakroom. I'm keeping the rest of mine." I hung my hat on a hook by the door, sat at my desk and fired up my PC. The hard drive wheezed to life with an awful groan. We did a few minutes of meaningless *how've-you-been-fine-and-you-fine* small talk, then I wrapped it up by saying, "What brings you to town?"

I looked at Goldman, and she looked at me. One of those who-goes-first moments. Beyond the rare email and an oddly awkward phone call, I hadn't communicated with the dark-haired agent in almost a year. For some reason, Goldman seemed reluctant to speak. She twitched and fidgeted, which was normal for Goldman, but I had never known her to be shy.

"What brings you to town?"

As if relieved to have been prompted, Goldman sat back and propped her pumps up on the corner of my desk, apparently oblivious to her skirt riding above her knees and showing off a lot of leg. Nice legs, too. *What was that Spencer Tracy line? She didn't have much, but what she had was choice.*

I averted my eyes to avoid staring. Almost instantly. No more than two or three seconds.

And they say chivalry is dead.

"Pay attention, Ranger Cable." She dug into her leather satchel, retrieved a document and sailed it across the desk at me. "I just made you part of the task force."

"Huh?"

"Task. Foorrrce." She drew it out, as if speaking to a slow child. "I need your help on a Chechen terrorist deal. I'll explain it all to you later, in simple words, but in the meantime, consider yourself part of the task force to track down and neutralize a terrorist threat."

"Chechen what?"

"Che-chen ter-ror-ists." Goldman rapidly twisted her fingers in an imitation of American Sign Language. "I don't remember you being this slow. You sure you don't need more coffee?"

"I've had a bad week. Why don't you take it from the top and clue me in? Maybe I'll catch up by the time you get to why I'm involved."

"It's easy. Pay attention and follow the bouncing ball. We have a CI who told us the Chechen mob got their hands on a bio-weapon. The informant said they—the Chechens—were testing this stuff here in East Texas, using a meth dealer as the conduit. With me so far?"

"Chechens? In East Texas? You're pulling my leg, aren't you?"

"I pull it not, I so solemnly swear." Goldman held up a mock Boy Scout salute.

"We've got meth heads out the wazoo. Offhand, I don't recall any of them having Chechen baby mamas, but I'll play along." I rolled my hand for her to continue.

"That's about it," she admitted. "Except for two names. Sergei Tarasov is the top bad guy, and he's using a local meth head named McVee to test out the weapon. Lethality, effectiveness, whatever."

I examined the PC monitor and idly traced my mouse pointer from icon to icon, mulling over what she'd told me. "Tarasov is a terrorist?"

"No, I didn't explain that well. Tarasov runs the local southern-based wing of Chechen OC for a day job. On the side, he's licking the heinie of the terrorists, seeing as he's a big believer in the cause."

"Which cause?"

"The jihadi cause."

"Organized crime involved with radical Muslims?"

"We don't use the word 'Muslim' in today's FBI," Goldman admonished. "It's frowned upon. You may use the term 'jihadist' or 'extremist,' if you wish."

I grunted. "Anything on the weapon? Anthrax? Bubonic plague? Is it area denial or anti-personnel?"

"No idea. Not. A. Clue. Could be a big frickin' white powder hoax like anthrax-in-the-mail scams, and our informant is fulla shit." Goldman paused and quirked an eyebrow. "C'mon, Cable. I thought you'd get a kick outta this. Get to run with the big dogs, bust some terrorists maybe."

"And you thought of me why?"

Her cat-ate-the-cream-filled-canary grin stretched across her face. "You are the local liaison between the federal government and the banjo-playing redneck brothers, cousins, aunts, uncles, and sisters of yours that infest these God-forsaken woods. I figured you could, you know, speak their language."

"Tell me about this." I held up the document she'd handed me earlier; an Excel spreadsheet of names, addresses, and vital stats. I recognized about three out of the twenty people listed.

"The DEA coughed up a list of known and suspected meth cookers from around here," Goldman explained. "The closest thing we got to a McVee is a guy named McVey, William F. I thought"—in her New York accent, it sounded like "I taught"—"we'd go check him out, see what's what."

"Willie McVey, huh?" I found his name on the printout. "I know Willie. He wouldn't know a Chechen from a chigger."

"Uh, let's see..." Rita consulted her folder, spreading it across her lap and digging through her pile of documents. "Mr. McVey was busted for possession with intent to distribute. He could be one of Tarasov's dealers so far down the food chain, he doesn't know he's working for them. A perfect fall guy if things went to shit."

"Well, I'm pretty sure I know where we can find him," I said. "You want to go see him?"

"Yes, I do."

"It's way out in the country. Wildlife and bugs everywhere."

Goldman lifted her chin in a superhero pose. "I go where duty calls. Wait. Are there snakes?"

"Thousands. Copperheads, moccasins, corals and really, really big rattlers."

"Your job is to shoot any snakes that sneak up on my cute federal ass." She stuffed her papers back in the satchel, fumbling a bit, not looking up. "I hate snakes."

"Believe me, Agent Goldman," I said, climbing to my feet and reaching for my hat, "they will feel the same way about you."

HARDESTON

Professor Bernie Hardeston arrived at the lectern, slopped his stack of papers down, and flicked a glance at the seventy or so vapid, clueless nitwits filling the classroom. He fought back a reactive sneer induced by the vacant expressions of his Biology 101 students, all of whom were absorbed in their handheld electronics. He'd seen this group maybe twice all semester, and if his teaching assistant weren't down with a stomach bug, he wouldn't be seeing them now. Freshmen frayed his nerves faster than people talking on their cell phones while on the toilet, texting at a movie or a fundamentalist Christian trying to justify creationism.

Although he might make an exception of the sweet little ginger in the front row. Farm-raised and milk-fed, with blue eyes and freckles, the girl wore a loose T-shirt that showed some decent cleavage. *She could text me anytime.*

He drew a deep breath and boomed out in *basso profundo*, "All of you have been marked for death. Your killers have no mercy, no remorse, and they number in the billions."

That stirred the phone-praying twits. A ripple of shifting seats, coughs, and tapping keys flowed across the room. Talking about megadeath always seemed to grip their infantile minds in a way cellular mitosis never could. The redhead leaned over her tablet, typing notes, revealing another inch of creamy flesh. Yum. *Those are truly epic tits.*

"In 1918," Hardeston continued after forcing himself to look away, "influenza removed over twenty million people from the planet. Smallpox has slain more than all the wars of this century. HIV-AIDS has devastated a generation of Africans and millions of Americans.

COVID-19 devastated several hundred thousand lives and brought the world economy to its knees. A miniscule organism, too small to be seen with a common microscope, killed sixty thousand soldiers during World War II. Sixty thousand is a figure not even George W. Bush or Donald Trump could rival on their best day."

Hardeston circled behind his desk, using the pause to keep a straight face at the glares from the hicks in the room. Here in the Great State of Texas—he always heard the capital letters in his mind—Dubya was a hero. Making fun of him was like wiping one's ass with the Bible. Even Ms. Ginger was frowning. He winked at the scrumptious little freshman. She wore loose running shorts; the hems rode up when she crossed her legs. *Smooth as fresh powder on a ski slope.*

"If you want the raw numbers," Hardeston said, "epidemics have killed—at minimum estimates—half a billion people since the turn of the millennium. Viral infections are mutating little monsters that suck out your DNA and replace it with their own. They learn from their mistakes, too." Hardeston sniffed and surveyed the room over the top of his reading glasses. At least he had their feeble little iPad-zombie attention. "When two different viruses attack the same cell, the viruses hash it out. The battle results in an exchange of RNA, and a mutation occurs. A new and better virus emerges. These adaptations grow stronger, much harder to kill. They become much more competent at cleansing the gene pool. It would almost seem that Mother Nature wants to be rid of us two-legged, planet-destroying meat sacks. And some day, she might get her wish."

Hardeston propped his butt on the shelf of the whiteboard. A warning crackle of stressed plastic jolted him upright—a reminder that he could stand to lose a few pounds. "All it would take to return the world to the Stone Age would be a combination of, say, a strain of Ebola mating with a rotavirus, thus giving wings to the limited transmission vectors of Ebola and allowing aerial transmission. Imagine an airborne hemorrhagic fever transmitted through a sneeze or a cough. As we have seen with COVID, one person's unprotected snot could kill hundreds of thousands, and that was at a measly two percent mortality rate. Imagine what the world would look like if COVID had a twenty or thirty percent kill rate."

His students, the post-adolescent get of East Texas farmers and roughnecks, exchanged glances and nervous smiles. Fingers were tapping, and more than one student had a cell phone propped up, recording him for later viewing. *Damned cameras are everywhere these days.* Not only did they have Big Brother, they had a billion Little Brothers, too.

"And that's nothing to sneeze at." Hardeston allowed himself a half smile at the small chuckle that followed. He scratched his beard and waited for quiet. "But don't go buy a year's supply of toilet paper just yet. That kind of *natural* mutation is nearly impossible from two such widely unmatched strains. Think of dumping a red puzzle and a green puzzle on the floor and mixing them together, then having a red piece accidentally be an exact match with a green piece." He held up laced fingers to illustrate a tight pairing. "No, that kind of superbug could only be created in a lab... and only then after much stringent, careful, and diligent hard work on the part of a *talented* virologist." He quirked a smile and flicked on the overhead projector. "However, we'll leave that topic for your senior year. For today's session, let us consider the lowly cold virus. If I may draw your attention to page sixty in your textbooks..."

Chapter 4

"YOU WANT TO FIREBOMB the town of Cedar Creek, California, population 2,600, with something called a fuel air bomb, the most powerful non-nuclear weapon in our arsenal. The way it works: it explodes, sucks in all available oxygen to the core, vaporizes everything within a mile of ground zero, men, women, children, and one airborne virus. Destruction complete, case closed, crisis over." – J.T. Walsh as Chief of Staff, in Outbreak

SEEING GOLDMAN STRUGGLE into the front passenger seat of my Expedition was akin to watching a penguin try to pole vault. I kept a straight face through her swearing and waited for her to get settled. She blew a tuft of hair off her forehead and asked me what part of my anatomy I was compensating for by having such a big vehicle.

"You need a booster seat?" I asked.

"Let's get the Starship Hi-Ho Silver on the road, smartass."

We headed north through the middle of Longview and left the city behind within minutes. I set the cruise control, and the countryside blurred by in one long, straight, green-lined tunnel. For every neat, well-tended house along the road, we passed two broke-ass trailers with overgrown junkyards and two-point-six derelict cars.

"No zoning out here, huh?" Goldman said.

"It's the country. People do what they want."

"Tell me about McVey," Goldman said after a long spell of quiet.

"Not much worth telling." I steered around a red hound loping along the shoulder. "McVey's not so much white trash as he is that sloppy-nasty stuff that falls out when the bottom of the trash bag breaks. From what I recall, he lives with his girlfriend out between Gilmer and Graceton. Mostly off her paycheck and whatever disability he can claim. For the life of me, I can't figure why Carrie hooked up with him."

"Carrie?"

"Carrie Porter. Works at a Stop-N-Rob outside Gilmer. Place has been held up so much, Carrie told me they were putting in an express lane, fifteen items or armed robbery."

The turn from Farm-to-Market 726 onto a narrow blacktop lane called Montgomery Road appeared before I expected it. I tapped hard on the brakes and slewed the heavy SUV to the left, boiling through the gravel shoulder and stirring up a red dust cloud.

Goldman shot me a narrow-eyed glare. "You flip us over, I'll shoot you in the face." After a pause, she added, "How's the shoulder, by the way?"

I rolled my left arm. "Still a bit stiff. Collarbone healed up, but the muscle tear pulls a bit." I had taken a couple of hits while in the process of losing my prisoner in the Gila National Forest. The wounds didn't bother me as much as my memories of Jade Stone. A bruise on a man's ego would last much longer than a bullet wound.

Before leaving Longview, I had confirmed Carrie Porter's address. She lived way out in the boonies on a half-acre plot of land that had once been somebody's farm, back before the Depression. Sometime after that, the land had been sold, cut up, and parceled out. Blacktop roads with more pothole than asphalt connected these little chunks of heaven to the rest of the world. Or in some cases, it wasn't blacktop but packed caliche-rock roads, as was Carrie's place.

I had not been out this way in over ten years, so it was through more luck than skill that I found it on my first try. I eased across the bar ditch and wheeled the SUV into the crushed-rock drive of a single-wide trailer home, where I parked next to a paint-challenged Dodge Neon in the shade of a hackberry. On the other side of the sprawling tree, a Chevy 2500 dually collected a Jackson Pollock paint job of bird droppings and tree sap.

I hummed the window down with a touch of the control and switched off the engine. The smell of Johnsongrass and milkweed rolled in, along with a faint trace of skunk. In the distance, a chainsaw buzzed and revved. A thin breeze, not enough to ruffle Goldman's frizz, sighed through the open window.

The Porter-McVey homestead wasn't bad, as such things were judged in East Texas. It wouldn't make the cover of *Better Trailers & Yards*, but it wasn't tetanus central, either. Barbed-wire fences on each side and south, along with dense woods to the back, bordered the half-acre of land. A covered porch clung to the front of the trailer, screened by a lattice of wooden strips—once white, now leprous gray. A scattering of clay pots with dying plants littered the steps.

Would a self-respecting Chechen terrorist be caught martyred in a place like this? I couldn't see it.

Goldman lasted for nine seconds of silence. "Hello, Earth calling Ranger. What are you now, the Hick Whisperer?"

"You need to relax, Miss FBI. Smell the honeysuckle."

"Makes me sneeze." She grabbed the door and climbed out. "Let's get this over with."

Goldman and I mounted the rickety porch steps. A wet-dog-food smell permeated the porch, although there were no food bowls or other signs of a dog around. Taking up station to the side of the entry, I used the meaty side of my fist to pound the storm door through a gap in the screen. I kept my other hand on the butt of my Kimber. "Willie! Carrie! It's Sam Cable. I need to see you!"

No answer. No noise. Even the chainsaw stopped buzzing.

I pounded again. Same answer as last time. The doorknob was firm. Locked.

Goldman tried looking through the high-set diamond-pane windows in the door. She grumped when she couldn't see inside.

I snickered. "Want me to find you a phone book to stand on?"

"Maybe they're gone. Dickhead."

The chainsaw wound up again in the distance. *Bzzz-bzz-bzz-bzzz!* The light breeze died, and the day went from comfortable to stagnant in the time it would take to shuck a pecan. My shirt stuck to my back as the sun climbed toward noon. "I'm pretty sure that's McVey's truck and Carrie's Neon, so unless they walked or went off with someone else..."

I thumped down the steps to take a look around back. Along the way, I tried to peer in the front window. I leaned in for a look, stretched on tiptoes, but it was too high. All I could see was the window frame. Oxidized paint left white spots on my fingertips.

Goldman chuckled. "Want me to find you a phone book?" A shiny green bottle fly barnstormed her face and made her jump back. "What the fuck kind of gamma radiation lab mishap was that?"

"That was a baby. Wait until you meet its mom."

The morning sun had burned off the dew, and heat radiated from the skin of the trailer home. A trickle of sweat threatened my eyebrow, so I took off my hat and wiped my forehead with a sleeve. A jay flitted through the tree line, a flash of bright blue among the greenery, but nothing else moved. A second later, a whiff of decaying meat caught my attention; a stench immediately identifiable and equally nauseating.

Human or animal? Please let it be an animal.

I pulled the .45 and held it down by my leg. I rounded the corner to the back of the trailer house and froze. The back door hung open. Carrie Porter sprawled at the base of the rear steps, her chunky body in rucked-up shorts and a faded cotton T-shirt. The beginning of lividity, dark-purple bruising, traced the lower parts of her exposed body. She had been dead more than a few hours.

"Goldman, back here!"

The FBI agent rushed up and stumbled to a halt next to me. "Holy shit on crackers."

Procedure said to go check the body for signs of life, but I'd been doing this long enough to know I didn't need to. Carrie hadn't seen a sign of life in many hours. Flies had already laid their eggs in her nose, eyes, and... elsewhere. One crawled out of the hem of her shorts and buzzed away. Whitish crud caked Carrie's lips and chin, and her face had warped into a spasm of agony. Whatever had killed her had hurt... a lot. Her entire body lay rigid and twisted, as if every muscle had locked up. It did not look like a natural death, yet there were no obvious wounds.

"Bio-weapon?" I asked.

"It could be."

"I thought you were full of shit, talking about WMDs in East Texas."

"I hoped I was."

"Let's back out of here and call it in."

"What about McVey?"

"You want to go looking for him?" I asked. "Go ahead. I'll wait here."

Goldman and I imitated statues. Me like a Greek god, of course, and she more like a plastic figurine with frizzy hair. Neither of us were in a hurry to get any closer to Carrie's body. *What the hell killed her? Did it transmit through contact or via airborne particle? Sprayed or consumed?*

The backyard held a couple of plastic chaise lounges with faded flower-print cushions. On one chair's arm sat an ashtray containing lipstick-stained butts. A round barbeque grill stood off to the side, upon which lay two charred hockey pucks I suspected had once been hamburgers.

I dug out my cell phone and stared at the screen as if an answer would leap forth. *Is there an app for bio-weapon containment?* "Damn,

Goldman, I forgot who we're supposed to call first for potential biohazard. FEMA, Homeland… What?"

"Umm." She glanced at me, and a smile twitched her lips. "Let's start with the Sheriff's Department. Mobilize enough deputies to contain the site. You do that, and I'll call my boss. He'll get the hazmat people in the chem suits. The CDC and whatnot."

"Good plan." With everybody using scanners, some things were best left off the police radio. I hit the speed dial on my cell phone for the Upshur County Sherriff, Bob Pike, and listened to it ring. While I waited for Pike to come on, I kept an eye on the forest at the back of the property. The unfenced backyard—a weedy lot, really—terminated at a heavily wooded stand of mixed oak and hackberry choked with vines and creepers about a football toss away.

Carrie and Willie owned one of those above-ground pools, which was set up close to the trees bordering their backyard. An adult could submerge in the pool but wouldn't be able to swim a stroke. One of the sidewalls had collapsed, leaving a muddy patch that extended ten or twelve feet. Reddish-brown wasps wheeled and dipped over the mud puddles.

Pike's voicemail came on, so I left a quick message and keyed off. I walked around the yard in a big circle, watching where I put my feet. I passed the grill and checked it with the back of my hand. Cold.

Goldman's voice rattled in the background, talking on her phone. She said, "I shit you not" quite a bit. I wandered toward the back of the property, stepping carefully. The farther I got from Carrie's body, the better I felt.

My phone buzzed with a call from Sheriff Pike. I ran down the situation, saying, "I shit you not" quite a bit. "We need a cordon around McVey's property," I said. "Call it a mile in every direction. Nothing gets in or out. We need to find McVey, too."

"I reckon so," Pike admitted with a sigh.

"And, Sheriff, tell your guys to be ready to shoot if anybody tries getting out of the area. Chances are the bad guys are already gone, but if not, and they're infected or carrying a biological agent..."

"Got it."

I killed the call and bent down to get a closer look at the muddy patch of ground.

"Sheriff Pike's on the way," I called out to Goldman. "He's going to broadcast a BOLO."

She nodded, sliding one finger down her phone.

A depression in the mud caught my eye. It looked like... "Hey, Goldman. Tracks."

She craned her neck and stood on tiptoe. "Lookit you. Daniel-fucking-Boone."

Impressed in the red mud, between patches of weeds, a set of footprints led from the crime scene straight toward the forest. They pointed at a gap—more of a tunnel in the brush, really—that looked like a real nightmare to get into. I would not enjoy digging my way through those briars. I angled closer to the opening in the creepers, but I couldn't see more than a couple of feet into the vegetation. The hole in the woods swallowed all light and looked like a rough and nasty place to stick my nose into. *Probably full of ticks, too.*

"I can't see shit back here."

Goldman said something I didn't catch, so I asked her to repeat it.

"I'm not going in that fucking jungle," she stated, loudly and clearly. "C'mon, Tonto, you first."

"No, Lone Ranger, Tonto's wearing Manolo Blahniks. You think I'm going a-hiking in these?" She held up one foot to show me.

A rustle of brush, a blur of motion, and somebody blindsided me at cruise missile speed.

I smacked the ground—really hard. The wind huffed out of me with a *whoof.* It was the toughest hit I had taken since high school football. My gun went flying.

McVey was about five-eight, two hundred pounds, and a little on the pudgy side. I had six inches extra height and a Texas Ranger badge. Even though he wasn't a big guy, McVey had momentum and a shopping cart full of crazy.

My hat flew off, and my skull bounced in the dirt, setting off flashing lights. My teeth snapped together. I hunkered over, trying to protect my eyes as Willie came at me. He used fists, teeth, fingernails, and the kitchen sink. It took everything I had to just to keep him from ripping my face off.

Jesus, he's infected!

Willie slobbered like the poster child for insanity, with red-rimmed, bloodshot eyes and debris stuck in his curly hair. Dirt, grime, and blood smeared his face and hands. He gibbered, and foam as thick as shaving cream frothed from his mouth.

Thump!

Crazy Willie's head jerked, his eyes fluttered, and he went limp, his loose weight covering me like a filthy blanket. Goldman stood over him, eyes wide, pistol out.

"Did you kill him?" I asked.

"No, I just slugged him the head. You all right? Did he bite you?"

"I don't think so. But he sure as hell failed to social distance himself."

I pushed McVey's dead weight off and lay there for a second, trying to get the earth and sky to stop spinning. Willie smelled of sweat and urine, mud and weeds, and blood and dried snot—a Port-a-Potty stench that made my eyes water.

"Go wash off," Goldman urged. "He could be contagious."

Now there's a cheerful thought.

A garden hose lay by the pool. I traced it back to the spigot and ran—not walked—to turn it on. Water spewed, brackish and warm at first, then cold. I clamped a thumb over the nozzle to make it spray hard and turned the hose to hit me full in the face. Then I shucked off my shirt and sluiced my torso, checking for bites or scratches.

"Your neck!" Goldman pointed.

I touched two fingers to a stinging spot on the left side of my neck. They came away red and dripping.

"Ah shit, Cable. He scratched you?"

I looked at the blood dripping off my fingers for a long moment. "Well... fuckmuppets."

Chapter 5

"I DON'T KNOW WHAT MY spirit animal is, but I'm pretty sure it has rabies." - Anonymous

"OW!"

"Quit your whinin', ya big baby." Goldman swabbed my neck with alcohol pads from the SUV's first aid kit. She proved she was lactose intolerant to the milk of human kindness by pressing harder than before. Pure solar fire rippled down my neck.

"They aren't deep," she said. "Barely broke the skin. You feel okay?"

"You mean do I have an urge to foam at the mouth?" I grunted. "No. Not yet. Give me that and go see if McVey is still handcuffed to that mulberry tree."

"Tonto lives to obey, oh mighty Ranger." Goldman dropped the pink-stained swabs in my hand and huffed away.

"Please," I added to her stiff back. Waiting under the partial shade of my SUV's open tailgate, I dabbed my cuts and inspected the result. No fresh blood appeared. I retrieved one of two foil packets of antibiotic ointment from the first aid kit, pinched off the end, and smeared the tan goo across the side of my neck. After a half-second's consideration, the second packet followed the first.

Man Law of Medication: If one is good, two is twice as good.

I mopped sweat with a sleeve and fanned my face with my hat. Midday sun, bright and hard, baked the yard. Far to the south, at the edge of my hearing, a late-sleeping rooster crowed.

From the other direction, a car engine howled along Montgomery Road. I glanced up at the blip of a siren. Sheriff Bob Pike slammed his cruiser into the front yard, bringing along clouds of dust and an aura of dread. Three additional blue-on-gold squad cars turned in behind him. The flickering LED bars and pulsing headlights of four cop cars turned Carrie's lawn into a psychedelic riot of red and blue.

Pike extricated his prodigious belly and buffalo-sized butt and shambled to where I waited. "Shit, boy," he rumbled, "you look like a squashed scrotum."

I held him back with a raised palm. "Stay back over there. There's a smidgen of a chance I'm contagious."

"No, can't be." He grinned. "Stupid ain't catchin'."

A state trooper wheeled up behind the logjam of police vehicles and added his light show to the chaos. The law enforcement contingent in Carrie's weedy front lawn was growing exponentially, and it would only get worse.

I squinted and pinched my temples. A headache had crept in from behind my eyes and threatened jihad on my brain. "Don't bust my chops, Bob. I've had a very bad day."

"It'll get worse. I hear the feds are coming."

I sighed. "They're already here. Who do you think got me into this mess?"

TRUE TO PREDICTION, more feds arrived. Fewer government employees had stormed Utah Beach than were in Carrie Porter's front yard. They invaded the Porter homestead in battalion strength and were equipped with enough gear to establish a new civilization on a distant planet. Come to think of it, the guys in the bio-suits crawling through Carrie's singlewide trailer resembled astronauts exploring a strange alien domicile. By five in the afternoon, we had four Hazardous

Evidence Response Team agents from the FBI, a guy from the Office of Health Affairs BioWatch program, two lab geeks and a passel of doctors from the Center for Disease Control and Prevention, an uncountable number of blue-jacketed FBI special agents, a henhouse full of squawking FEMA people, and one mysterious spook-type super-secret agent in a gray suit who stood off by himself and talked into a satellite phone. It took all of Pike's deputies and two shifts' worth of state troopers to keep the law enforcement traffic moving along an overflowing Montgomery Road.

Goldman appeared from the crowd and plopped next to me on the back deck of my Expedition.

"Aren't you afraid I'll infect you?" I asked when she plopped down.

"Ah, hell, I'm already infected by you Texicans. I'm starting to say *y'all* and shit."

"Next thing, you'll be eating grits and barbeque."

"Ew." She made a face. "Not together, I hope."

We watched the circus, complete with clowns and juggling acts, spill across the half-acre of ankle-high Johnsongrass. Goldman swung her feet in short arcs and drummed her thighs with quick bursts of energy. Her dark eyes darted everywhere, and a thin smile curled her lips at the corners.

I bumped Goldman's shoulder. "You know what you call Jesus Christ acting like a federal agent?" After a beat, I added, "Role reversal."

"Har-har. Now who's this?"

This turned out to be a doctor from the CDC in a biohazard suit with the hood thrown back. Dark skinned with salty hair and steel-framed glasses, he carried a small plastic case in one hand. A patch on the left side of his chest identified him as Dr. Tancredi.

"You're the one who was scratched by the subject?" His eyes shifted from me to Goldman and back.

"That's correct," Goldman popped off. "I had to save his dumb country ass from a beating."

I flicked a look at her. "As if."

"Ah, well then." The doctor blinked, and his bottom lip pulled into a frown. "Officer...?"

"Texas Ranger Sam Cable."

"Ranger Cable." He tapped the plastic case. "We feel it would be prudent to give you a shot of Bayrab right away as a prophylaxis. We were told you'd washed the wound thoroughly and treated it with antibiotics, which is perhaps the best preventive measure, however—"

"Preventive of what?" I said.

"Excuse me?"

"What are we preventing?" I indicated the case. "What's Bayrab for?"

"Ah. No one told you."

I checked with Goldman, who shrugged and pulled a "beats me" look.

"We think," Tancredi said, "we believe, that is, though of course we won't be sure until the autopsy, but the evidence suggests the victims died of rabies."

"Rabies," I barked.

"Wait," Goldman interjected. "*Victims*? You said victims, like in plural form."

"Yes." Tancredi's eyes bounced back and forth between us, as if not sure who to answer first. He picked Goldman. "Both subjects have expired."

Expired. As if past their date code. "From rabies?"

"We think." Tancredi focused on me. "We won't know until—"

"The autopsy is done," Goldman supplied.

Tancredi's eyes shifted to her. "That's correct."

"The Bayrab is what?" I asked.

His eyes bounced back to me. "Human rabies immune globulin."

"Which you carry in your toolbox?"

He volleyed over to Goldman. "The CDC stocks treatments for as many known viral agents as possible. That includes a supply of HRIG."

I bumped Goldman's shoulder again. "In case there's a wild-dog epidemic."

"In case we need to treat a victim of a rabies outbreak, yes." Tancredi was beginning to look a little flustered. CDC doctors generally didn't care to be ping-ponged with questions.

"Jeez, cowboy"—the small woman bumped me back—"you got rabies. You're gonna hafta get those shots, y'know? The big, long frickin' needles right in the belly."

"That is no longer the treatment, Agent," the doctor huffed. "There is a further series of injections, but they are intramuscular."

Goldman cackled. "In Cable's case, that means his head."

"I—"

"Just jab me, doc," I said. "While you're at it, see if you can find an immunization against wiseass Yankee dwarves."

Tancredi swabbed a spot near my scratches with an alcohol pad and stabbed me in the neck with his hypo. "We will set up an operations base at the Longview Regional Medical Center for the duration of the crisis," he told me. "If we discover this is indeed rabies, you will need to come in for follow-up injections to continue the course of inoculations. Treatment of rabies is almost always one hundred percent effective when the patient is presymptomatic. The HRIG injection may make you feel tired and sore, but that should dissipate. If it does not and you develop flu-like symptoms, such as headache, fever, muscle aches and pains, you should report for treatment immediately."

"How contagious am I?"

"Not at all," Tancredi said then hastened to add, "*If* it is rabies. Rabies is transmitted via a bite or scratch from an infected animal or person. It is not airborne and cannot be passed through casual contact."

"And after people show symptoms?" Goldman asked. "Can they be treated?"

Tancredi—who had already proven he had the sense of humor of a mollusk—turned even more grave. "After the onset of symptoms, rabies is fatal in virtually all cases."

And on that cheery note, he went back to join his comedy troupe of CDC buddies, who were lugging the bagged remains of Carrie and McVey to their van's lab. He detoured around Bob Pike, who tromped our way, trailed by a scrawny deputy with jug ears.

I muttered an aside to Goldman, "No Barney Fife jokes, you hear?"

"Who? Me?" She tried for shocked. "I would never."

"This is Deputy Sewell," Pike announced. He stood where Tancredi had, thumbs hooked in his maximum-strength utility belt. "He saw some interesting shit out this way the other day. Tell 'em what you saw, Randy."

Randy Sewell gawked at my FBI partner like she was a unicorn. The sheriff's command filtered through his cerebral cortex, and he snapped to. "Oh. Right. Day before yesterday, I was coming out this way on a call from Gladys Hargrove. Lives down there a ways?" Sewell made it a question and pointed to the south. "She called in a noise complaint, said there was a bunch of motorcycles charging up and down the road. She said she was afraid they were Hell's Angels. Anyway, as I came along Montgomery, a bunch of bikers pulled out of McVey's place and blew past me. Right out of there." He indicated the driveway entrance, now torn to shreds from a dozen or so official vehicles running in and out of the property.

All of us examined the spot, as if a clue would leap out of the mud and jump in our laps.

"Could you tell who they were?" I asked.

He shook his head. "Never seen 'em before. Their colors all showed, like, an ace of spades? On the back?"

"Aces High," I said.

"Aces what?" Goldman asked.

"Motorcycle gang, mostly stay to themselves, out east of Longview. Tool around the back roads on their Harleys and scare the tourists."

"Tourists?" Goldman's eyebrows shot up. "Here?"

I nodded my chin at Deputy Sewell. "What were they doing?"

"Couldn't say. They weren't breaking the law, so I let 'em go."

"McVey's been a pissant meth dealer for years," Pike said. "Nickel-and-dime-bag stuff."

"You think the Aces were buying dope?"

"Wouldn't surprise me none." Pike snorted and spat to the side, downwind. "Them bikers chew meth like it's gummy bears."

Goldman and I shared a look.

"I wonder if dope is all they bought," she said.

"You want to go see some bikers?"

"Rabid bikers? Sure. Better than sittin' around here."

I hopped off the SUV's back deck and pulled on my hat. "Let's go then, before I start foaming at the mouth."

I navigated the SUV out of the yard without hitting a federal agent—tempting as that was—and pulled onto the blacktop, then threaded the Expedition through a double line of vehicles parked along the shoulders. A mile shy of FM 726, the logjam cleared, and I built up some speed. I flipped the air conditioner on max. Cold air chilled the sweat on my face and neck.

We were ten miles away before I thought to ask, "Was there a senior agent you were supposed to check in with back there?"

"Guy named Fiegenbaum's in charge." Goldman shrugged. "He knows how to find me."

"Fiegenbaum?"

"Yeah, a real speed demon behind the wheel. If you ride with him, be sure and take some No-Doz. At least you don't dawdle around."

I took US 259 south, toward Diana. A yellow school bus from the New Diana Independent School District lumbered by in the opposite direction, half full, with its windows up, down, or part-raised, as the students preferred. I had a quick impression of festive afterschool shouting and bouncing youngsters.

"Rabies," Goldman said. "Rabies doesn't make a lot of sense. You know what I'm saying?"

"A weapon of mass distemper?"

"What are they doing? Injecting a bunch of dogs?"

"We're jumping to a conclusion. Might not be rabies at all. Might just look like it." My scratches tingled. I stopped my hand from touching them at the last second.

Goldman made a noncommittal noise in her throat. "What looks like rabies, but isn't rabies?"

At Texas Highway 154, I gunned it through the yellow light and turned east. The setting sun, an hour above the horizon, lit the interior of the Expedition through the rear glass. I tilted the rearview mirror to keep the reflection from blinding me.

"How far is this place?" Goldman asked.

"We'll get there about dark."

"Rabid bikers in the dark. Lovely."

After a lengthy silence, I asked, "Ever see that movie *28 Days Later?*"

"Can't say that I have."

"There's this virus that infects people, turns 'em into attack zombies from hell. A person would get bitten, and in a few seconds, they'd turn into this... this wild creature that wanted to eat your face off."

"Sounds like family dinner at Ma's house," she deadpanned.

"All the time I was trying to keep McVey off of me, that's what I was thinking. He was like some attack zombie."

"You think—?"

"No, I don't believe the Chechens have a super-zombie virus. For one thing, no virus works that fast. And secondly, both Carrie and Willie died from it. They weren't running around trying to eat people's faces. Willie was just... unhinged."

I slowed behind a lumbering semi and spent fifteen frustrating minutes trying to pass it. Every time there was a passing zone, oncoming traffic blocked me. When there was no traffic, I was in a no-passing zone. I began to loathe the name of the trucking firm stenciled on the trailer door: Abel Yeager Trucking, McAllen, Texas. I finally toggled the lights and siren and zoomed past as the trucker eased to the shoulder.

"You Texans are too polite," Goldman said. "I'd've done that first."

"Damn truckers think they own the road."

I jogged south at Marshall, then back to the west on Interstate 20, then south again for a bit on Texas 43. Goldman surprised me by nodding off about the time I hit the interstate and not waking again until I slowed for the turn into the Aces High clubhouse. She came to with a yawn when I hit the blinker.

"Damn car rides in the country. Always make me sleepy."

The bikers lived in an old Victorian-style farmhouse set off from the road by a gravel drive. To the left, a modern steel barn with sliding doors faced the drive. A razor-thin slice of orange sunlight rimmed the western skyline, pitching the yard into darkness. Heavy forest surrounded the property, gloomy and spooky as all hell. A lone firefly signaled its way across the yard.

Nothing else moved. At. All.

"Well, ain't this peachy," Goldman said. "You got a plan, there, Sherlock?"

"Sure do." I shouldered open my door and stepped out. "Go knock on the front door and say howdy."

Chapter 6

"ALL GIRLS LIKE GUYS who are tough. Obviously, riding a motorcycle. I don't want to say that there's a bad-boy quality, but there's definitely a tough and macho thing about a guy who rides a motorcycle and that element of danger. That's really sexy." — *Marisa Miller*

HARLEYS, HARLEYS EVERYWHERE. Flatheads, Softails, Dynas, Big Bears, Fat Bobs, choppers, and other Harley offspring that had no given name. All of them littered the yard, the drive, *and* the porch. Not a Honda or a Suzuki anywhere in the bunch. Near the open metal doors of the barn, a '67 Cuda fastback squatted on bloated rear tires, its front end resting on jack stands. I parked the Expedition behind the only other four-wheeled vehicle in the yard, a late-model Bumblebee Camaro.

I circled back to my SUV's cargo compartment and rummaged around until I found a package of disposable gloves, a pair of N95 HEPA masks, and a small tube of Vicks VapoRub. I handed a mask and a set of gloves to Goldman and tucked the rest in my back pocket. Then I clicked on a Mini-Mag flashlight and held it down by my leg.

I touched the yellow Camaro's hood on the way by. "Warm."

"So somebody's here, huh?"

"With all these toys out in the yard?" I detoured around a chopper with tall handlebars and a tear-drop tank painted in an American flag motif. "I surely hope so."

Not a single light shone from inside the farmhouse, giving it the look and feel of a remake of *The Texas Chainsaw Massacre* or the kind of place where Freddy Krueger and Jason would keep a basement full of body parts. A railed porch wrapped the front of the house, anchored by bay window turrets on each end. Paint-chipped wooden steps split the middle and led to the front door.

I cocked an eyebrow at Goldman. "The place smell like an auto shop to you?"

"That and toe jam."

A motorcycle engine hung from a hoist to the left of the stairs. Enough spare auto parts and tools were scattered across the porch to outfit a NASCAR team. In what had once been a flower bed on either side of the steps, red-and-white Budweiser cans sprouted thicker than geraniums. In one window, a POW-MIA flag acted as a curtain.

I mounted the steps and approached the front door. The glass panes in the top half had been replaced with plywood. A few flecks of white paint clung to the bare wood of the lower section. A board underfoot squalled as I paused at the door and knocked on the plywood section. The door swung open without resistance. The smell of death rolled out and punched me in the face.

I drew my Kimber and said, low and quiet, "Mask up, then clear your piece, Goldman."

My Mini-Mag picked out a pair of boots, followed by the legs then the torso of a dead biker. His body lay in the central hallway, as if he had decided to take a nap on the soiled carpet runner. Grungy hair, bad teeth, mechanic's jeans, and a Nine Inch Nails T-shirt. No visible evidence of trauma marked the corpse. The man appeared to have been dead for hours, so there was no reason to suspect a killer might be hiding in a closet inside the spooky old mansion. Then again, I had no reason *not* to suspect it, either.

"Ready," Goldman said, her voice muffled.

The N95 masks were rated for particulate matter. Short of a fully self-contained breathing system, no mask would completely stop a virus, but it made me feel better. And it provided a way to control the smell. I holstered my piece, put on a mask, then smeared some Vicks on the outside, near my nose. I handed Goldman the tube and waited for her to do the same. The menthol tamped down the reek from inside the house, making the rotting-meat stench at least bearable. Pistol in hand, I called out, "Police! Anybody here?" *Alive, that is?*

"Or any zombies?" Goldman yelled, echoing my thoughts.

I slid past the door, stepping carefully around the corpse and into the hall. Rooms opened to either side through arched lintels. I swept the light into each. A pool table covered in boxes with Castrol and Quaker State logos took up most of the space in the room on the left-hand side. In the room to the right, a big-screen TV dominated the front wall. Across from it, a dark-brown leather sofa ran along the back.

Covered in a tan acrylic blanket, a dead man huddled on the sofa, staring at the blank TV. Gray-speckled gunk—saliva remains—had dried around his lips and down his chin, the same as Carrie and Willie. Except for that detail, he could have been the brother of the man in the hall. He had the same lank reddish-brown hair, ratty beard, bad teeth, and biker boots.

"Déjà-fuckin-vu," Goldman said.

The warm Camaro outside worried me. Somebody had arrived at the house in the past few minutes, so where were they? Hiding from the cops was not the behavior of the pure and the just.

"Hello! Police!" My muffled voice sounded as though I'd called into a cavern or a deep mine shaft, one recently opened after a collapse. As if there was no one left to hear but the dead. My breath tasted sour under the surgical mask—menthol and decay, with an underlying taint of halitosis. I glanced at Rita. "You bring any chewing gum?"

"I look like a 7-Eleven to you?"

Straight ahead, the hall continued another two dozen feet, ending in a plain door with an old-fashioned glass knob. To the right, a closed door waited at the midway point. On the left, stairs began at the end of the hall and angled up from the back to the front of the house.

My flashlight beam revealed a greasy light switch on the right-hand wall, just past the pool room. I flipped it. Nothing.

"Somebody forget to pay the electric bill?" Goldman's normally scratchy voice had gone quiet. Even the tough-as-surgical-steel federal agent seemed a little freaked out by the gloomy house and dead bikers.

"Maybe their generator ran out of fuel, and nobody's alive to refill it." I met her eyes and winked. "Or the zombie fairy paid a visit and blew all the fuses."

"Zombie fairy." Goldman's eyes crinkled in what I recognized as her default smirk. "Funny guy."

I eased forward, flashlight probing, gun down by my leg. "Police!" I yelled again. "Anybody home? Anyone need assistance?"

The floor creaked, and grit crunched under my feet. The Aces High were not the most fastidious housekeepers. The last vacuum cleaner to touch this hallway had been sold by a door-to-door salesman. Stains of unknown origin blotched the peeling print wallpaper. Trash littered the edges of the baseboards—french fries, crushed spark plug boxes, spent .22 shell casings, and the other debris of modern biker life.

"Oh my God," Goldman muttered to my back. "I feel like I need a full-body condom. People live like—"

The door at the end of the hall banged open. A dark figure loomed in the frame. I held the Mini-Mag like I wanted to stab someone. Its beam slid across a shoulder, a neck, then a face. Male, mid-thirties. He flinched when the light hit his eyes. A bright flash exploded from his hand, and my hat jerked backward and flew off. The concussion of the gunshot slapped me in the face. He triggered a second round, and sheetrock erupted overhead. White dust showered me.

I lined up the three dots of my Kimber's sight. One-handed, no time to brace. My gun kicked. Two shots. Center mass. Dead, solid, and true. A golfer would know a perfect stroke by the sound of the ball leaving the tee. A quarterback would know a perfect pass when it left his hands. I knew a perfect kill shot the instant I fired.

The gunman staggered back. Collapsed.

Goldman shoved against my side and stood next to me, gun raised.

Over the ringing in my ears came the sound of the squeaky porch board by the threshold. I pivoted. A second man filled the entrance. He was huge, blocking the opening from side to side and top to bottom. He had a gun.

I dropped the Mini-Mag and braced my shooting hand—

Light flared from his pistol, and Goldman yelled.

I lined up on the giant.

Goldman spun away, dropping to the floor.

The Kimber barked once, twice. Both shots were solid hits to the center of the big man's chest. A .45 slug would hit with over four hundred foot-pounds of force, the equivalent of a heavyweight boxer's punch delivered into a half-inch of surface area.

The gunman barely flinched.

His pistol traversed right, centering on me.

I fired again.

Solid hit. Again. Again. Again. Each round slapped the giant man and jolted him a half-step back. Six 185-grain, jacketed hollow-point slugs in .45 caliber hit the man square in the chest, but he refused to go down. His pistol, at least, had been knocked off target as he absorbed the energy from the bullet strikes.

My slide locked back.

Thumb release, mag drop, strip new magazine from holder, drive it home—

The gunman raised his weapon.

—toggle slide release.

I walked it forward, triggering a round with each step. Muzzle blast flared brightly, as if sparks flew from Vulcan's hammer. Concussion thudded the walls, echoed, and slammed my ears. Slide locked back. Mag drop. Strip. Insert. Toggle.

The doorway was clear.

The glow of my dropped flashlight revealed a pair of giant shoes, soles facing my direction. One foot jittered as if electrified. It rattled against the porch then stopped.

Goldman—

I retrieved my Mini-Mag and hustled to where the small woman sat on the floor. She pressed a hand under her right breast.

I dropped to a knee beside her. "Are you hit?"

"Fucker nearly shot my boob off," she growled. Popping the top button of her blouse, Goldman pulled it aside to reveal a lacy bra and, under the cup, a red two-inch-long welt where a bullet had burned across her flesh. Small dollops of blood oozed from the angry wound.

The vise gripping my chest relaxed, and I breathed in, heedless of the menthol, decay, and gunpowder reek. I grinned behind my mask. "Pretty small target then. Nobody's that good a shot."

Her eyes narrowed. "Watch it, buddy. Help me off this floor. I'm probably catching ptomaine just sitting here. And my clothes... *holy fuck!* Look at this blouse!"

"Let's make sure that's all of them," I said. When I lifted Goldman to her feet, she steadied herself with a hand on my forearm. Indicating the SIG dangling from her other hand, I asked, "Did you get a shot off?"

"Hell no."

"Good," I said. "Less paperwork for you."

I retrieved my mortally wounded hat and clamped it back on my head. Goldman and I cleared the next room on the first floor—a dining room—and hit the final room, the one where the original shooter had appeared in the doorway. It turned out to be a kitchen, empty except for the dead gunman—a dark-complexioned, black-haired white male in his early thirties. Two red flowers the size of peonies bloomed on his muscle shirt, a half-inch apart, left of the sternum. Heart shot. The guy hadn't bled much.

Goldman whistled. "Good shooting, Tex."

"Thank you, loyal sidekick." I tossed the words out nonchalantly, past the sick feeling in my stomach. It was a righteous shoot, but two more dead men would now be added to a growing list of midnight visitors.

Reversing course, we tiptoed around the corpse in the hall and approached the open door. I poked my head outside and swept the narrow beam of my flashlight around the yard. Invisible ants crawled over my skin at the thought of more shooters hiding outside the range of my puny flashlight. Nobody shot at me, which I took as a good sign.

The second attacker was sprawled on the porch. His eyes failed to react when I shined my light in them, remaining glassy and fixed on a horizon only the dead could see. Blood soaked the giant from neck to crotch.

"If this guy blinks," I muttered, "I'm running for the truck."

"Oh my God," Goldman rasped. "How many times did you shoot him?"

"Enough." After a long beat, I added, "I hope."

"See if he's got any ID."

"Thank you, FBI. Never would have thought of that on my own."

She blew me a muffled raspberry from behind her mask.

A wallet in the dead man's trouser pocket yielded a Texas driver's license and credit cards belonging to Anton Mikhail Saidullayev, of Dallas, Texas. His ID listed him at six foot seven and two hundred sixty-five pounds. If he was an ounce under two hundred eighty, I would eat my hat, which now had a bullet hole in the crown. I handed the docs to Goldman.

"Saidullayev," she mused. "Could be Chechen or Russian. I'm betting Chechen."

I tucked his pistol—a Glock—in my waistband at the back. "Let's go see about the other guy."

Returning to the kitchen, Goldman read the second ID under the light from my Mini-Mag. "Muhammed Ibn al-Khattab. Lives at the same apartment complex as his buddy, Anton, on Hall Street in Dallas."

I slipped al-Khattab's weapon—another Glock, identical to the first—into my pants, next to Anton's. I had to loosen my belt a notch to accommodate all the hardware. The techs would have a conniption when they found out I'd moved the guns, but I really hated leaving weapons out when the scene wasn't secured.

"What do you think?" I asked. "Chechen or Russian?"

"Chechen. Has to be."

I panned the flashlight around the first floor. Nothing but dead bodies anywhere I looked. "We should get out of here, call this in."

"What about upstairs?"

I sighed. New dampness joined the stale sweat under my arms. The post-shooting jitters were capering around the edge of my control; it wouldn't take a lot for me to sit in the corner and shake for a while. I wanted out of this house, and soon. "I guess we should check, huh?"

"Could be somebody alive." Goldman's shoulders moved in a shrug, dimly visible in the reflected light of my small flashlight. The movement must have pained her ribs; she let out a hiss and dropped an atomic-sized f-bomb.

I held up my .45. "They better not be related to Anton. I only have seven shots left."

"I'll protect you, big guy." The small woman patted my shoulder. "C'mon."

At the base of the stairs, both of us froze. Goldman's eyes shone back at me. "Did you hear that?"

I nodded. Something was definitely alive up there, something big enough to make a very heavy thump when it hit the floor.

Chapter 7

"HAVE YOU EVER MET ANYBODY you didn't kill?"

"Well, I haven't killed you yet." - Danny Glover as Roger Murtagh and Mel Gibson as Martin Riggs, Lethal Weapon

I PUSHED PAST GOLDMAN and piled up the stairs like an uphill avalanche. At the second-floor landing, there was a closed door on the right. A hallway went left. At the end, another closed door waited. I chose Door Number One, pulled it open, and slipped inside, low and fast.

Stench hit me in face. A powerful smell of bloated death and human waste made my eyes water, despite the Vicks. In the narrow beam of my flash, I gathered a mental picture of a room big enough for a game of handball. A sitting area on one end featured grimy floor-to-ceiling windows. A lengthy bedroom took up the remaining space. Decorations *a la* Harley covered the walls. A king-sized bed was near the back. Piles of dirty laundry were heaped on the floor.

No. Not laundry.

Goldman crowded up next to me. "Are those…?"

"Dead bikers?" I said. "Yeah."

I counted seven heaped forms rolled in damp bedding—sleeping bags, mostly—with slack, waxy faces and eyes locked in death. Some lay in or near their own vomit, and the reek of loosened bowels told the story of people too sick to leave their beds.

One of the piles moved. I would have shot it if Goldman hadn't grabbed my arm.

"Someone's still alive." She holstered her piece and brushed past me. "Hold the light over here."

I followed the small dynamo of determined federal agent to a prone form near the bed. I shined my light on the victim while Goldman snapped on latex gloves and knelt. The Mini-Mag revealed a heavyset woman—biker chick, I guessed—in stained T-shirt and panties. Wide at the hips, with scraggly hair molded into a briar patch by sweat, the woman appeared to be in her late thirties. Her yellowy skin was scattered with pock marks. The former probably had something to do with the disease eating at her insides.

The woman shuddered when Goldman touched her cheek.

"Get me some water," Goldman told me.

The sick woman became agitated and let out a strangled gasp. Her eyes rolled in terror, and her throat worked as if she were trying to swallow a golf ball. "No... no wah—" A trembling hand spasmed in the air.

Goldman caught it and held it in her own. "No water? Okay, relax, sister. What happened to you? How'd you get sick?" Goldman asked. To me, she said, "We need an ambulance out here."

"On it." I was already punching 9-1-1 on my cell. I connected with dispatch and reeled off the details of what we needed—which was basically the entire circus from the previous crime scene.

The scratch on my neck itched.

Rita stripped the blanket from the soiled bed and wrapped it around the sick woman, who shivered uncontrollably. Goldman held her hand, speaking soothing words of encouragement while I played lamppost. The woman's shivers subsided, but her breathing remained tortured. Her chest heaved, and air whistled, as though through a straw.

Tired of doing nothing, I poked around the room. I wanted to sit down, but that would mean putting my butt in contact with a petri dish of live virus. I shifted my feet and remained standing. My mask and rubber gloves suddenly seemed very flimsy.

In the glow of my light, I recounted and confirmed six dead in this room alone. Including the two downstairs, that equaled eight motor-heads killed by an infectious agent—*probably* an infectious agent—and one very sick woman. No doubt more rooms waited on the far side of the house. Were there more dead or dying that we hadn't seen yet? Or had some of the infected bikers ridden off before becoming fully symp-tomatic, spreading the disease along the way?

And what were the Chechen shooters doing here?

I prowled around a room full of corpses, as useless as a park statue, while Goldman murmured and a dying woman wheezed.

QUARANTINE SUCKED.

As a genuine action figure of a Ranger, I hadn't been given the op-portunity to shelter in place during the whole COVID crisis, so my ex-perience with sitting around doing nothing was limited.

The CDC put us up in two FEMA trailers they'd off-loaded at the Aces High property. Identical white cracker boxes on wheels. Function-al, utilitarian, and as homey as a concrete bunker.

"Which one do you want?" I asked Goldman.

"Ooh, I want the French Provincial. You take the ranch style, as be-fits your heritage."

People in spacesuits delivered food—takeout pizza and frozen din-ners—while we twiddled our thumbs and waited to see if we would die. More spacesuit people took our temperatures, our blood, our waste, and our dignity.

The trailer came equipped with a small TV, internet, and a laptop computer. We could Vudu, Hulu, Netflix, and Amazon Prime ourselves into a media-induced coma, if we wished. In reality, we spent hours in teleconference after teleconference with investigators, doctors, and supervisors from every three-letter agency in the government directory. The sessions lasted well past midnight and would have gone on longer if Goldman hadn't lost her temper and told everyone to fuck right off because she was taking a shower and going to bed.

A team of media relations stooges from the FBI crafted a fake news report, which was relayed by local authorities. News outlets reported a disinformation piece about a rabies outbreak in rural East Texas: people should remain wary of stray animals, don't go around petting skunks and possums, and report any dogs acting strangely. The death toll was kept quiet. A dozen bikers and meth heads weren't sufficiently missed to create a public uproar.

I called Goldman on my cell the morning after our incarceration. "I'm bored."

"No shit, cowboy. I'm going nutso-crazy in here, bouncin' off the walls."

"How long they gonna keep us?"

"The fuck if I know?" Goldman rapped out. "Not long, I imagine."

"Super-quick incubation?"

She snorted. "Look at the timeline." Goldman paused, and I could picture her ticking off points on her fingers. "Barney Fife tells us he saw the bikers, uh... he said day before yesterday, so that would be—"

"Monday."

"Memorial Day, yeah. So they get... infected or whatever on Monday. By Wednesday night, eight of 'em are dead, right?"

"Nine. My boss said that woman—Cindy Thornton was her name—died early this morning."

There was silence from Goldman.

"I'm sorry," I added.

"It's okay. It's nothing." She cleared her throat. "Okay, so figure one or two days, tops, we'll know if we're infected."

"'Cause we'll be dead."

"Or howlin' at the moon, yeah."

I settled back on my industrial-grade sofa, pinching the phone with my shoulder. The trailer had the basics in one room—sofa, a recliner, small dining table with two upright chairs, and a mini-kitchen. A narrow hall led to a closet-sized bathroom and a bed so short, my feet hung off the end. In the shower, I felt like a raccoon stuck in a drainpipe.

"Did they give you the shot?" I asked. "The HRIG stuff?"

"Guy said the vaccine on hand was expired. They were gonna bring some in from somewhere."

"What the hell?" I snapped. "Tell them to get their collective federal head out of their ass! That's bullshit."

Goldman barked a short laugh. "My tax dollars at work."

"This stuff hits faster than a freight train. I've never heard of a virus that incubates in hours."

"Somebody made this. It's the only thing that makes sense."

"And they tested it on McVey and Carrie, and the Aces."

"Then two Chechen mofos come to see how well their stuff worked on the Aces..."

"We show up..."

"They panic and try to blow us away." She gargled a laugh. "Which is when you go all John Wayne and shit. Blam-blam-blam. My ears are still ringing."

"And you nearly got a boob shot off."

"Don't remind me!" Goldman laughed again. "It's not like I have any to spare."

Silence settled over us. I remembered her on the floor of the Aces High clubhouse, holding her blouse open, and the dainty, lacy bra underscored by a red welt.

"Well, then..." I started.

"Yeah. Well."

"Talk later?"

"Sure."

"Bye."

"Bye yourself."

I thumbed off the phone and tossed it to the side. Morning sun painted a parallelogram on the floor, above which dust motes spiraled and died. I watched them dance and listened to the silence.

HARDESTON

Hardeston enunciated powerfully to overcome the background noise inside the Running Duck—a carbon copy of the type of college bar he'd visited a thousand times. "The militaristic establishment sucks young Americans in with sentimental nonsense like Memorial Day in order to fuel their war machine." Hardeston pushed his glasses up with a forefinger and leaned against the table to make his point to the adorable young brunette sitting across from him. "They perpetuate this jingoism to appeal to young men full of testosterone so they"—he used air quotes—"*die for their country* rather than think for themselves."

The beginning of a tiny frown pushed up the young woman's bottom lip, a sure sign that she either had a thought cross her mind or she needed to pee. Pretty enough, though a little heavy in the hips and round-faced, the girl had the type of bosom biologists and other men of science referred to as "*humongous melons.*"

Under normal conditions, Hardeston could impress a girl like this with his academic credentials and his notoriety as an uncompromising, free-thinking, anti-establishment lightning rod. Freshmen and sophomore girls, even a few juniors and seniors, found his radical politics exciting, titillating, and more than a little sexy. The bar noise made it hard to be as persuasive and charming as he would have liked. It was hard to sound intellectual when one had to shout. Plus the girl's two working brain cells clearly struggled to keep up with his lecture.

His cell phone buzzed on the table, indicating he'd received a text message. When Hardeston reached for his phone, the brunette—*Stacy? Cathy?*—made an excuse and headed for the ladies' room. Hardeston watched her butt sway, thinking she had another two years, tops, before that fiddle bottom turned into a bass cello.

The message read: *Meet me outside. Back lot.*

"Fuck," Hardeston muttered under his breath. *What colossal bad timing. Nothing for it, though.* Some people, he could keep waiting. Others needed more... delicate handling. He finished his beer and left the table without bothering to call for the check. Stacy-Cathy would get it.

The night air cooled the sweat on Hardeston's forehead as he turned left and made his way to the rear of the building. A stiff wind blew in from the southwest, ruffling his Hawaiian shirt and cargo shorts. He touched the joint in his shirt pocket and thought about lighting up. He could have used a hit to calm his nerves.

Better not. This is Texas. Probably get the death penalty.

The bar's parking lot ran a narrow strip along the flank and opened into a wider space in the rear of the building. A high fence dotted with signs proclaiming it as a tow zone surrounded the lot. The single halogen light on the roof's back corner painted the cars in monochrome, like something out of an old noir movie. The breeze carried the faint reek of dumpsters and fried food. Traffic on Peach Street whisked by, and a siren warbled far in the distance. The sound never failed to give Hardeston a slight chill. More so these days. *If the cops only knew...*

He paused under the security light and squinted into the dark.

A figure leaned against the door of a Porsche Panamera at the far side of the lot, parked away from the light. The man whistled a poor imitation of a Broadway show tune. Hardeston recognized the person, the whistling, and the car. Heart thudding, he circled behind the vehicles parked between them and ambled up to meet his visitor. *Or is it summoner?*

"David." He didn't bother trying to shake the younger man's hand. David Rogers didn't like being touched.

"Dr. Hardeston, it is good to see you this evening." Rogers spoke English without a trace of accent, but his diction was often stilted and formal, as if he'd learned the language from books rather than growing up speaking it. "I am happy you could join me on such short notice."

As if I had a choice. "Glad to." Hardeston tried on a grin, but it felt wrong, so he dropped it. "How can I help you tonight, David?"

"The test was very successful. I—"

"About that," Hardeston interrupted. His eyes had adjusted to the darkness, and he could make out Roger's ultra-handsome face crease into a frown. One eyebrow shot up, disappearing into the strategic fall of jet-black hair. Pierce Brosnan playing James Bond couldn't have done it better. The professor rushed on before his courage evaporated. "We agreed on something from the start. You remember?"

"Yes, I think. But remind me."

"Only military and high-value government targets. Remember? Our fight isn't against the common people. It doesn't get much more common than bikers and rednecks."

Rogers shifted and folded his arms. "We share objectives, Professor. The... subjects were chosen based on opportunity, not their socio-economic status."

"I just—I don't..." Hardeston ran a hand through this hair and tugged on his ponytail.

Crickets gathered against the back wall of the Running Duck. A dozen of the black insects were scattered on the wall, and twice that number hopped or crawled across the sidewalk. A pile of cricket corpses had drifted against the curb. *An omen?*

"I didn't spend all that time in the lab to have the results used indiscriminately."

After a long pause, Rogers said, "There is no disagreement here. We are prepared to strike as we have discussed. It is time, Dr. Hardeston."

"Time?" The professor pretended not to understand, trying to overcome the feeling stirring in his gut.

"Time to enter the mass-production phase."

"Ah. Of course."

"The *fooling around* is done." Rogers peeled his lips back in a humorless grin. "The time is coming to strike the establishment, Professor. The moment you have long awaited is within your grasp. Are you ready to act, or are you going to remain a-a *talker* and not a *doer*? Are you prepared?"

The crickets' mating song intensified. The musky smell of so many of the bugs together momentarily overcame the dumpster stink. The professor wrinkled his nose and looked away.

This is how it begins. The fate of a bloated, overgrown military-industrial giant is decided in the parking lot behind a goofy little bar in Podunk, Texas. So long, Exxon. Goodbye, AT&T. Sayonara, Raytheon and Boeing and the planet-killing pigs in Washington.

Bernie Hardeston stood a little straighter, and his mouth tightened. "Yes, David. Let's do this."

Chapter 8

"DON'T WORRY ABOUT THE world coming to an end today. It's already tomorrow in Australia." – Charles Schultz, illustrator

THEY LET US OUT OF our cushy FEMA trailers Sunday morning. My boss, Captain Les Marshall, waited at the bottom of the trailer steps, hat cocked back and gray eyes appraising me with a gunslinger squint. Five foot eight in tall boots, Marshall had been a Ranger since Moses's river cruise in a reed basket. He was also as thin as telephone wire and twice as prickly.

"Boy," he greeted me, "are you dumb as a fucking stump?"

"Depends on the stump, I suppose."

He shook his head and spat a bullet of saliva from between his teeth. "You go off lollygagging around a house full of dead people, mighta been killed by the bubonical plague, and nearly get yourself shot by a couple of Chechen gangsters."

The morning sun was topping the trees to the east, casting long shadows from the farmhouse across the yard. Dew sparkled the grass, and the smell of pine trees mixed with the stink of portable generators.

"We know for sure they're Chechens?" I asked.

Goldman waved at me before ducking into a generic Bureau car with three other feds. The vehicle wheeled a bumpy circle in the churned-up yard and drove away. Other than a CDC van with a couple of medical techs and a deputy in a patrol car, Marshall and I were the only two people left on the property.

"They're Chechens, all right," Marshall said. "Got the rap sheets of a pair of muscle boys. Killin' 'em did us all a favor. Speakin' of which, DA's reviewed the case, decided not to present to the Grand Jury. You still gotta dance for the Inspector General."

"Aw hell."

"Don't get your Underoos in a wad. Since you ain't dead yet, I'm keepin' you on active duty. Pending review."

"Do we know what caused it?" I didn't need to specify which *it* I meant.

Marshall tapped out a Marlboro Red and lit up. Blue smoke rolled from his nostrils. "The sainted feds will enlighten us poor rubes tomorrow. We got a briefing in the morning with all the gubbermint asswipes in Texas. Gonna tell us how to mind our bidness." The captain tipped his head toward my SUV, which had been moved to a corner of the yard. "Get on home, change your damned clothes, then show up tomorrow at the Longview cop shop. Eight ayem sharp."

Marshall stalked away to his dusty Crown Vic before I could draw breath to say anything else.

I followed his example and climbed into my vehicle. The keys were still inside, and I fired it up. Letting the engine run, I stared at the scene through my windshield. The motorcycles had all been towed to impound and locked up. The Chechens' muscle car was gone, as well, towed yesterday to join the motorcycles. Yards of yellow tape wrapped the porch, fluttering in the breeze.

Goldman had told me her informant had mentioned Tarasov's people wanting to "test" a bio-weapon. It looked like the CI was right. The terrorists had somehow targeted and delivered a biological agent to Carrie and Willie then to a motorcycle gang.

Over the previous three days, I had watched from the trailer's window as hazmat-suited techs removed one blue plastic body bag after another—fifteen in total. All dead as a result of a *test*. How many more would die if they actually managed to deploy it? This thing would make COVID look like a mild summer flu.

"God help us." I slapped the shift selector into Drive and headed for home.

SUNDAY EVENING, I ANSWERED my doorbell and found Goldman holding a takeout pizza box and a six-pack of Shiner Bock. She wore jeans, loafers, and a lemon-yellow button-down shirt. Her hair hung loose and looked softer than normal.

"Hey, Cable. Want a beer?"

"Uh, sure. Twist my arm." I let her in, conscious of my Sunday-afternoon grubbiness. I had on a tank top and basketball shorts, and a full day's growth of whiskers. Luckily, I'd picked up my dirty socks and washed the dishes earlier that day.

"Set the pizza on the coffee table," I said. "I'll get some paper towels."

"Sure."

In the kitchen, I dug out a bottle opener, a bottle of Tabasco sauce, and a shaker of dried parmesan crumbs that had lived in the fridge since the last presidential election and required banging on the counter to loosen it up. I unscrewed the green lid and took a sniff. It seemed okay. If it was bad... Well, that was what the Tabasco was for. After tucking a roll of paper towels under my elbow, I carried everything back to the living room. Goldman had taken my one good chair, leaving me the prime spot on the sofa, in the corner under the lamp.

I set out the condiments and used the bottle opener for its intended purpose.

Goldman held the Tabasco. "What's this for?"

"It makes pizza better."

"You're such a liar."

We got down to the serious business of making the pizza and beer vanish. The pizza had Canadian bacon and mushroom on one half, sausage and onion on the other. Goldman had to act fast to get a slice with bacon.

When I slowed down, I said, "How's your... your..." I gestured vaguely at her chest. "Your wound?"

"Sore, but better. I think it's gonna leave a mark."

"Cool. You can show the other FBI analysts your scar. They'll be so jealous."

"You kiddin' me?" She snorted. "Ain't none of those dweebs seeing my tits."

I left that line alone by stuffing a slice of pizza in my mouth. I concentrated on chewing without looking at the assets in question. Thinking about Goldman's boobs disturbed my equilibrium. The woman was so far from my ideal dating partner, she might as well have been male. She had a mind powered by Intel, packaged in a small, lean body. She carried a cinderblock chip on her shoulder for the world in general, and the ignorant in particular. Goldman could strip bark from a pine tree with her voice then chop it down with her razor-sharp tongue. Having felt that lash, I pitied the poor guy who would have to endure that Ginsu knife flaying on a regular basis.

I, on the other hand, tended to date blond women who were stacked and wore a nametag to work.

Neither of us made eye contact. The silence grew.

"Good pizza," I said.

"Yeah, it's not bad, for Texas." Goldman wiped her lips with a napkin then took a swig of beer. "Of course, the best slice is Joe's Pizza, down in the Village."

"I'm kind of partial to Papa John's."

Goldman rolled her eyes. "Heathen."

We talked about the Aces High, rehashing things we'd already covered. The conversation was going nowhere special, but it was soothing just the same. Then I told her about my attempt to bust Rashad and how he'd run fast enough to create a sonic boom. She gave me a rundown of her regular assignment in New York—following terrorists' money trails—half of which went over my head.

Goldman glanced at her watch and brushed her jeans, preparing to stand. "Well, it's getting late, and we have to get up early for the briefing."

"You okay to drive?" I indicated the empty Shiners on the table.

"Yeah, I'm good." She flicked a smile, on and off. "I paced myself." At the door, she said, "I had a really nice time."

I looked at my socked feet, my toes flexing into the carpet. "Yeah. Me, too."

"Maybe we—"

"Well, I—" I smiled. "Sorry, you first."

"Naw, that's okay. Nothing that can't wait."

"Oh, okay, then. You take care, y'hear."

"Yeah, you, too, cowboy."

I hesitated. She reached out, and we hugged like relatives meeting for the reading of our uncle's last will: awkward and self-conscious. I watched her butt move in her tight jeans all the way to the car. Firm, round, and tiny. *Yikes.*

"Sam," I said to myself. "Don't. Just don't, okay?"

MONDAY MORNING, I STOPPED by the evidence room to retrieve my Kimber, which had been processed by the ballistics people. Dub Miller, the property clerk, had been hired by Sam Houston and moved with the fragile care of a glass robot.

He acknowledged that "Yes siree, your pissel is roun' here somewheres," and shuffled off into the stacks and racks. I would have be-

lieved the old man had died back in there but for the occasional muttered curse and the sound of rattling snot as he cleared his sinuses.

"Here ya go." Dub came back into view, moving slightly faster than
evolution, with my .45 in a plastic bag. The magazine and remaining
ammo were in separate bags. "Heard ya kilt a buncha terrists with dis
here pissel."

"Two Chechens, Dub. I don't know if they were terrorists or not."
I signed all three evidence forms and escaped before Dub processed
the question on his face into words. I called back over my shoulder,
"Chechens are like Russians, Dub."

"Oh. Commies."

In my office, I ran a bore brush down the barrel of my "pissel" and
followed that with a few patches soaked in cleaning fluid. I lathered,
rinsed, and repeated until the patches started coming through clear. I
popped a fresh magazine in the .45's butt and racked the slide, then I
topped up the magazine and reinserted it. I clamped the Kimber in the
high-rise holster on my right hip, slipped on my corduroy jacket, and
ventured out to the briefing room.

Conference Room B-101 was filling up fast. Goldman had saved
me a seat, and she waved me over when I walked in. She wore a creamy
blouse with navy slacks; a matching blazer decorated the back of her
chair. The white camisole showing under her opaque blouse brought
back an image of a lacy brassiere filled with apple-sized breasts.

I shook off the memory and settled into the swivel chair. Somehow,
I was going to have to stop thinking about Goldman's boobs.

"Meetings," I muttered from the side of my mouth.

Goldman quirked a smile. "Stupidity is proportional to the number of attendees." She sniffed. "You smell like gun oil."

"Chanel de Hoppes Number Forty-five."

"Oooh, my favorite."

More people filed into the conference room. I nodded to some of
the locals around the table, such as Ferdinand Reyes, a detective from

the Gregg County Sheriff's Department, and Darren Winston, a detective from Upshur County. The bulldog Reyes contrasted sharply with Winston, a black guy cut from polished granite with a V-shaped torso and a gleaming skull. His tailored suit undoubtedly cost more than my entire wardrobe, while Reyes was dressed in black jeans, cowboy boots, and a bowling shirt.

My boss, Captain Marshall, leaned against a back wall, chewing a toothpick to splinters in place of the Marlboro I was sure he would have preferred. He acknowledged me with a microscopic movement of his chin.

Goldman touched my arm and whispered, "Here comes Fiegenbaum."

A gray-haired, gray-suited fed stirred the room by taking a spot near the white screen up front. A junior agent followed him with a laptop, which he proceeded to attach to the projector on the table. A third man, the doctor who'd injected me at Carrie Porter's place, entered last.

I leaned over and asked Goldman, "What's his name again?"

"Tancredi," she supplied.

Dr. Tancredi found a place in the corner. He fidgeted, tapping a handful of index cards against his leg, adjusting steel-rimmed glasses, and tweaking the knot of his red-and-blue-striped tie.

The junior agent got the projector running with amazingly little fuss, and a title slide lit the screen: Interagency Taskforce June Bug.

Goldman scrawled on her notepad and tilted it where I could see. *First, we'll do a round of introductions.*

"Ladies and gentleman," Fiegenbaum started. He cleared his throat and waited for the murmur of conversation to die out. "First, I think we should do a round of introductions…"

Here is today's agenda, Goldman wrote after everyone had identified themselves and their organizations. I counted eight federal and twelve local agencies represented.

Fiegenbaum clicked a handheld device, and the projector advanced. "Here is today's agenda."

The meeting waddled along at the pace of an IRS audit. Fiegenbaum brought the group up to speed by recounting in government-speak the events of the past few days. I perked up when he said, "And now I'd like to turn the meeting over to Dr. Tancredi of the CDC, who will cover the details of the bio-agent as we understand them. Dr. Tancredi?"

Another round of shuffling and throat clearing traveled through the room while Tancredi took the remote and clicked it. The screen filled with a grainy picture of a spiky capsule-looking critter.

"This is our enemy," the doctor said in his humorless voice. "A recombinant virus constructed from elements of both the Rhabdoviridae—rabies—and Orthomyxoviridae—influenza—families, in addition to some components which we've yet to identify. At eighty-five nanometers in diameter, over one hundred million can dance on the head of a pin."

The CDC doctor advanced to a slide showing a picture of a very sick dog. "The base component is rabies, but make no mistake, this virus has been engineered in a lab. Someone created this for the purpose of killing organic creatures—humans and animals—indiscriminately. There is both good news and bad news in the way the virus operates. Bad news—rabies is virtually incurable once symptoms have presented. Fortunately, the method of transmission is inefficient. A pandemic of rabies would be difficult to engineer. Imagine trying to bite a city full of people. Impossible, right?"

"Zombie apocalypse," somebody stage-whispered, and a chuckle rippled through the group.

Tancredi didn't smile. "However, here is where we get into trouble. The creator of this virus is a very talented clinician. Somehow, he or she has managed to couple the rabies virus with a variant of avian flu—H1N1—that is highly contagious, airborne, and easily transmissible, much like we saw with COVID-19. Good news, bad news: either by design or accident, the virus has an accelerated incubation period. Unlike COVID, the victim, once exposed, has a very short time to obtain treatment before becoming symptomatic. As little as twelve hours. With flu-like viruses, patients may be symptomatic for quite a while before they need hospitalization. This situation is good for us."

"How is that good?" one of the Homeland people asked. I thought his name was Ramirez.

"It's good because the virus also burns out quickly. A small pocket of infected will become sick and die before they can transmit the disease. Real pandemics only occur when those who are exposed spread the contagion before seeking treatment, becoming incapacitated, or quarantined. Avian flu spreads via casual contact for several days before the victim becomes too sick to move. COVID spread like wildfire as people went about their daily lives, believing they merely had the flu. With this...ultra rabies, what we will see is local flare-ups. They will be intense and devastating to those impacted, but they will be brief and unlikely to spread."

"So no zombie apocalypse?" Detective Winston asked. He caught my eye and winked.

Tancredi shifted his feet and pursed his lips before replying. "There is one unfortunate side effect of rabies infection, one which we have already seen play out." The doctor gestured in my direction. "The Ranger here experienced it firsthand. In about eighty percent of rabies cases, the victim will undergo periods of delirium, paranoia, and aggression related to hydrophobia. They will lash out and often attempt to bite others during these episodes of violence in classic, ah, foaming-at-the-mouth fury."

I growled under my breath, and Goldman slapped my arm.

"Down, boy," she said, which brought on another round of hollow chuckles.

The meeting dragged on for another hour without anything else of consequence being discussed. I passed the time doodling on my notepad until Fiegenbaum adjourned the meeting. Captain Marshall caught my eye as I stood and stretched. He twitched his head to the side in a come-hither gesture and left the room without speaking.

"Your master calls," Goldman quipped. "You better heel."

"Woof-woof."

What Marshall wanted was to hand me a scrap of paper with a name and address written on it. "This is something even the feds don't have," he warned me. "And I don't want 'em to have it, neither. Not even that she-devil from New York you hang out with, Goldfish."

"What is it?"

LEOs of all persuasions were spilling from the conference room, creating a cop-jam in the hall. The captain led me away with a jerk of his head. We turned a corner and stopped by a water fountain.

"We got a call from the campus cops over in Kilgore. At Jeff Davis College." Marshall spoke so low, I had to lean down and strain to hear him. "That yeller Camaro belonging to Sudafed—"

"Who?"

"One of them Chechen pukes you shot, Anton Mickie-something Sudafed. Remember? Anyway, this Sudafed got a parking ticket over there last week."

I squinted. Anton Mikhail Saidullayev. The T-Rex that had required a full double mag dose of .45s to drop. "A Chechen gangster? At a college?"

The captain tipped his hat back and nodded. "It's a puzzler, all right."

"How come the FBI doesn't have this yet?"

"College system..."

He paused as Fiegenbaum and his junior agent rounded the corner, heads together. They failed to acknowledge us. I was shocked and hurt by this and made a mental note to snub Fiegenbaum at the next meeting.

"The college computers ain't tied into the state database. They're barely outta the Stone Age over there, far as technology goes."

That was coming from a man who still had his emails printed for him.

"And we have it because…?"

"Because the campus police"—Marshall pointed at the note in my hand—"called it in to our office when their chief recognized the name from the news." The cagey old lawman wrinkled his eyes in a grin. "Which means we got it and the feds don't. Now, quit jawin' and get your ass down there. Find out what a kinner-garden dropout like Sudafed was doing at a college."

I touched the brim of my hat in salute and walked away.

Chapter 9

I MET JOSHUA BOUCHE in his office located on the first floor of the Jefferson Davis College administration building. The Chief of the JDC Police stood six foot two and had a wrestler's physique—big chest, meaty arms—with quiet brown eyes and a Cajun burr in his speech.

"You pronounce your name *Boo-shay*," I said. "You must be from Louisiana?"

"True dat." He grinned, flashing bright teeth. "Seems ages ago I swam the Caddo and sneaked across the border into Texas."

"We have open borders with Louisiana now. Didn't you hear?"

His office was bland, modern, and sterile, like one of those places people filled out loan documents or discussed deductibles and whole life options. A window overlooked the common area of the campus. We had a view of the Student Union and an open park with benches, shade trees, and concrete paths. Students loafed in the park—some even studied. A young man jogged past, iPod cords dangling from his ears. He dodged a group of three kids cutting across the grass with backpacks and Starbucks cups.

"Tell me about Anton's car," I said. "How'd it stand out?"

"It was the man's name more than his car. I review the daily activity logs, and that one stuck out to me when I saw it. Had to work at pronouncing the damn thing. Then when he popped up on the news, being dead and all, something... clicked, you know?"

I did. Every once in a while, when two pieces of information floating around in a cop's brain made a connection, it was almost something tangible, like puzzle pieces snapping together under a thumb.

We paused to study a slender girl with a blond ponytail as she bounced across the grass on New Balance shoes, wearing a midriff T-shirt and pink running shorts. Her sport socks had pink trim around the ankles. We watched carefully until she was out of sight.

Clues could be anywhere, after all.

Bouche focused on me. "What was I saying? Oh, yeah. I pulled the video feeds from all the cameras we have on campus for the time frame, but nothing doing. Saidullayev doesn't show up on any of them. No big surprise. It's not like cop shows on TV. We don't have cameras everywhere."

"Yeah, ain't that always how it is?" I stared out his window, picturing myself as a campus cop. Pink-trimmed socks. Parking tickets. Almost zero chance of having to kill somebody. "Where was his car ticketed?"

"Spenser Hall, a week ago last Friday."

"Can I see where it was parked?"

"Sure. Marta's the one that wrote the ticket. I'll get her on the horn, and we can meet her over there."

A thought had been bouncing around the empty space in my head. "Who's your big dope dealer here on campus?"

"This is a college, man. Who's *not* dealing would be easier to answer."

"How about meth?"

Bouche's face scrunched up in a frown. "We mostly get weed. Some X. The occasional roofie. Meth is around, 'specially during finals." He crossed his arms and tugged his bottom lip in thought. "I believe it mostly comes from in town, but there was a prick enrolled here... I'm tryin' to remember his name..."

While I waited for Bouche to dredge his memory, I tried to picture a hulking brute like Anton Mikhail attending a rural East Texas college, sitting in class with his black turtleneck and satin sport coat, gold chain dangling and a Glock tucked into his pants. It didn't compute. *No, Anton was here for something else.*

"Rogers!" Bouche blurted. "David Rogers. Graduated a year or two ago, and, man, I was glad to see him go."

"Why's that?"

"Pretty sure he beat up a girl—named Megan something." Bouche sighed. "Pretty thing. Came to the clinic all bruised up, said her boyfriend, Rogers, did it. Told the nurse he was running meth all over campus. By the time I got there, she had changed her story. Sobered up and got scared. Wouldn't press charges."

I kept quiet and let the information soak in.

"I believe," Bouche continued, "this Rogers cat was tied in to OC somehow. Never could prove shit, but he seemed to run with some tough pals, as I recall."

"Organized crime? The Chechen mob, maybe?"

The campus cop shrugged. "Not that I know of. Could've been Chechen, could've been Russian—hell, could have been Martian, for all I know. I never could get close enough to find out. Never enough probable cause, and there was always another fire burning hotter that I needed to put out."

"Where is he now? Rogers?"

Bouche tapped some keys on his computer. He leaned back and pinched his lip again, waiting for the screen to refresh. "He used to live over on Maple, just off campus. I don't know if he's still there. What's this about, anyway? There's more going on than some Eastern European bangers fuckin' around out here in the sticks."

"I can't tell you… directly." I pushed up from the chair and stretched. Bouche would have gotten the same cover story as the rest of the world, but he wasn't buying it. Puzzle pieces were shifting around behind his eyes, trying to connect. "I can't, however, prevent you from deducing certain conclusions if you were to assist me in my investigation. Want to go have a look and see if Mr. Rogers is still around?"

The campus cop's brown eyes appraised me for a long moment. "Yes, I believe I do."

WE MET OFFICER MARTA Ruiz in the gold-sticker parking lot of Spenser Hall. A big-boned, broad-shouldered woman, the campus officer carried an impressive amount of equipment on the belt around her chunky hips.

I asked her what the stickers meant, and Ruiz told me the gold lots were for faculty and staff only. She showed me the spot where she'd ticketed the yellow Camaro. It was one of six spaces along the curb that were personalized with names; Anton had parked in one belonging to Gischler. In the spot next to it was a Chevy pickup.

"Whose truck?"

Marta was quick. She said without hesitation, "Dr. Banerjee, teaches physics."

"And this guy?" I indicated the space on the other side, marked Hardeston.

"Dr. Burning Hard-on." The cop's tone carried a sneer. "He's a time-warped refugee from the sixties."

A four-story-tall cube of concrete and glass, Spenser Hall clashed with the more stately and Southern-influenced architecture of the JDC campus. It was located at the very edge of the grounds, next to Eighteenth Street, with no dormitories anywhere close. Jaywalking students crossed the four-lane road to a strip mall featuring a seedy, worn-out

Taco Bell and a seedier Laundromat. Had the Chechen stopped here to grab a Burrito Supreme? Or get his turtlenecks washed? I saw nothing that would prompt someone like Anton Saidullayev, having driven here from Dallas, to park next to this building on the west side of the campus.

I resettled my hat and wandered around to Spenser's front entrance, which faced inward toward the center of the college. Bouche and Ruiz followed me, no doubt impressed by my superior policing skills.

An engraved plaque near the door dedicated the building to Robert B. Spenser, noted physician. In big letters, it proclaimed: "For the furtherance of knowledge in the field of life sciences."

"They teach science here?" I asked Bouche.

He nodded. "Yup. Mostly biology and chemistry. Botany. Virology. Physiology. All them other -ologies."

"Hmm." I took two more steps before his words hit me. "Wait. When you say 'virology,' you mean you have classes on viruses?"

"True dat. It's what virology means," Bouche said. His eyes narrowed. "That mean something special?"

"What about research?" Puzzle pieces whirled. "They do research on viruses here?"

This time, it was Ruiz who answered. "One of the best virologists in the south is that letch, Hardeston." She sniffed. "He's brilliant. It's too bad he's such a tool."

Virologist. Chechen mobster.

Click.

RITA

Over the past few days, Rita's Yankee-trained ear had tried to regain her ability to interpret a thing Sam Cable said. Listening to him was like listening to a record played at half speed. It surprised her when she answered her cell and understood what he meant when he said, "Git a peyn 'n' rat this dowyn." *Get a pen and write this down.*

Translation was simple, once she'd tuned her ear to the country station.

"What's the mattah?" Rita snagged the pen from over her ear and flipped to a clean sheet in her notepad. "G'head."

"Bernard Hardeston. PhD," Cable said. "He's a virus guy with an anti-government attitude, and Anton may have been by to see him last week, before we met him at the Aces High clubhouse. We need to crawl so far up this old boy's ass, we can see what he had for lunch. Deep, deep background. Here's his vitals." Cable recited Hardeston's date of birth, address, social security and driver's license number, and current address, speaking as if reading from a form. The ranger added, "I went looking for him, but the doc's not in his office, his lab, or his house. His TA said he hadn't heard from Hardeston in the last two days."

"And we—"

"Wait. I ain't finished." Cable said something to another person on his end, and a keyboard clattered. Rita counted to eleven before Cable resumed. "Here's another one we need to dig into. Ready?"

"I'm dyin' here, I'm so ready."

"David Clifton Rogers. He took a class with Hardeston his senior year, and he's maybe a meth dealer, maybe connected to OC." He rattled off Rogers's information, though "rattled" to him meant one slow bump over the cobblestones at a time. She managed not to grind her teeth while taking dictation. Cable continued, "I'm headed over now to see this fellow, Rogers. Hmm? What's that?" The last bit was in response to a deep voice that rumbled too low for Rita to catch the words. "Oh, right. After we see his ex-girlfriend, Megan Stewart. You get that, Goldman?"

"Megan Stewart," she repeated. "Is that Stewart with a 'w-a-r-t' or a 'u-a-r-t'?"

"A what?"

"Is that with—?"

"I gotta run. I'll catch you later." And he hung up.

Rita checked her phone display to confirm that Sam Cable had, indeed, disconnected. "Now what the hell was all that about?"

Phones rang, and voices chattered around her borrowed cubicle inside the Longview Police Department. Members of the task force were digging into Chechen dirt with the furious intensity of gophers on speed. She had at least twelve browser windows open on her laptop, following money trails so faint, it was like trying to track a penny downhill by its smell alone.

And no one had gotten jack-fucking-shit so far.

"Goddamn him." Rita glared at the phone in her hand, torn between calling Samuel-frickin'-Cable back and throwing the device against the carpeted wall of the cube. It went to screen saver and blanked out before she decided.

"Bernard Hardeston, let's see what's up with you." She opened another screen and started typing, muttering under her breath. "And if that cowboy thinks I'm gonna play Miss CSI for him all day long, he better think again."

WE FOUND MEGAN STEWART, a pretty girl with lustrous blond hair and brown eyes, in King Hall, a coed dorm on the east side of campus. Bouche had called ahead so we could meet her downstairs, in the common room, a sitting area with chairs and sofas arranged around an old TV. A gaggle of girls crowded near the set, watching a daytime soap, so we took up a far corner away from the chatter.

Megan wore tight shorts showing leg all the way up to her unmentionables, and a replica Dirk Nowitzki basketball jersey that hinted at freestyle boobs, swaying at every movement. Being the keen observer I am, I suspected she wore nothing underneath.

"Megan," I began, "do you know David Rogers?"

She gave a startled look, like a fawn caught in the open. "Uh, yeah."

"Do you know if David sold methamphetamine while on campus?"

"I don't know anything about that." And just like that, she started lying through her perfect white teeth.

"Megan," Bouche said, "we didn't come to see you just out of the blue. We didn't just point at the phone book and say, 'Let's go see Megan Stewart.' We have a pretty strong reason to believe that you might have been... close to David at one time. Do you still see him?"

"Uh-uh," she said and looked away.

"Do you have any knowledge of what he's up to?" I asked. "How he makes his money?"

"Nuh-uh. I don't think so."

"Has he ever been associated with any Chechens?"

"Chechens? I don't know... Maybe." Megan sat back and hugged herself, both arms crossed in front of her. It did interesting things to her Mavericks jersey. Being a good detective required practicing my observational skills at all times.

"Are you afraid of David?" I asked.

"Afraid of David? Why would you say that?"

"Is David dealing dope?"

"Not to my knowledge."

"Ever see him do dope?"

"See him do dope?" she repeated. Her eyes met mine for an instant then shot away to examine her knees.

"Yes," I soothed. "Even just smoke a joint, maybe? And trust me, Megan, we aren't here to get you in trouble. We don't want to lock you up, ruin your record, make you lose time in class by having to deal with legal issues. We just want to stop people from getting hurt. You don't want people to get hurt, do you, Megan?"

She hesitated then managed, "No."

"Some bad stuff is coming through the meth pipeline here in East Texas. People are getting hurt. People are dying, Megan. Folks who are dealing meth are mixing it up with... with poison. It's killing people. I think maybe David has something to do with that, but I'm not sure. I just need to know if David is a meth dealer, or does he just use a little from time to time? He's a dealer, isn't he, Megan?" I'd moved too fast and hurried the question. I knew I'd screwed the pooch the instant I said it.

Megan's body language closed down. She turned her eyes to the TV and wouldn't look away from it. "I don't know anything about that."

I tried a couple of different lines, but Megan refused to look at me. I gave up after about ten more minutes of patter, working every rationalization I could think of to get her to open up. Megan Stewart obviously wasn't the key to the whole thing, but if I could get her to spill the beans on Rogers, maybe I could get enough for a search warrant, bust the guy on a dope charge, and see what happened from there.

In the end, it wasn't meant to be. "Well, Megan, if you get in any trouble or if you need help, just give me a call."

She took my card but didn't say anything as we left.

On the steps out front, Bouche put on his sunglasses. "Wow," he said with a straight face. "It's always a pleasure to watch a real-life Texas Ranger at work."

"I hope you took notes."

Chapter 10

BOUCHE DROVE HIS SHINY Dodge Charger Police Interceptor into a time warp. About a mile from campus, I goggled through the windshield as we transitioned into a *Leave it to Beaver* neighborhood of comfortable houses with big porches and natural stone facades over-looking velvet lawns. Canopies of ancient oaks blocked the sun. Flower beds exploded with variety: dianthus, verbena, azaleas, and, of course, roses. Reds, yellows, and pinks, in palettes of whispering pastels and screaming primary hues, they graced trellises, ran amok in disorderly profusion, or lined gardens in trimmed precision.

The houses had been built in an age when a single car was the norm, so the brick-lined driveways were narrow, often leading to de-tached garages. Excess cars, many with JDC parking stickers on the back windows, jammed the curbs. Elderly residents tended their yards while youths cycled by, carrying backpacks, their ears plugged by buds connected to smartphones. The neighborhood breathed the aroma of exuberant youth spiced with stately age in a way only a college town could manage.

That this neighborhood existed in the same town as Chantina Moore's Soviet-style apartment complex said something profound. What, exactly, I wasn't sure. But profound, nonetheless.

Bouche rolled his cruiser to a stop in front of a two-story classic house with a brick first floor and a wood-sided second story. "This is the place. I think." He had stopped in front of the last known address for David Rogers. As a lair for a dealer-terrorist-Chechen gangster, the house needed a bucket of sinister poured over it.

"Looks like it popped out of 1956," I said.

"People in Kilgore don't believe in change." The toothpick poking from Bouche's mouth twitched when he smiled. "And it don't believe much in them, neither."

"You think Rogers is trying to assimilate or hide in plain sight? A dope dealer would stand out in this refuge of Norman Rockwell Middle America."

"Half these places are rented out to college kids, Ranger. Grad students, mostly. None of the wild crowd of first-years or frat houses. But still. People here are used to students coming around day and night. Transient and anonymous as a Philadelphia flophouse."

"Huh." I shrugged. "Let's go see if Davey can come out and play."

Cracks zigzagged the concrete path from the sidewalk to the front door, though the grass edged either side in a laser-straight line. Cicadas wailed their scratchy song, and music thumped from a nearby house. The scent of meat on a barbeque grill seasoned the air, reminding me of the hockey pucks burnt to a cinder in Carrie Porter's backyard.

I rang the bell and stepped back. Bouche took up position on my right.

The door swung open.

At some point in his life, the man in the doorway had driven fence posts... with his face. He had a linebacker's build—square shoulders, square jaw, and square demeanor—with features only a dentist could identify. He reminded me of Lurch, from the Addams family.

I held up my credentials so he could see the shiny badge.

"Cops," he grunted.

"Aw, what gave it away? We need to see David Rogers."

The troll's left eye twitched. "Wait." He closed the door.

I leaned over to Bouche and stage-whispered, "What classes do you think *he* takes?"

"Advanced Brutality with Professor Fist."

Square-cut greenery flanked the porch and bordered the front of the house. To the left, a hose bib dripped water in steady, slow plips, soaking into damp soil. A mosquito stabbed me in the jugular and died in a wet smear under my palm. I wiped the remains on the doorframe.

When the door opened again, Lurch had been replaced by a male model fresh from a cologne ad. Tall, black-haired, and olive-skinned, David Rogers shamed the student ID picture Bouche had pulled from the school's records. Broad, athletic shoulders filled a maroon V-neck shirt made of a slick, buttery-smooth material that looked as soft as a baby's thighs. His designer jeans had been artificially lightened on the front, and Rita Goldman would have a jealous conniption if she saw the loafers on his feet.

"Can I help you?"

Silky voice, too.

Rogers lifted an eyebrow in a classic Mr. Spock imitation, regarding us with eyes the color of weak tea.

"You mind if we come in, ask you some questions?" It was always better to presume consent and see how far that got me. I stepped up close, as if going inside was a foregone conclusion.

Rogers didn't budge from the door. "Yes."

"Excuse me?"

"Yes," he said, "I mind if you come in and ask questions. This is an inconvenient time." He leaned against the doorframe and waited while Bouche and I exchanged a look. "I'm entertaining guests at the moment, so I would much prefer for you to make an appointment."

At my side, Bouche swelled up, no doubt preparing to unleash a magnum-force verbal assault on the smirking prick in the doorway. I touched the chief's shoulder and backed him down with a look. I said to Rogers, "No problem. We'll catch you next time. C'mon, Josh, let's leave the man to his guests."

I tugged Bouche's arm, and we retreated to his cruiser. Rogers watched us get in with a thin frown. I touched the brim of my hat in salute, and Megan's former boyfriend disappeared behind a firmly closed front door after shaking his head.

Bouche regarded me with hooded eyes. "The hell? We jus' gonna kiss his ass and walk away?"

"It was a mistake," I said. "Coming here, I mean. Now he knows we're on to him."

"Then he made a mistake, too."

I grunted. "True. He should have let us ask questions."

"Fin' out what we know by what we *axe.*"

"You know," I said, "you get excited, you use more street lingo than a chief of campus police should."

"You observant." The chief quirked a smile in my direction. "Should be a detectiff, or sumpin.'"

"I sent away for the course."

Bouche cranked the ignition, and the Charger rumbled to life. He pulled into the street, lifting two fingers from the wheel in a casual wave to a female student passing by on a bicycle. She waved back with a grin.

"Kids here seem to like the cops," I said.

"This ain't Portland. What are you going to do about Rogers?"

The quaint neighborhood of Mayberry houses fell away as we returned to the land of the strip mall. A used car lot flashed by, and it reminded me of JC Fortney, widower of Senate candidate April Maree Fortney and someone I hoped to never see again. The cold hand of repressed memories touched my neck. A double lungful of air hissed through my puffed lips like escaping steam.

To Bouche, I said, "I'm going to chant a spell and invoke a certain little frizzy-haired demon in a skirt who will ram a federally approved cattle prod up David Rogers's ass, with both force and vigor." I finger-combed my sweat-damp hair and resettled my hat. "If that doesn't work, I'll get creative."

ROGERS

David Rogers closed the door on the two cops and returned to the backyard patio, where the thuggish Marat glowered at their guest, Professor Hardeston. The virologist's pudgy body strained the capacity of a wicker patio chair. He was seated in dappled shade, under the spreading branches of an untrimmed crepe myrtle. One of the tree's pink-tinged blossoms had settled on the fringe of the professor's hair, over his ear, secretly typecasting the old hippie as a flower child.

"Who was that?" The old man's hands rattled a plastic baggie containing four pre-rolled spliffs. He shook one loose and popped it between his lips.

"No one." Rogers resumed his seat across from the professor. His glass of tea remained untouched on the low table between them. No doubt by now, it had gone too cold to drink. "When will the product be available in quantity?"

The professor's eyes shifted back and forth from Rogers to the hulking Marat. Hardeston's disposable lighter *skritched* three times before flaming up high enough to almost singe the old man's eyebrows. Flame danced, and the weedy smell of burning marijuana drifted through the backyard. The doctor took a deep drag and held it.

"You know," Hardeston said through exhaled smoke, "it's not like making a cake, dude. Can't throw some Betty Crocker in a pan and set the timer on the oven. No way, Jose. Each batch has to be cultured from the original seed stock, one dish at a time. You get too far away from the original, and mistakes creep in. Like making a copy of a copy of a copy, you know?"

Rogers folded his hands in his lap to restrain himself from slapping the academician hard enough to make the man's brains flow through his reddened bulb of a nose. *Patience. We need the stupid pig for a few more days.* Instead of striking out or speaking precipitously, Rogers cocked an eyebrow.

"I'm, ah..." Hardeston took another hit from his joint. Held it. Blew it out. "I'm on schedule for the end of this week. Friday. For sure by Friday. No later than Saturday."

"We can take delivery Friday, then?" Rogers kept his voice mild, a cool river flowing over concealed rocks.

"Friday. Absolutely. But look..."

Rogers waited.

"Ah, look, David..." Hardeston fortified himself with a deep toke, which he held for an eight count. "I have to know the plan, man." He wheezed. "It's, like, are we in alignment, goal-wise, dude?"

"Alignment?" Ice formed on the riverbanks of Rogers's mild voice.

"When we talked about this, we agreed we'd hit the fat cats first, right?"

"We've discussed this many—"

"I know, dude, I know." The professor tugged his gray ponytail, and the wicker chair creaked when he scooted onto the edge. "Look, I just have to be sure, man. This isn't about the money for me, right? You know that. This is about sticking it up the ass of the establishment—"

"Enough!" David Rogers shot to his feet, tipping over his chair. "Professor Hardeston, the time for quibbling over who we target is long past. Your ends will be achieved, the same as ours. I have discussed this enough with you and will discuss it no more. Deliver the product on Friday, Professor. Not one day later."

"But..."

"No buts," Rogers stated. Fire flushed his neck and heated his face. *This stupid... stupid little man.* "You may leave now."

Rogers turned his back and stalked away, waving to Marat to deal with the idiot. He closed his ears to the old man's bleating, lest he lose what little control remained on his temper. He went to the kitchen and relit the burner under the kettle. A glass of tea would help settle him.

When Marat found him after showing the doctor out, Rogers said, "I don't trust that hippie moron. Follow him. Find out where he goes. Call the boys for support, if you must.. I want a twenty-four-hour watch placed on that cunt. We are too close to having the weapons to let his idealistic impulses ruin everything."

Marat nodded and left.

Rogers waited for the kettle to boil, staring through the kitchen window without seeing anything. Would Hardeston hold up his end of the bargain? Would he produce the weaponized biological agent in sufficient quantity to satisfy Tarasov's urge to kick the Great Satan in the nuts? If not, would the lack of results blow back on him, David Rogers, for instigating the plan in the beginning?

When he'd cultivated Hardeston in the early days, Rogers had played on the radical professor's hatred for everything from the fat cats of Wall Street to the religious rightwing ideologues of the American heartland. Once he realized his biology professor was dabbling in gene-engineered viruses, it only required a few nudges in the right direction to dedicate the man's lab work to creating a killer plague. Promises of targeted strikes on Exxon, Dow Chemical, and GOP headquarters had fired Hardeston's imagination, and the 60s throwback had set to work with a will. His adolescent dream of an agrarian, egalitarian society in tune with the rhythms of nature had blinded the professor to the reality of Rogers's agenda. Only a few of their goals were actually aligned. Hardeston wanted to kill off the rich pig capitalists; Rogers wanted to kill all Americans. But now some of these harsh truths may have intruded into Hardeston's pot-fogged brain. Rogers worried the old man might be getting cold feet.

The kettle whistled, pulling Rogers from his thoughts. He fussed with making tea until it was steeping in a ceramic pot.

One thing, he must do, tomorrow if not today. He must go see his uncle before Hardeston had a meltdown. No way in hell did he want Sergei Tarasov blindsided by the old flowerchild's attack of conscience. His uncle's temper was legendary, and once unleashed, it could easily catch David Rogers in its blast radius. And that would not be good.

"No," he murmured. "That would not be good at all."

I WANTED TO ASK RITA what she'd found on Rogers and Hardeston, but when I got back to Longview, the taskforce personnel were swarming to the main conference room for an emergency meeting. I joined the flow and followed along like a good lemming. The only spot left was a seat on the far side of the table from Rita. We traded nods like two colleagues at the office, nothing more.

One of the feds had brought multigrain bagels with tubs of flavored cream cheese, fruit, and coffee. The coffee came in a box. *What'll they think of next? Spam in a sack?*

"Where's the doughnuts?" Darren Winston asked. The detective from Upshur County wore an immaculate charcoal suit with a bold red tie. At zero-point-one percent body fat, Winston looked as if he hadn't eaten a doughnut since grade school.

"Cops and doughnuts. You're perpetuating a stereotype, Winston," I told him. "That's a slippery slope to racial profiling."

"I am the epitome of diversity, Cable." With a straight face, the black detective pointed to the pile of strawberries on Ferdinand Reyes's paper plate. "Damn, Reyes, you people supposed to pick those, not eat 'em."

Putting on a heavy Chicano accent, Reyes said, "Touch my strawberries, and I *keel chew*."

Rita cackled.

Fiegenbaum bounced in like a puppy with a new toy. "We found the Chechen leader. We got lucky with gang intelligence from the Dallas PD. They spotted Sergei Tarasov leaving a private terminal at Love Field and followed him. Tarasov is staying at a condo in Dallas rented under a shell company's name."

"Way to go, DPD!" I got up to try out the boxed coffee.

"Indeed." Fiegenbaum grinned and fiddled with setting up his laptop. I dumped some fancy raw sugar in my coffee and flicked a glance at Rita, who looked away. She was in black today. Black suit jacket and black slacks, with a sapphire-blue blouse. I may have imagined it, but I thought I saw a blush color her cheeks. It looked good on her.

Nah. Not in a million years.

While Fiegenbaum connected his laptop to the projector, his underling handed out packets of documents. The senior agent put up a surveillance photo showing a modern, ground-level condo complex—one in a block of identical square condos—in a tree-shaded neighborhood.

"Mr. Tarasov is staying in the uptown area of Dallas, just off Highway 75 and Lemmon Avenue. 2012 Oxmoor Drive." Tarasov's place had a recessed front door on a narrow footpath next to a two-car garage. "There's a map and floorplan in your handout. We have a no-knock arrest warrant for Mr. Tarasov at this address. We also have a search warrant for the premises, specific to drugs, chemicals, and any DNA, fibers, and material evidence related to biological weapons. Please turn to page one of the ops plan."

I sipped at my coffee while Fiegenbaum laid out a detailed plan for the execution of the arrest and search warrants. Unsurprisingly, the feds had assigned me and the local cops the job of covering the back door. I had to sneak through the alley to the rear of the property and play catcher while the federal agents glory-hogged the entry.

Rita was awarded the number-three position on the stack. She would go in third behind Fiegenbaum and an FBI agent named Jackson.

We finished the planning process, and the meeting broke up. Everyone jammed up at the door as we filed out.

"Excuse me, Ranger." Rita passed me in the shuffle. Her butt brushed my thigh, and an electric jolt shot directly to my groin. When I grunted, she smiled and flashed me a look that I couldn't read before heading in the opposite direction.

I caught myself—again—watching her rear end as she strode away. "Have to stop doing that," I said under my breath. "Have to, have to, have to."

Chapter 11

"None yet."

"Pity. I'm getting so I miss my morning coffee and corpse." — Ed McBain, Cop Hater

I RODE TO DALLAS IN a van with Reyes and Winston, the only local guys on the task force. Reyes drove, and I sat next to him. On the way, we finished off takeout hamburgers, stinking up the inside of the van with a meat-and-mustard smell. The sun's orange light stabbed us in the eyes as we drove into the dying day. Using the visors didn't help, because they didn't cover the lower part of the windshield. Reyes squinted and shielded his eyes with a hand.

The scenery rolled past, mile after mile of green forest giving way to prairie and farmland the closer we got to Dallas. This part of Texas was so flat, you could roll an armadillo for miles.

"Damn feds are screwing us." Reyes snorted up some of his takeout Coke. "Giving us the back door? That blows."

"I know one fed would give Cable a screwing," Winston chimed in from the back. "And maybe a blowing, too."

"Jesus, Winston," I said. "Are we in high school, or what?"

"You damn near wag your tail when she whistles."

"Bullshit. Can I help it if women swoon at my feet?"

"I think the chloroform has something to do with that."

"You really got the hots for that Smurfette?" Reyes cracked the window and fired up a cigarette.

"No." I looked out my window. We passed a barn painted to resemble the Texas flag. It was better tended than the home next to it. "I don't know. Possibly I'm merely suffering from hormone overload. It's been a while."

Winston laughed. "Ms. Special Agent Goldman, she a steel-plated ball buster to everybody exceptin' the cowboy here. I seen one guy try coming on to her, whoo, man. He might as well have dipped his balls in battery acid. And yet, when my man here comes around, she rolls over, purrs, and shows her belly."

"Yeah, yeah, real funny."

"I only noticed because I was checkin' her out my ownself. Right off, I could tell it was a lost cause." Winston slapped Reyes on the shoulder. "Only guy she looks at is the Longgg Ranger here."

"I..."

"Don't worry, Kemo Sabe," Reyes said. "Your secret's safe with us."

"Yeah. Right. I feel so much better now."

RITA

Rita Goldman counted only two other women at the briefing in the Northwest Patrol Division of the Dallas Police Department. Both were DPD cops, stout women with blocky body armor turning their upper bodies into trash-compactor shapes. The women hung out together, their body language throwing up an invisible shield that said, "Don't fuck with me." Through hooded eyes, they seemed to regard the whole raid as a supreme dose of boredom.

This was Rita's second takedown. The first had been of a *memzer* nicknamed Snake. She had stood in the weedy woods, dripping with rain, and covered the rear of a shitty little house near Dallas. She'd gotten lucky when the guy busted out the back, trying to get away. This time, she would be in the front door stack. She swallowed hard, and the acidic remains of bad coffee burbled in her stomach.

Half an hour before midnight, jazzed on caffeine and adrenaline, she was very aware of Sam Cable standing three feet away with his buddies Reyes and Winston. The black detective caught her eye, leaned close to Cable, and whispered a comment behind his hand. Cable grinned and elbowed Winston in the ribs.

Boys. Do they never grow up? Pfft.

A whiteboard covered one wall of the briefing room; a decade of dry-erase scribbling had left behind a rainbow of faded colors. Hard plastic chairs were laid out in rows, and fold-up tables lined the back wall.

The room reeked of leather, sweat, gun oil, and testosterone.

Fiegenbaum stood at the front, dressed all in black, from his combat boots to his flak jacket, which had "FBI" lettered in yellow on the back. He wore his sidearm slung low and carried an assault shotgun with an attached flashlight. He looked like Bob Barker in tac gear. The remaining federal agents, including Rita, wore similar equipment. The bulky vest and bloused cargo pants made her feel like she was playing dress-up in Daddy's clothes. The pants did nothing for her legs at all, and the shoes... *Oh my God, the shoes.*

Rita overheard Winston's next whispered comment. "I feel underdressed amongst all these here Spiderman ninja federal muthafuckahs."

The Ranger smothered a laugh and put a hand over his mouth. He and his two amigos wore regular street clothes with Kevlar vests and POLICE-lettered jackets. They looked relaxed and slightly bored.

Cable glanced at Rita and winked. She flipped him the finger but couldn't hold back the smile that went with it.

"Ah, true love," Winston muttered, and Cable elbowed him in the ribs again.

Rita felt her face heat.

Fiegenbaum went over the ops plan again, restating that Jackson, Goldman, and the other FBI agent, Pete Schmidt, made up the front-door stack. They passed around and tested small radio packs with ear-buds and throat mics, courtesy of a low-bid federal government procurement contract.

"You think these'll work?" Winston asked Cable.

"Only when you need it," the ranger muttered back.

"Listen up, people." Fiegenbaum called everybody to attention. "We believe Mr. Tarasov to be a dangerous character with an unknown number of bodyguards, some of whom are ex-military. Also, he may be in possession of a bio-weapon of almost one hundred percent lethality."

One of the cops farted, and someone else said, "My bio-weapon beats his bio-weapon."

Groans and laughter followed. Fiegenbaum looked pissed. "This is our only lead to this dangerous substance. If this stuff gets out into the population, we'll have rioting in the streets like you've never seen before. COVID was a bad day at the office compared to this stuff." He ended with "Let's be careful out there."

A DPD cop snorted and said, "Yes, Mom."

"Hey, did you used to be on TV?" another DPD cop asked Fiegenbaum.

The graying FBI agent flicked his head, and the federal team filed out of the room and headed for their waiting cars.

REYES, WINSTON, AND I rode out to the condo complex, which was called the Sterling Heights, in a Dallas squad car with a twenty-year veteran of the DPD named Lillingston. The man dipped Skoal and left the window down so he could spit when he slowed down or went around corners. He didn't say much, and the rest of us kept our thoughts to ourselves.

We followed a line of squad cars and drifted to a stop around the corner from the target condo. Everyone climbed out, easing doors shut rather than slamming them. Bugs danced in the streetlights, and bats slashed through the swarms. A small yapping dog barked like a machine gun from the backyard of a nearby condo. As a rule, I liked dogs, but I drew the line at yappers. This one made enough noise to wake up the entire city of Dallas.

"Call Animal Control," Reyes said. "Get some tranqs for that mutt."

Rita and the feds, along with our band of brothers from the DPD, headed off in a jingle of equipment.

My watch showed five minutes till two as we followed Lillingston through the alleys of Sterling Heights to the rear of 2012 Oxmoor Drive, where Mr. Tarasov presumably slept the peaceful sleep of a Chechen mobster while visions of tortured sugarplum fairies danced in his head. The alley presented us with a valley of wooden privacy fences broken up at intervals by gates. Green trash bins with hinged lids guarded every fence. Metal numbers screwed onto each gate told us the street number of the residence.

We assembled by the gate labeled 2012. All of us stood back, gawking at a fence as tall as Fenway's Green Monster. Fully twelve feet high, with the crossbeams on the inside, it was impossible to climb without a ladder.

The crackle of the comm bud in my ear startled me.

"Alpha ready," Fiegenbaum said in my ear. The feds were set to breach the front. I pictured Jackson with the ram, Fiegenbaum and Goldman braced to enter, followed by the DPD SWAT team and the remaining feds.

Lillingston reached toward the gate latch.

Standing next to me, Lillingston announced through the comm, "Beta ready. Do it."

"No!" I shouted.

Too late.

A thud from around front was followed immediately by a babble of raised voices. The radio jammed into a snarled mess of howling static. A drumline of gunfire thundered from inside the house, hammering the night with stunning, sudden violence. I snarled at Lillingston. "Why'd you give the ready signal?"

Gunshots popped. The takedown team had jumped directly into a firefight, and we stood in the alley with our thumbs penetrating our collective ass, unable to assist. The rattle and bang of gunfire inside the condo announced a small war going on in there.

"Fuck," Reyes barked, "they hit a hornet's nest!"

My heart thudding, I shoved Lillingston aside and slammed the latch down. I rammed the gate with my shoulder—and bounced back.

The gate was locked.

A chain wrapped the latch from inside, holding the gate closed. More shots popped. My people were in trouble. Rita was in trouble. *And this freaking gate, this stupid collection of wood slats and nails is—*

In!

My!

Way!

I reared back and kicked the gate with my boot heel. Wood splintered and cracked around the latch. The gate sagged loose. Not loose enough to open, though.

"Dammit!"

"Move over! Stand clear!" Winston racked his shotgun.

Boom! Boom! He pumped two rounds point-blank into the gate latch. Wood and metal chips exploded. I lashed out with my boot, smacking it with everything I had. More slats broke, and the thing hung by a stubborn metal thread.

"Shoot the fucking chain!" I yelled.

Winston stuck the barrel of the shotgun directly against the chain with one hand and ducked away.

With a flash and a boom, the chain popped loose. I kicked it again, and the gate skittered open a foot then stuck on something. Lillingston hit it with his shoulder at a dead run. The gate sprang open, and he fell through.

I jumped over the Dallas cop and ran through a small backyard. A table and chairs occupied a postage-stamp patio. Lengthwise blinds covered the glass of sliding doors leading inside. I couldn't see inside, but nothing banged or flashed anymore.

Was it over?

I grabbed one of the metal lawn chairs, wound up like a slugger at batting practice, and slammed it into the glass. It imploded with a bang. The chair hung up in the blinds. I kicked it free of the mess and went through before the shards stopped falling from the doorframe.

Code word! What the fuck was the code word? Dying by friendly fire would majestically suck. "Ruby, ruby, ruby!"

Clearing the blinds with a sweep of my arm, I barreled in hard and fast, nearly tripping over an easy chair next to the door. Stumbling in the darkened room, I took cover and swept left to right with a flashlight braced under my Kimber.

The fight was over.

The living room of the condo reeked of gunsmoke and shit. A dead Chechen lay in a spreading pool of blood, splayed across the floor, automatic weapon close by. The others on the entry team called out the countersign "Diamond!" and filtered back into the front room from a hallway on the left. Flashlight beams danced around as people moved. I counted heads until I saw a short and frizzy one—

Rita.

Somebody found a light switch, and the sudden illumination made me flinch. Rita trailed Jackson, engaging the safety on her weapon and slipping it back in the holster. She looked up and saw me there.

"Hey, cowboy, where were you? Getting coffee and doughnuts?"

"I had to *pahk* the *cah*," I said in my best attempt at a New York accent.

"You from Boston, now?" She came over and punched me lightly in the chest. She had a manic, slightly crazed cant to her eyes. "What took you so long?"

"The gate was locked."

"'The gate was locked,' he says. Hey, Ferdinand, you believe this guy? I thought Rangers were tough. He says the gate was locked."

Down on one knee, Ferdinand Reyes studied the dead guy in the floor. "Chica, I thought he was going to tear that fucking fence down with his teeth, the guns started going off."

"So what happened?" Winston reloaded his Rossi, having negotiated the debris in the entrance. The man looked spotless, like he'd just stepped out of *GQ*, the Guns & Ammo edition.

Fiegenbaum gestured and spoke to the DPD guys, pointing at this and that and generally acting in charge.

"We hit the door," Rita said. "And the Fourth of July happened."

"The *fort* of July?" She spoke so loud and so fast, I had a hard time following her.

"Smartass. The fourth, Cable. Listen to me when I'm tawking to you." Rita gestured at the guy in the floor. "This guy must have been on guard or just hanging here in the chair. Soon as we went in, he's up and shooting. I think Jackson caught a couple in the vest, because he went down, then everybody was shooting at everybody else. Guys started shooting from the back, and we blew one up in the hall and one in the bedroom. Tarasov's gone. Not here."

"How's Jackson?"

"He's fine, Cable." Fiegenbaum came up to our group. "Okay, our scene's too packed with people here. We need to get out and let the evidence guys do their thing. Goldman, I called the boss, and he's sending out somebody to run lead on the shooting investigation. I'm sure you know the drill by now. You'll need to surrender your weapon for testing once he gets here."

"Sure, no problem. Not for nothing, but it won't help. I couldn't shoot around you guys in front of me, so I don't think I hit anything but wall."

Fiegenbaum, distracted, just nodded. As the adrenaline high leaked out of him, he looked jumpy and wild-eyed, like a horse in a thunderstorm. "Once the crime scene guys get here and do their thing, we can look for the biological agent and anything else on the warrant."

"Look for the biological..." My jaw fell open. "Are you shitting me? You found nothing? No beakers of brimming, bubbling rabid death lying around?"

"We haven't found anything out in plain sight yet, Cable," Fiegenbaum snapped.

No virus. No Tarasov. Our leads were drying up, and the bad guys knew we were on their tail. They would have to act soon, and they knew it. Tarasov had to know his timetable had just been hijacked.

Winston said, "Let's hope we find that shit soon. I'm not going sleep well until we do."

"Amen to that," I told him. "Amen to that."

Chapter 12

"I'M THE POLICE, AND I'm here to arrest you. You've broken the law. I did not write the law. I may even disagree with the law, but I will enforce it, and no matter how you plead, cajole, beg, or attempt to stir my sympathies, nothing you do will stop me from placing you in a steel cage with gray bars. If you run away, I will chase you. If you fight me, I will fight back. If you shoot at me, I will shoot back. By law, I am unable to walk away. I am a consequence. I am the unpaid bill. I am fate with a badge and a gun. Behind my badge is a heart like yours. I bleed, I think, I love, and yes, I can be killed. And although I am but one man, I have thousands of brothers and sisters who are the same as me. They will lay down their lives for me, and I them. We stand watch together, a thin blue line, protecting the prey from the predators, the good from the bad. We are the police." – Jake Gyllenhaal as Brian Taylor, End of Watch

WHEN CITIZENS ARE SHOT and killed by police—even citizens firing fully automatic AK-47s—the system wraps the officer in red tape from head to toe. Tuesday dragged into Wednesday, which crawled into Thursday, while we chewed our way out from the bear trap of bureaucracy. Statements, reports, depositions, and review boards were all accelerated—*accelerated!*—by the circumstances of a potential terrorist strike being planned by the Chechens. Even so, time ticked away without active progress being made.

I was one of the first cut loose, in the wee hours of Thursday morning. Goldman and the remaining feds would be back to work Friday, so

I had a little time to kill. I used it to look for Rashad Phillips, suspected murderer of Taniqua Johnson. The DNA report on the skin and hair particles recovered from Taniqua had come back as a solid match for Phillips. She had fought back against her assailant, which put Phillips in the crosshairs. Putting him in jail would pull at least one thorn from my paw.

I stopped at the All State Tire and Battery in Tyler, and Phillips's tire-busting coworkers gave me another possible lead on where to find Rashad. They said he sometimes stayed with a family friend he called Aunt Jessie, who lived in Whitehouse, not far from Lake Tyler.

Aunt Jessie turned out to be Jessica Malverna Martin, address 525 Olive Grove. I cruised past the house—a two-bedroom frame-and-termite structure on the outskirts of a half-dead town. A hundred yards past the property, I rolled into the red-gravel lot of an abandoned body shop, cut a big circle, and stopped next to the wasp-infested carcass of a 1982 Dodge Aries with no tires, wheels, or window glass. From where I sat, Aunt Jessie's screened-in front porch was visible between the trunks of scattered pines and Southern live oaks.

The neighborhood consisted of houses spaced every dozen yards or so, set back from the road by gravel drives. Among them were scattered tire swings and worn-out cars. Metal lawn chairs rusted in place under the shade of pine trees. Sagging clotheslines made of eight-gauge wire sagged over red dirt and weeds. Gardens and chicken coops were mixed in with the weeds and welfare. Old men smoked and grew older while watching the world pass from their rickety porches.

A scrawny ten-year-old boy and his ragamuffin little sister picked their way along the side of the road. The girl squatted every few steps to inspect a treasure before she ran to catch up with her big brother. She had on pink shorts with a dusty bottom and a white T-shirt, fitted tightly. Beads were braided into her cornrows, and her hair clattered when she ran.

At ten o'clock in the morning, the temperature had already achieved wretched, on its way to steamy and disgusting. The air lay as heavy as a quilt soaked in used engine oil. It carried the smell of rust with it when I rolled down both windows. A train's air horn moaned from a distance, overlaying the sound of someone pounding metal.

The post-adrenaline crash and lack of sleep had left me groggy. I yawned and toyed with my cell phone, scrolling through my contacts list over and over. I kept stopping at Rita's number then clearing the display. Two minutes later, I would find her number again, my thumb poised to connect the call.

"This is stupid." I stabbed the button and held the phone to my ear.

She answered with "Hey, cowboy."

"Hey."

"Whatcha doin?"

"Police stuff. Catching bad guys."

"Wow. By yourself?"

"Yeah."

"Oh my. I *am* impressed."

I listened to her breathe.

"Anything new?" I finally asked. "On the Chechens."

"Nah. Nothin'. Tarasov's a ghost. He slipped surveillance before we hit his place, somehow. But he'll turn up."

"Hopefully not too late."

"Hopefully."

Sweat trickled down my neck. I cleared my throat and shifted in the seat.

"What's that background noise?" Rita asked.

"Somebody's beating sheet metal."

"Oh."

"Hey," I said. "Anything on Rogers or Hardeston?"

"Shit. I forgot all about them."

"Understandable."

"I'm kidding. But to tell the truth, I didn't get very far before the shitshow came to town. I'll do it today."

"Too many coincidences, all bumping into each other."

"Yeah, you're right, I'm sorry. I'll get on it."

"No problem." My phone had heated against my ear, and sweat coated its glass surface. I wiped it on my sleeve and shifted it to the other side. I took a breath and let it out. *Shit, this is worse than high school.*

"Anything else?" she asked.

"Yeah. Um, I was thinking—" Through the pine trees, Jessica Martin's screen door slapped open, and Rashad Phillips shuffled into the front yard. His shorts hung low, showing a swath of plaid boxers. He wore no shirt, and his V-shaped upper torso looked oiled. "Oops. Gotta run. My prom date just showed up."

"Be careful, stud."

"Careful is for sissies."

She laughed and disconnected.

I found a different number on my phone, dialed it, and waited.

WHEN I WHIPPED THE Expedition into Jessica Martin's front yard, Rashad Phillips did what I expected. He lit off like a bottle rocket, leaving a Road Runner dust trail around the side of the house before I could even get the car door open. Two Whitehouse Police Department squads, LED bars glittering, boiled into the yard behind me.

I stepped out, stretched, and put on my hat. Closed my car door. Two young bulls, bulky in Kevlar and weighted down by a thousand pounds of police gear, thundered past me. Shouts echoed from the rear of the house. I followed the parade around the side yard, taking my time.

The unfenced backyard was half weeds, half vegetable garden. The two Whitehouse cops from the front joined their brothers, who had lain in wait at the rear. By the time I rounded the corner, the four of them had Rashad on the ground, cuffed, face in the zucchini.

Delegation. The key to success.

"Hello, Rashad," I said. "Remember me?"

He angled his face to the side, squinted at me with one eye, and spat out something dusty and green. "Fuck you, Buck Rogers."

One of the uniforms, red-faced with coppery hair—Personowski by the name on his tag—bounced Rashad's face off the ground, not gently. "Watch your language, fuckwad."

I crouched beside Rashad so he could see me better. "You mean Roy Rogers. Buck Rogers was a spaceman. Okay, listen up now. Rashad Phillips, you are under arrest for the murder of Taniqua Johnson. You have the right to—"

"I din't do nothin'!"

"—remain silent. You have the right—"

"Gets me a goddamn lawyer!"

"—to gets you a goddamn lawyer. If you cannot afford—"

The back door banged open. A black woman of unusual size, in a sack dress and pinkish slippers, glared from the top step of the porch. "Y'all git the hell out my squash! Rashad, what you done now? Don't think I got the money to get yo skinny ass out the jail no mo'."

"I din't do nothin', Aunt Jessie!"

"Boolshit, you din't do nothin'! Wouldn't be no poh-lice in my garden, you din't do nothin'. Don't you 'Aunt Jessie' me!"

One of the Whitehouse cops went to hold off Aunt Jessie while I finished reciting Rashad's Miranda rights. We would do it twice more before we sat down to question him, once in writing, but it never hurt to do it first thing. Considering how Aunt Jessie squalled loudly enough to alert the National Guard about the invasion of her garden, I doubted he'd heard a word of it.

Officer Personowski hauled Rashad to his cruiser, the boy's bare chest covered in weeds and dirt. His shorts fell around his ankles, and nobody bothered to pull them up for him.

"I'll see you soon, Rashad," I promised then shut the cruiser door on his sullen face.

I told Personowski I would come by the county lockup to question Rashad in the morning. "Something I need to do first."

"Knock yourself out. This boy ain't going nowhere soon. He tries to run with them pants, he's gonna fall on his face."

HARDESTON

Bernie Hardeston checked his rearview mirror frequently while he drove to his—cue the maniacal laugh—secret lab. *Secret lab.*

Even the idea of having a secret lab made him giggle, even though paranoia bugs crawled up his spine. They were generated either by a cocaine hangover or the real possibility he was being followed. Late-afternoon sun threw shadows across the rural two-lane highway. Browsing cattle nosed grass on the other side of barbed-wire fences while turkey buzzards overhead wheeled and soared, lifted on warm air currents.

The absurd humor inherent in his possession of a "secret lab" thereby casting himself in the role as a mad scientist never failed to bring a sneering smile of self-derision to his lips. Yes, Bernard Hardeston, PhD Molecular Biology, PhD Virology, former Associate Head of Virology at Harvard's Program in Virology, former executive committee member of Emory's Immunology and Molecular Pathogenesis Graduate Program, former professor at the University of Maryland Baltimore's Molecular Microbiology and Immunology Graduate School, had a secret fucking lab. All he lacked was a hunchback assistant to complete the picture of an evil-genius loony scientist.

As labs went, his was... less than perfect. It was constructed in a metal building next to a rock quarry deep in the asshole of the world known as Texas. He'd bought the property with the last of his savings. His bank account, so robust back in the heady days at Harvard, had been pillaged by one unjustified termination after another and the subsequent periods of unemployment. He had been forced to pilfer, purloin, or otherwise fraudulently procure the equipment and instruments he required from the pathetic Jefferson Davis Biology Department, which he now headed.

His deep baritone rumbled in the quiet interior of his Prius as he deliberately misquoted a famous verse from the Book of Samuel. "Oh, how the mighty have fallen, and the weapons of war *have* not perished!"

Not hardly. Not yet, anyway.

Hardeston glanced in the rearview mirror again. The highway remained clear as far as he could see. For several days, he'd been unable to shake the impression of being watched. Followed. With more frequency than coincidence could explain, a black Cadillac SUV had appeared and trailed him for miles before disappearing.

Were his investors getting nervous? Would Rogers have him tailed? He snorted. *Are Catholics closet cannibals?*

They wanted his product. They wanted Siren's Tears. And Friday, they were coming to get it.

"But will I let them have it?" he asked himself. Again. That question had haunted him more and more often lately. His first impression of Rogers had turned out to be completely wrong. Instead of a resistance fighter like himself, equally committed to breaking the stranglehold of capitalism wrapped around the necks of the working people, Rogers had revealed himself to be in tune with the anti-Western values of the radical mullahs, motivated by the more bloodthirsty passages of the Koran. In other words, Roger was an Islamic terrorist.

Although many of their goals were similar on the surface, Hardeston had no patience for religious fundamentalism of any stripe, be it Muslim, Baptist, or Wiccan. *And just how did someone named David Rogers become aligned with—and radicalized by—fundamentalist Islamic terrorism?* Hardeston grunted and shook off the thought. It didn't matter. Facts were facts.

He checked the rearview mirror. *Clear.*

If Rogers took delivery of the three dozen canisters of aerosolized virus, as promised, would he target Wall Street and their complicit parasites in the government, or would his victims be more... indiscriminate? Terrorists had a tendency to favor soft targets. Average citizens. The very people Hardeston intended to free from their oppressors with precise, targeted strikes.

The entrance to the rock quarry was coming up. Hardeston slowed and put on his blinker. He tapped the brakes and waited for a pulpwood truck to blow past from the other direction. The truck's pressure wave rocked his little car, and he hissed at the blundering giant before pulling in and stopping at the chain-link gate.

What was it to be? Give them what they wanted and stand by while they killed innocents with his life's work? Or hide the canisters and deny the terrorists their new weapon? Hardeston wasn't certain he had the fortitude or resources to carry out the strikes himself. He definitely preferred not to. Using Rogers's network had seemed the perfect solution—Bernie's brains and David's muscles. Hardeston knew he was no action figure, being more the cerebral genius behind the scenes than the cutting edge of the war against the one percent.

But now he was having doubts about his tactical partners. Serious doubts.

He unlocked the gate and swung it back on squealing hinges. "Decision time, Bernie."

ON THE WAY BACK FROM Whitehouse, I detoured through Kilgore. A few doors down from the charming Colonial lair of the handsome and smug David Rogers, I jockeyed the Expedition into a space barely big enough to fit the big truck. The sun had burned off all the clouds overhead, and only the shade of the post oak I parked under saved me from baking into a biscuit. A line of dark thunderheads built up in the west, so far away they were only a prayer of rain.

Three houses past Rogers's place, a team of men mowed and edged a lawn with casually efficient speed. The roar and buzz of their equipment filled the street with noise.

I didn't have a plan. The best I could hope for was that a big truck with a sign proclaiming "Bioweapon on Board" would pull up in front of Rogers's place and drop off a shipment of test tubes filled with weaponized rabies. I was either wasting a colossal amount of time while melting into a puddle of goo, or I would come up... ah, Aces High on surveillance. I was hoping to repeat the luck I'd had with Rashad.

The afternoon ground toward evening, with no stunning clues dropping from the sky. The letter carrier walked her beat in shorts and a sweat-blotched blouse. Two hours later, the lawn men packed up, shared some water from their orange cooler, and drove away, pulling a rattling trailer of equipment. Shadows seeped across front yards as the sun dropped behind dark clouds. A steak broiled over an open fire, and I slow-roasted in my own juices and waited. The mysterious grill man had more meat on the flames, and my stomach was complaining about it. Reba McEntire's "Turn on the Radio" wailed from a nearby house.

At dusk, Rogers came out of his house, jingling a set of keys in his hand. I climbed out of the Expedition and stood next to the fender, where he couldn't miss me. Rogers made a beeline for a Corvette parked on the curb, but when he glanced my way, he did a double-take and stopped. He jiggled the keys in his hand for a moment, watching me, then started my way.

I leaned against the hood and waited while Rogers weaved between parked cars. He wore khaki cargo shorts and a green polo. Topsiders on his feet, no socks. *No doubt what all hip twenty-something Chechen drug dealers are wearing these days.*

He stopped an arm's length away. "You were at my house the other day. What do you want?"

I stared into his brown eyes for a beat, hoping for a tell or a flicker. Something to show me I had him agitated. I tilted my head to one side and squinted. "Visiting your beautiful neighborhood, Mr. Rogers."

His eyelids twitched in confusion. "Why are you here? Seems like a waste of taxpayer dollars, keeping Myrtle Street safe." His black hair ruffled in the slight breeze and fell perfectly across his forehead.

"Can you say 'rabies,' Mr. Rogers?"

"Rabies—" Another eye twitch, this one looked more like surprise. "What?"

"Sorry that wasn't clear." I spoke slowly, as if to a small child. "Do you know anything about a bioweapon being produced that causes rabies?"

He put his hands in his pockets. Playing it cool. The pulse jumping in his throat gave him away. "I have no idea what you're talking about."

"Uh huh. I don't believe you, son."

Rogers smirked and shook his head. "If you're going to arrest me, go ahead. If not, I have places I need to be."

It was tempting. *Arrest him now and look for evidence later? Would a judge give me a warrant based on the rumor this kid was a meth dealer and might have a connection with a biology professor? Would pigs build a spaceship and fly to Mars?*

"No," I admitted. "I'm not arresting you. Not yet."

He smirked. "Have a nice day."

Rogers pivoted and sauntered back to his Corvette, looking both ways before he crossed the street.

Clearly, I had terrified him.

Chapter 13

FRIDAY MORNING, I FOUND Rita in the task force conference room, hunched over her laptop. I paused in the doorway and watched her for a beat. She had tamed her bushy hair with a white clip, pinching it into a bunch at the back. A sleeveless white blouse contrasted with her olive-toned skin, and a small Star of David dangled from a gold chain around her neck.

She registered my presence with an arched eyebrow. "You gonna hold up that doorframe all day?"

"Just wondering if you beat solitaire yet."

"FreeCell. I'm ninety-five percent on FreeCell."

"Not without cheating."

I settled into a chair across the table and gave her a rundown of my adventures of the previous day, ending with Rashad Phillips's arrest. "By the time I got back to Rashad, his public defender was already talking plea deal with the ADA."

"Good for you," she said with real sincerity. Given her penchant for dry sarcasm, it was sometimes hard to tell when Goldman was on the level. "I found a couple of interesting things while you were out playing cops and killers."

"Tell me."

Rita tapped keys so fast, it sounded like Chiclets spilling from a box. "I did a criminal history, civil history, UCC filings, sexual offender, credit header..." She trailed off, lost in cyberworld, and I stayed quiet to let her concentrate. Dark eyes flicked back and forth across the screen, processing information at light speed. Her lips were puffed out in a slight frown, looking full and ripe—

Jesus wept. Stop, stop, stop. Goldman had somehow become an itch in an uncomfortable place. Scratching it, though, could lead to real trouble.

"Here it is." Rita read from her screen without looking up. "Dr. Hardeston has been a bad boy. Two hits for possession, one with intent to sell, probation, no jail. One hit for rape, pled down to assault. One for theft of property, no time served."

"Good Lord, how'd he get a job as a teacher?"

"He's been fired from one job after another, bounced around the country." She shrugged. "You look at it like this: he was a big shot at Harvard, and now he's teaching at a jumped-up junior college in East Texas. Maybe that's punishment enough, right?"

"Anything else?"

"Property records show he owns a rock quarry on County Road 294." She looked up at me. "Where the fuck is that? And why would a biology professor need a rock quarry?"

"Where on 294?"

"I look like a Michelin guide to East Bumfuck? Here." She tapped laptop keys, paused, then swiveled the machine to show me a map.

I squinted. "Not far from Lake Cherokee."

"And not far from this airport. What's this? East Texas Regional? Yeah, East Texas Regional. Wonder if they have anything bigger than a biplane out there."

"What say we go take a look at this rock quarry? Or would you rather stay here and collate reports?"

"I love reports. What's wrong with reports?"

"I thought you wanted to be an action hero, like me."

Goldman snorted. "Sure, I'll go. You wanna call some of the guys, bring some backup? Oh, no, wait. What am I saying? I forgot my head there." Rita grabbed her jacket and pulled it on. "Come on, cowboy. Let's go see a rock quarry. Another thing off my bucket list."

THE QUARRY GATE STOOD open, pushed all the way to one side. *Open gate's an invitation to come visit, right?*

Gravel crackled under the Expedition's tires when I pulled off the blacktop highway. The satellite map I'd seen on Goldman's laptop showed the tree-lined drive carving a path from the road for about two hundred yards. A dog leg at about the halfway point curved right then left. I couldn't see what lay ahead until I turned the final curve and came to an open, unpaved yard. A metal warehouse reflected the afternoon sunlight, an eye-burning shade of bright white. A black Escalade was parked in front, facing out, next to a green Prius.

I tapped the brakes and crunched to a stop. The instant I did, a guy stepped out of the Escalade. He swung around the Cadillac's door, bringing up an automatic weapon.

"Down!" Rita yelled.

We both ducked for cover at the same moment. Our heads cracked together across the console. Bullets smacked the Expedition like hail, shattering the windshield and hammering the front of the car in a deadly rattle.

Rita barked a curse.

"Hold on!" Bits of glass showered me.

I slapped the shifter into reverse and floored it, fishtailing backward. Piloting with the backup camera, and thanks more to luck than skill, I made it out of the direct line of fire. Steam poured from under the hood. The spiderwebbed safety glass obliterated my view through the windshield.

I popped my head up long enough to look back and slide the big SUV around the first curve. Speed, gravel, and adrenaline beat me on the second turn. The Expedition slid across the road, bounced off a tree and came shuddering to a halt among the trees. The engine clattered, wheezed, and died. Hazy smoke leaked into the cab.

I smelled smoke.

"Get out!" I snapped at Rita, but she was already moving, pistol in hand.

I went over the seats and wiggled into the back compartment. I had a weapons case bolted into the storage compartment, locked with a keypunch to make it easier to open. I stabbed the code, opened the case, and scooped up my LaRue Tactical in .308 caliber and a vest filled with spare mags.

Like a dumbass, I'd left my HK on the kitchen table, disassembled for cleaning. I vowed right then to never leave home without the HK. I bailed from the back of the Expedition's lift gate.

Rita's 9mm barked out a steady rhythm, punctuated by the chatter of a military rifle on full auto. I slapped in a thirty-round magazine and pulled the bolt, racking a round. Peeking around the side of the SUV, I glimpsed movement through the trees—a flash of a guy in a suit, running with a weapon in his hands. The carbine banged my shoulder three times. The guy went to ground. Maybe hit, maybe not.

Heart thumping, I kept an eye on the spot where he dropped.

"Rita! You good?"

"Peachy!"

Her voice came from somewhere to my right, on the other side of the smoking Expedition. White-and-black clouds billowed from under the hood and through the open rear hatch. A flickering glow from the passenger compartment indicated a merry little blaze had started there.

Possibly a fuel line had taken a round and sprayed gas on the exhaust manifold. Possibly it was just a bad day for me.

My cell phone sat in the cup holder between the seats.

I scrambled toward the driver's door, going for the phone. Bullets pinged the side of the car and drove me back. I ran around the other side, keeping the SUV between me and the shooter. Inside, the center console was empty. My phone had tumbled God only knew where inside the car. Dig into a burning car for a missing phone?

Skip it. Use Goldman's phone.

Rita had snugged up behind a deadfall. She scanned forward, pistol tracking like a turret, studying the forest, focused and intent. What a deadly little warrior she was turning out to be. I ran over and flopped down beside her.

"I think there's four of them," Goldman said. "They're moving in good cover formation."

A burst of fire chewed bark and clipped leaves a foot over my head. I ducked. Rita never moved.

Crack! Crack! She snapped off two shots. Someone cried out, and Rita bared her teeth in a feral grin. Voices called in a Slavic language. *Russian, maybe? Or Chechen? Do Chechens have their own language? I'll have to look that up. Later.*

"I think we found the bad guys," I said. "Where's your phone?"

"In my bag." She never moved her eyes from downrange.

"Where's your bag?"

She jerked her head toward the car. "In the backseat. Why?"

The Expedition picked that moment to go up with a boom and a whoosh. Flames roiled skyward. Heat and pressure washed over us.

"That's why."

"Well, don't this suck." She cracked off two more shots. "Fuck. Missed."

Another burst probed our position. The zip and crack of bullets passed close overhead, smacking into the trees around us, setting my teeth on edge.

"These guys are mutts; I can tell you that," Rita said.

"Nuts?"

"Mutts."

Bullets smacked our deadfall barricade. Two goons jumped from concealment, ran a few paces, and dove to the ground. They were up and down before I could draw a bead. Moments later, they popped up from a different position and fired a burst while the other two scrambled forward. They were coming from left and right, spread wide to make targeting harder.

"These mutts seem capable," I said. We had minutes left maybe before we would be flanked, pinned down, and shot to shit.

Rita snorted. "Let's hope they don't have grenades."

"Goldman, some days you can be such a Suzy Sunshine."

We had to move to break up the assault, and by not giving the bad guys a single position to outflank us. I low-crawled to the right, behind and past Rita, and moved deeper into the forest, breathing in the damp musk of pine needles, dust, and leaves. I snaked my way behind an enormous oak. Its base surrounded by secondary growth offered concealment, if not protection. I eased the LaRue into firing position. Forcing deep breaths, I let myself go loose. Poised and wary. One guy with a buzzed haircut, in a dark suit, burst from cover then juked right. He dropped before I could fire. I lost him in the undergrowth. I scanned the brush with my scope. A flash of pale skin amid the green caught my eye. I zeroed in on Buzz as he eased sideways.

Only the top half of his head was visible. Forty yards. The crosshairs jittered then steadied. *Breathe in. Half out. Squeeze.*

The rifle bucked. Pink mist sprayed. Recoil obliterated the sight picture. I dropped to the ground as return fire chopped the leaves and vines around my hidey-hole. Bits of vegetation sprinkled down. I hunkered behind my tree.

It was a beautiful spring day in the woods. Moderate temperature. Light, fluffy clouds in a blue sky. Refreshing breeze bringing the smell of green and growing things.

Bap-bap-bap-bap!

Gunfire.

"Another beautiful day in the forest," I muttered.

Lead hornets zipped past me. My sheltering tree shivered with hits, and more leaves pattered down. The probing burst might have been seeking my flesh or attempting to flush me out. I decided to flush.

"Goldman! Tactical retreat!"

"Gotcha!" Her voice echoed through the trees.

"Go!" I poked the LaRue around my sheltering tree and squeezed off steady, evenly spaced shots, not aiming. I sensed more than saw Goldman dash and dodge away through the woods. With nothing but a flicker of motion, she was gone. The volume of fire from the goon squad tripled. Controlled bursts rattled out from everywhere, forcing me to pull back as my oak took a pounding.

"Cable! Go!" Rita's SIG started to bark.

I jumped up, took two running steps—

Whap! The side of my head took a mule-kick wallop and—

I was face down in the dirt. *What the hell? What just happened?*

I shouldn't be on the ground. This isn't right. I have... somewhere... I need to be.

Blood splattered the carpet of leaves and twigs. The right side of my head flashed from frozen numbness to a blinding white heat.

Who's bleeding?

Why am I...?

I pushed up on one arm. The earth tilted. I rolled over. For such a bright, sunny day, night had fallen quickly. The canopy of rustling greenery grew dark.

I needed to catch my breath. *I'll lie here for a while... then I'll move.*

I OPENED MY EYES. NAUSEA clenched my stomach, and vomit threatened to come up. Above me, a green kaleidoscope whirled. The ground seemed liquid, like a waterbed. My head throbbed as though pulsing rubber mallets thumped the inside of my temples. I had been unconscious; that much was obvious.

How long?

Gunfire nattered like angry woodpeckers, out for blood. It took a real effort to remember where I was and who was shooting at me. I couldn't have been out long, or I would have woken up dead.

Oh, no. I rolled to my side in the nick of time, ralphing up my breakfast.

A harsh laugh froze me to the spot. Stepping from the trees, a small guy in a poorly fitted black suit held a cut-down AK-74, the commando model of the popular AK-47. He grinned, showing me bad teeth, and said something nasty in his own language. The bore of his weapon lined up with my forehead.

I tried to move. *Nope.* All lines between my brain and body were tangled. I managed a feeble flopping.

Four ounces of trigger pull, and I would be dead.

Crack!

A black hole appeared in the Chechen's forehead. He dropped like old laundry.

Rita rushed out of the brush, pistol in one hand. She grabbed a wad of my shirt with the other. She tugged. Her feet went out from under her, and she fell on her butt. A laugh wanted to bubble up past the queasy, spinning sensation in my guts.

"C'mon, you big ox," she panted. "Give me a hand here, would ya?"

Bullets slapped the air over our heads. Groaning, I rolled onto all fours and baby-crawled a few feet before I could get my feet under me. Rita shoved her shoulder under my arm, and together, we stumbled deeper into the forest.

We ran maybe ten feet before—

"Rifle!" I said. "I forgot my rifle."

I turned to go back for the LaRue, and the tree next to me exploded, bark chips flying as bullets slapped it.

"Fuck the rifle," Rita snapped.

"Fuck the rifle," I panted. "Agreed."

We found a deep cut leading to a creek, about four feet deep, overgrown with briars and covered by fallen limbs. Perfect shelter if you were on the run from Chechen terrorists in East Texas.

I played that back in my head: *Chechen terrorists in East Texas? Un-frickin-believable.*

We wriggled and grunted, sweated and cursed until we settled into our makeshift foxhole. We faced back the way we'd come, weapons ready. Goldman changed magazines, and I readied my pistol, steadying my aim across a brace of timber. I blinked sweat and blood out of my eyes, gasping hard for air. The trees wobbled in and out of focus, and my head throbbed.

"The hell happened?" I whispered.

"You got shot in the head," Goldman muttered without looking at me. "That's the good news and the bad."

My hat was gone, the scalp over my right ear burned, and hot spikes of pain fired into my skull. I touched the wound gingerly and winced. Blood soaked the side of my head, wet and tacky. At the range once, I'd fired a .223, and the super-hot spent shell had ejected, bounced off a support beam at some crazy angle, and snagged behind my ear. That burned half as bad as this did.

I touched it again. "Ow!"

"Shh," Rita hissed. "And stop touching that."

Brush moved to our front as one of the Chechen killers glided forward, sliding from cover to cover like some kind of Spec Ops character. He was at long range for a pistol, so we let him come on.

He had my LaRue slung over his shoulder.

Now that *pisses me off. You are so dead.*

I tried to regulate my breathing and focus over the three dots of my sight picture.

He froze about thirty yards away, reacting to a barked command from the rear. His answer sounded like a Slavic version of "Aw, c'mon, Mom, just let me play a little while longer?"

The response displeased him, because he threw an angry glare in our direction then retreated as cautiously as he'd approached. Common sense said I should stay put. I was in no shape for a gunfight. I should wait. Right here.

Rita grabbed my sleeve and hauled me back when I started up. "Be still, cowboy," she hissed. "We're a little outgunned here."

I settled back, and we waited in silence for five minutes, then ten. My head cleared as minutes passed. A car engine revved then receded in the distance, leaving the forest in peace and quiet. A mockingbird settled in the brush to my right, twittering like mad, calling us names in bird-speak.

"You think they're gone?" Rita broke the stillness, her voice barely a murmur.

"Why don't you go see?"

"I'm the girl, Cable. You go see."

"Since when are you a girl?"

Creeping and crawling, it took us almost thirty minutes to make our way back to the clearing at the quarry building. The smell of burnt plastic drifted by, and a trace of smoke in the air indicated my car still smoldered. No black Escalade waited in the gravel lot, and the office door stood wide open. The Prius sat on four flat tires.

"Finally, we're alone at last."

"Funny guy, Sam. Don't quit your day job."

"And give up this excitement?"

We swept into the office hard and fast, like a real life professional law enforcement team. A bare and empty office greeted us. It swayed and twisted under my feet. I braced a hand on the desk and held on to whatever was left in my stomach.

The warehouse attached to the office was empty, as well.

Except for the guy taped to the chair.

The one bleeding all over the floor.

Chapter 14

"YOU ASK, 'WHAT ABOUT the innocent bystanders?' But we are in a time of revolution. If you are a bystander, you are not innocent." – Abbie Hoffman, Revolution for the Hell of It

"I THINK IT'S HARDESTON," I said.

"The professor?"

"Or the Chechens have killed Santa."

He was strapped to a rolling chair, between racks on one side and tables of lab equipment on the other. His head lolled back, his scraggly hair standing out as though he'd been shocked. Blood stained his beard, and his upper body was a nest of white hair saturated with blood. More blood stained his beard. Scraggly hair stood up from his scalp, as if he'd been electrocuted. The chair sat between racks on one side and tables of lab equipment on the other. A rash of burn holes on his chest and belly showed he had been tortured before they shot him. His fingers were swollen and purple, like they'd been crushed in a vise.

I thought he was dead until blood pumped from a hole in his chest.

Goldman beat me to the old man's side. "Cable, see if you can find something to compress this wound." She pressed her palm against the pulsing hole in his chest.

I plucked a lab coat off the back of a chair, wadded it up, and handed it to Goldman.

"Who did this to you?" I looked into his eyes, but they were vacant and lost.

He was going fast, face pale and beaded in sweat. He mumbled something I couldn't catch.

I put my nose up close to Hardeston's ear and yelled so he could hear it, no matter which dark tunnel he traveled. "Where's the virus?"

His head lolled to the side, and he looked at the empty shelves and slurred out, "Gone. All gone."

"Who took it? The guys that shot you?"

Blood soaked through the lab coat Rita pressed over Hardeston's wound. The guy was as white as a cotton ball. A wad of keys, a wallet, and other pocket crap lay jumbled together in a pile on the table next to him, along with, wonder of wonders, a cheap prepaid cell phone.

I snagged the burner phone off the pile and glared at the tiny screen. "Dammit. This ain't my day."

"What?"

"No service."

"You gotta be kidding me."

"Help?" Hardeston whispered the word, looking bewildered. His eyes glazed over. The old man was on the big old Slip'n Slide to hell.

"What happened here?" Rita said. "Why'd they shoot you?"

"I tried," he whispered.

I leaned closer to hear.

His breath puffed against my ear. "I tried... tried... to hide it..."

It was three or four miles to the closest phone. An hour walk, at least. The professor didn't have sixty seconds, let alone sixty minutes.

"Hide the bioweapon?" I asked.

"Siren's... Tears..." he gasped out.

Rita and I traded a shrug. "The virus?" she asked. "You call it Siren's Tears?"

He responded with a weak, jerky nod.

"You created it?"

Another nod.

"We need to get some help, Rita. 'We' meaning you." My legs shook. I wouldn't make it to the end of the driveway without passing out.

"I'll go." Goldman gestured for me to take up the pressure on the wadded lab coat while she took Hardeston's phone, which she tucked in a pocket. "Maybe I'll pick up a cell tower on the way."

"Worth a shot."

As she jogged out the front, I checked Hardeston. His life force was fading. Blood squished under my hands as I adjusted my grip on the wadded cotton mess. I gave up and tried to make him comfortable, cutting the tape off his arms and legs with my pocket knife and easing him to the ground. I folded the coat to a clean spot and reapplied it to the wound.

"How much was there, Hardeston? How much of the virus?"

His eyes focused on me, as if seeing me for the first time. "Thirty-six." He coughed. Blood coated the inside of his mouth and stained his teeth red.

"Thirty-six what? Ounces, grams, pills?"

"Cans."

"How much is in a fucking can?"

A faint smile, lips pale. "Enough... to end... the oppression." His raspy voice was barely audible. Another coughing spasm gripped him, and his eyes grew wide. Blood fountained from his mouth and splattered his face.

"Hold on, Hardeston. Don't die on me." I pushed on the sopping cloth, but there was something major nicked inside him. All the pressure in the world wouldn't save the man. The pulse in his neck twittered at high speed; his heart hammered to pump blood that wasn't there. My voice shook, and my eyes turned hot, trying to burn a hole through the man's pupils and light up whatever humanity remained inside. "How much, Dr. Hardeston? How big are the cans?"

The old man rolled his head to one side and jerked his chin to point. I followed his direction and saw a silver canister lying under the shelving. Similar in size to a can of WD40, it had a weird nozzle on top, with a dial that looked like a timer.

His breath rattled, his mouth moved with unsaid words. Hardeston died then with the confused look of a child whose balloon had floated away. All the pity I had bled out in the face of the horror this man had caused. All I had left for him was contempt.

"Stupid jackass," I told his corpse. "I hope they find a special corner of hell and roast your testicles for a few thousand years."

THE SHELVES INSIDE Hardeston's lab were as barren as a politician's promise. Half-empty bottles of bleach. An opened box of disposable gloves. Junk.

On the lab side of the building, a worktable ran the length of the room from front to back, lit by a bank of fluorescent strips. High-tech equipment covered the table, of which I recognized only a centrifuge and a rack of test tubes. A machine with stereoscopic lenses and adjusting knobs might have been a microscope, assuming a microscope had carnal knowledge of a Cray supercomputer and had produced Roboscope of the twenty-second century.

In the back of the warehouse, I found a living area with a kitchen, a cot, and a bathroom, complete with shower. I washed my hands in the sink and splashed water on my face. The goon in the mirror spooked me. The skin over my right ear bled from a slash as long as my finger. Caked blood covered the right side of my face and stained my shirt collar. Cleaning the wound would tear open the dried and congealed mesh, and that would hurt worse than getting my nuts caught on a barbed wire fence. I left it alone. Instead, I wandered to the sleeping area, foot-heavy and drained. I slumped on the cot...

And a paramedic shined a light in my eyes and asked me how many fingers he was holding up. I showed him one finger—the middle one—and he said over his shoulder to someone else, "Probably a concussion. Let's get him to the hospital."

And that was the last I knew about anything for a while.

AT THE HOSPITAL, THEY shaved the side of my head into a one-sided Mohawk and installed a zipper over my ear. Thirty-two stitches. I looked like a punk rock Frankenstein. They kept me overnight to see how many times they could wake me up in a twelve-hour period—a lot—and determine if my pupils reacted correctly to light—they did—and that my insurance would cover the bill—that was questionable. It must have been close enough, because they let me keep the stitches.

My head throbbed, and a permanent ache had settled behind my right eye. I wore a hospital gown and needed to pee. I had no car, and the pill rollers had told me not to drive anyway, so Goldman said she would drive me home. I couldn't remember when she'd appeared at the hospital, but she was in my room when I opened my eyes.

"Nice haircut," she said, and went back to flipping through the pages of a hospital copy of *Vanity Fair*. At some point, she'd gone home and changed into jeans and a V-neck blouse with the sleeves pushed up to mid-forearm.

"Where do we stand?" I croaked. I drank water from the sippy cup and tried again. "Where do we stand with the case?"

Goldman tossed her magazine to the side. "With our thumbs up our butts, cowboy." She puffed a lock of hair off her forehead. It fell back. "We have to infer Tarasov and his people have Hardie-boy's little spray cans full of misery and destruction. If the empty canister we found in the warehouse is typical, then they're all equipped with a time-release gizmo, which means they can set it and forget it. They leave the can in a shopping mall's air vent or on the subway, set the dial, and walk away. Ten minutes later, the air is scented with rabies."

"And hundreds of people die."

"Thousands, more like." Goldman toggled her head from side to side. Her neck crackled like popcorn. "Good news is, the eggheads don't think it'll spread too far. It burns out so fast, infection'll be limited. According to the paper trail Hardeston left behind, they think the mad doctor designed it to take out very specific targets, like Exxon's headquarters, or maybe set a few cans off in the Capitol Building in D.C. He was a hippie of the Abbie Hoffman, Saul Alinsky stripe. Power to the people, even if you have to kill a few along the way."

"Any leads?"

She shrugged. "A few. Nothing solid enough to jump on yet. I put Fiegenbaum onto your guy, Rogers. Maybe he'll find a link there we can use."

"Do me a favor? Go ask the warden how long they plan to keep me here. We need to get moving."

Goldman gave me a fishy look but said, "Sure," and left the room.

I set about climbing out of bed and tottering into the washroom. Damn, I was weak. The room tilted, and the floor felt uneven. I held on to my IV pole and shuffled barefoot. Nausea stalked me from around the corner. I made it to the bathroom in one prolonged totter. Mission accomplished. The walk back seemed to go better, but I was still happy to lie down and let the thumping in my temples recede from kettle drums to bongos.

The bedside clock told me it was ten o'clock on Saturday morning. Our little drama at the rock quarry had gone down sixteen hours ago. The Chechens could be anywhere from Albuquerque to Atlanta by now, armed with thirty-six cans of time-released terror, and here I was, quivering in a hospital bed, trying not to let my head fall off my neck.

Is Rogers the connection we need? If he is, how do we find him? And how long do we have before the terrorists release their deadly spray of weaponized rabies and kill thousands of people?

THEY CUT ME LOOSE AT noon. A friend of mine—a fellow DPS trooper—brought me a change of clothes from my apartment, along with a box of .45 ammo and some toiletries. I washed up in the tiny hospital shower while holding firmly to the rail and keeping my stitches dry with a shower cap. I was in no condition to carry a weapon, but no one stopped me, so I strapped up like always. Cleaned, dressed, properly armed, and mildly medicated, I was ready to get the hell out of the hospital.

A male nurse pushed me out to the patient dump-off area, and we waited for Goldman to pull up in her—

"You gotta be kidding me." My lower jaw came unhinged.

"What?" Rita Goldman stood by the door of a miniature yellow roller skate. Her eyebrows perked up in a look of innocence. "You don't like my Solstice? C'mon, get in."

I folded myself into the tiny car, my knees around my ears and head touching the liner. I felt like GI Joe stuffed in a Tonka toy, joints twisted every which way. We took off at Mach 1.2, my butt zooming about two inches off the ground.

"You hungry?" Goldman asked.

Oddly enough, I was. The queasiness had left me, and my head seemed to want to stay glued together. I gave her directions to a burger joint in downtown Longview.

Rita drove with all the care and deliberation of a hamster on crack. She had a steel-jawed determination to get in front of every knot of cars and powered us into tiny gaps, leaping from lane to lane. My head kept banging into the window, setting off concussion grenades inside my skull.

Manfully, I refused to whimper.

"That guy, Rogers," she said after slipping in front of a Volvo SUV with enough room for a sheet of paper, "has crook written all over him. Fiegenbaum called me, all excited 'cause he thinks the kid might be a blood relation to Tarasov."

"Seriously?"

"As a coma, cowboy."

"Don't mention comas. I was too close to one already today."

We stopped at a red light. When it turned green, Rita bolted away as if shot from a gun. My noggin banged the seat back, and I groaned. Goldman ignored my plight. "He's supposed to call me back in a few. Fiegenbaum. Let me know what's what."

"Over there." I pointed.

Goldman slapped the gearshift and power-slid the little car around a corner of the town square. We braked to a stop in a slot in front of the restaurant. I braced a hand on the dash to keep from being thrown through the windshield. My headache was back—with a vengeance.

"Gawd," she said. "I'm starved."

"Funny, I'm not so hungry anymore."

We went inside and captured a booth by the front window. The midday sun warmed the seat and helped burn away the chilly after-effects of a near-death experience. My stomach grumbled at the smell of frying food and meat sizzling on the grill. Rita flashed me a look with her dark-brown eyes that sent a tingle down my back.

It's good to be alive.

Goldman's phone rang, and she glanced at it. "It's Fiegenbaum. Maybe he has something."

Chapter 15

GOLDMAN PUT HER PHONE on speaker and held it between us. "G'head," she told Agent Fiegenbaum.

"I don't know how you found him, Ranger, but David Rogers is definitely connected to the Chechens." The senior agent's baritone squawked out, tinny and overly loud in the quiet restaurant. Goldman turned down the volume, and we huddled over the phone in time to hear him say, "Get this: he is the nephew of Sergei Tarasov."

Goldman's eyes widened, no doubt matching my own.

Fiegenbaum continued. "Tarasov's sister, Yelena, married Akhmad Rostopovich in 1960 while still in Chechnya. Akhmad legally changed the family name to Rogers when he emigrated to Houston in 1982. Ever since then, the newly created Arnold and Elaine Rogers have kept a very low profile, paid their taxes, joined the country club, and stayed off our radar screen. Their firstborn son, David, attended Jefferson Davis College, graduating last year with a degree in business. Obviously, this is where he made a connection with Hardeston and, if the rumors you heard are true, where he currently oversees the Tarasov drug business in East Texas."

"Wait one." Our food arrived, and Goldman put the special agent on hold while the waitress set out our plates. The smell of grilled hamburger hit me with primal intensity, and my mouth filled with saliva. Hamburger. Good. Man eat now.

"Here's how I think the dots connect," I said once Goldman toggled off mute. "David Rogers goes to work for Uncle T, running meth and buying into the old man's radical Islamic fundamentalism. Is Daddy part of the equation, or is it just little Davey? We don't know, right? Somehow David recruits his hippie-dippy college professor under a false flag, claiming he wants to 'strike a blow' for the people. Sound right so far?"

"Agreed," Fiegenbaum said, and Goldman nodded.

"Hardeston creates the virus then gets cold feet. Maybe he wants more money. Maybe he decides mass murder is bad... For whatever reason, he tries to hold back on the delivery, so Rogers and his people torture the old man into giving up the virus." A thought occurred to me. "By the way, Hardeston called it Siren's Tears. That make sense to anybody?"

After a pause, Fiegenbaum's voice intoned, "'What potions have I drunk of siren tears, distilled from limbecks foul as hell within...' Shakespeare."

Rita's jaw dropped in exaggerated surprise. "Fuck me," she mouthed. I was surprised as well; I didn't see the senior agent as a Shakespeare buff.

"And for Final Jeopardy," I said, "where has David Rogers gone, and what do he and his uncle plan to do with thirty-six canisters of time-released virus?"

"We're sitting on Rogers's house now," the senior agent said. "We'll give it until five o'clock today. If he doesn't show up by then, we'll execute a search warrant and tear the place apart. If we're lucky, we'll find answers to those questions, Ranger Cable."

"Five o'clock," Goldman said. "We'll be there." She thumbed off the phone and set it aside.

I was already digging in to my basket of fries, clamping together six at a time and stuffing them into my face.

Goldman's lips quirked in mock disgust. "Getting shot must give you an appetite."

"Breathing gives me an appetite," I said around a mouthful.

Goldman took a bite as savage as my own, except without the snarling and dripping. Take away the woman's hangup over clothes, and she was feminine as a Craftsman wrench.

"Did you always want to be a fed?" I asked after I'd punished my lunch enough to think straight.

"Nuh-uh. I wanted to be a marine biologist, but it turns out that I get seasick in the bathtub."

"That must have been a blow."

"No, it was in calm water, no telling what would happen in a blow..."

"Yer fun-nee," I said in my best hick imitation. "Seriously, why FBI?"

"What's a nice girl like me doing in federal law enforcement?" Rita smiled. Sipped her iced tea. She looked outside and spoke to the window. "I was getting my law degree at NYC when I saw the Towers go down. I never saw nothin' like that, Sam. Nothin'." She glanced at me, at the table, then the restaurant, eyes darting around. "You gotta know, I grew up in Queens, on the flight path to La Guardia Airport, a neighborhood so rough, the cockroaches carried high-caliber weapons. You grow up hard in a neighborhood like mine. But nothing makes you strong enough to see something like that."

"Must have been a bad time."

She snorted. "I lost friends that day. After that, I just wanted to make a difference, ya know?"

"Yep."

"I applied for the FBI next day. I knew they liked accounting degrees, so it was easy. I must have filled an EEOC quota, huh?"

"Jewish American Princess? That's an Equal Opportunity category?"

"Yeah, right? Who knew?"

I fiddled with the three-sided advertising thing on the table featuring pictures of apple and key lime pies and something called Death by Chocolate cake. "Hey, I never said thanks, by the way... for saving my ass out there at the quarry." I took a sip of tea.

"What? We keeping score now? I think we're past that stage, don't you?"

"Yeah, I guess."

I must have made a face, because Rita asked, "What's a matter, cowboy? Don't like it when a woman saves your macho ass?" She patted my hand. "Don't worry, sweetie. It'll be our little secret."

I glanced at her hand, where it still rested against mine, and she pulled it back. She had red-lacquered nails and long fingers too elegant to be playing with guns. I sneaked a look, but Rita paid no attention, watching the other diners. Her thick black hair was loose again today, falling to her shoulders in a shaggy pile. A simple pearl stud gleamed from her earlobe when she pushed her hair back. The impulse to run my fingers through her hair came over me. I shook it off. *What the hell is wrong with me?*

"Wah... uh-hum—" I cleared my throat and tried again. "Well, thanks anyway."

She smiled and pinned me with her dark eyes. "No problem."

The waitress cleared away our empty plastic baskets filled with their residue of oily red-and-white-checked paper liners. We declined dessert but took a refill on iced tea.

Rita regarded me with a speculative look. "So tell me, cowboy..."

"What?"

"Why aren't you hitched, huh? I'm picturing some big-breasted *shikseh*, barefoot and pregnant, raising a yard full of little Cables."

"Jeez, Goldman, I don't know. How about you, huh? Where's Mr. Goldman?"

"Huh." She shook her head. "In New York. A doctor."

I sat back. "Really?"

"Well... ex-husband. Steven Silverstein. I knew him since high school. Like all good Jewish girls, I dated a boy my parents approved of. We got married our first year in college. A more boring man I have never met."

I played with my straw. "So what happened?"

"What happened? Nothing." She stared out the window, speaking in a subdued voice. "Three years of nothing. A big fucking yawn of a marriage. I think it's all my fault, y'know? Why he's not interested. Then I catch him doing a nurse, at the hospital. We fight, we break up, he sweet-talks me back, yada yada yada." She waved a hand in the air. "You know the rest."

"He did it again?"

"It was either divorce him or shoot him. Close there for a while, but I decided he wasn't worth the bullet."

"Hmm." The comment clearly showed my depth and intelligence. I sucked at my empty cup, draining some of the melted ice water in the bottom. Rita and I traded looks then glanced in different directions. Her presence pulled me like a magnet. Maybe she exuded addictive pheromones that acted on a subliminal level, but I couldn't help thinking about... things I shouldn't have been thinking about. It was deeply disturbing.

Rita scrabbled in her purse and dug out a wad of keys so big, she looked like a maintenance man at a lock factory. "Well, okay, cowboy. By the time we get to Rogers's house, the boys will be about ready to go in. What say we crash that party?"

"Only if I can drive."

"No way in hell."

DAVID ROGERS

Uncle Tarasov had told him to make the first strike loud and ugly. When David presented his plan, his uncle had lit up like a man discovering a one-hundred-dollar bill in an old pair of pants. The dour old bastard actually smiled.

Seven men, all citizens with unassailable identification papers, all committed to jihad, were recruited. David put them on standby two weeks prior to the delivery of the viral agent and sent them to lay low in separate motels in the Dallas suburb of Irving—the city where the stadium of America's Team had once stood. With their prepaid cells always close to hand, the men were told to raise no alarms, cause no trouble, and devote themselves to Allah for victory prayer.

He issued each of them code names, whimsically choosing another icon of American pop culture as source material. His uncle had complained, "You are too flippant, David. Not serious enough for the fight."

"Nothing could be further from the truth, Uncle," he'd argued. "The fire of Islam burns as deeply in my breast as it does in anyone from the Old Country. I would gladly give my own life to further the teachings of the prophet Mohammed and the will of Allah, the Almighty God." He smiled, turning on the charm. "Does Allah command men be grim and humorless? Do his teachings enjoin us to find no joy in irony?"

In that moment of whimsy, he codenamed his fighters Dopey, Grumpy, Sneezy, Bashful, Doc, and Happy. The leader of the strike team, Sleepy, was aptly described because of his hooded eyes and his half-awake appearance. He would provide logistics and support for the six soldiers as they deployed and recover them afterward.

Now, weeks later, Rogers gathered the men for the first time in one of his father's empty rental houses. When he told them the objective and the weapon they would use, the men grinned as one. He went over the outline of the plan then said: "And you will be recovered. This is not a martyr's mission...unless you're caught in the act. If that occurs, you are to spray the contents of the container directly in your face and breathe deeply. You will achieve martyrdom long before the pigs will have a chance to extract information." The double meaning of the word "pigs" sailed over the heads of the gathered men.

Rogers sighed. He had no illusions about the chances of a completely clean mission—some of these men would die. Some might be captured before achieving martyrdom. He had to assume he was burned, either way. He and Marat would not be returning to the house in Kilgore and would forevermore be off the grid, administering and overseeing the deployment of Siren's Tears throughout the United States. *Allah be praised.*

After that, he would fight until caught or killed.

He gestured to Marat. The tall, extremely ugly man issued each of the warriors a canister of Siren's Tears disguised as a can of air freshener. Following that, he added a metered time-release aerosol dispenser. The latter, Rogers had purchased over the internet from a cleaning supply company for forty dollars each. The original intent of the mechanism was to squirt sweet scent to cover the stink of the infidels' shit so their too-polite noses wouldn't be offended.

"If stopped and questioned by the TSA agents," he continued, "explain to them you have trouble with hotel smells and you use the freshener to mask them. If they refuse to allow the dispenser, you must abort the attempt to pass through security and go to the fallback plan. You must continue the mission without passing through security, even if you will be exposed to the pathogen." Rogers instructed the team on how to set the dispensers for five- to fifteen-minute intervals, whichever seemed most appropriate, depending upon their individual targets.

Next, he handed out six sets of e-tickets on various airlines, round trip from Dallas-Fort Worth International to multiple destinations and for random return dates. All departures were scheduled for Monday morning, the day after tomorrow.

"Do not board the planes," he explained again. "Exit the terminals, meet with Sleepy, and return here, where you will be given new IDs and transportation. At some future point, we must assume that you will be identified by agents of the enemy, so you will be hunted night and day. If compromised, you will join Allah by the most expedient means available. Avoid capture at all costs."

A ring of silent, committed faces regarded him. None had spoken. Rogers met the eyes of each man in turn and read nothing there except total conviction. These men would not fail.

"Now," Rogers continued, "here are your individual mission goals."

SPECIAL AGENT FIEGENBAUM jumped the gun, entering Rogers's home a full two hours in advance of his five-o'clock deadline. When Rita and I arrived at Myrtle Street, we found it clogged with FBI and police vehicles from one end to the other. She parked on a side street, hopped from the Pontiac Torture, then waited while I unfolded much more deliberately, moving with an old man's stiffness. Leaning against the car, I dug out the packet of pills they'd given me at the hospital and dry-swallowed a painkiller. A baboon with a rubber mallet pounded me silly whenever I moved my head too fast.

Rita's face scrunched like she was examining a tomato for soft spots. "You okay?"

"No." I straightened with an effort and joined her on the sidewalk. All around us, people stood on their porches or gathered in clumps, watching the live *Cops* episode unfolding in their quiet corner of heaven. "But I'll dance to the tune until the band quits. C'mon."

We found an exhausted Fiegenbaum in front of Rogers's home, directing the removal of boxes of evidence. If he were traveling commercial, the airline would have forced him to check the bags under his eyes as excess luggage. His steel-gray hair had sprung loose from its hardened shell. When he glanced up, I could tell the news wouldn't be good.

"Anything?" Goldman asked.

"The place has been sanitized." The special agent compressed his lips in a grim line. "We're a day late and a million dollars short. All the computers and electronic media are gone, including the phones. No books, no papers. They even cleaned out the shredder."

I indicated the boxes being carried out by guys in FBI windbreakers. "What's all this?"

"Some personal shit," Fiegenbaum said. "Electric bills, water bills, things like that. It's not much, and I don't expect it to lead us anywhere, but it's all we got. Rogers got his bioweapon from the professor, and he's out of here, off to kill some Americans."

"Dammit." An ice ball solidified in my gut. "This is my fault. I spooked him."

Rita laid a hand on my arm. "You don't know that."

"We wouldn't have had the lead at all without your work, Ranger Cable." The elder FBI agent perked up a little. "At least we know who, what, and how. All that's left is finding out where and when."

"What are those?"

A pair of agents came from the house with an armload of trophies, the tall kind that have a gold statue of an athlete on top and marble-looking pillars on the base.

"Martial arts trophies," Fiegenbaum said. "Apparently our boy Rogers is a master at tae kwon do and kung fu and a whole bunch of other fighting styles."

"Heh," Goldman grunted. "Mr. Lethal-fucking-Weapon. Go figure."

"Lethal in more ways than one, now."

WE HUNG AROUND WHILE the FBI searched Rogers's home, waiting longer than smart people should, hoping a clue would leap from the pantry, the den, or the garage and tell us where the kung fu master of Islam had gone. It was after ten o'clock when we gave up and Rita drove me home.

Inside her rocket sled, I swallowed another pill and closed my eyes. A few seconds later—or so it seemed—my Tasmanian Terror coasted to a somewhat gentle stop in front of my apartment door.

"You 'wake?"

"Yup," I mumbled and yawned. "Sorta."

"C'mon, pilgrim." She mangled a Western drawl. "Saddle up and move out."

"Yippee-kai-yay."

She helped me out of the car, which kind of resembled a beagle pulling a Great Dane. We stopped together at my door. I turned to her, my hand on the doorknob. Big brown June bugs danced around the overhead light, blindly thumping the glass housing with little ticking sounds. My heart suddenly pounded in four-four time, and I wondered why, until my brain caught up with my hormones. I was standing on a front porch with a woman, one I had recently entertained carnal thoughts about.

Ask her in? Am I nuts? What does she want? What should I do?

"Do... uh..." My brain froze solid.

Rita's eyes were dark. Unreadable. She stood so close to me, the heat from her body warmed me and the scent of her perfume short-circuited my brain. Without conscious effort, without thought or act of will, I gathered her in my arms. Small and light, she molded into me so that we were one body. Her full lips were mine to taste. At that moment, the hard, brassy shrew disappeared, replaced by sweetness, tenderness, and warmth. I wanted to hold her gently and crush her into my body at the same time. She smelled of gardenias, and I drank her in like dusty earth soaking up water. The muscles of her back flexed under my hand like velvet-coated steel, and her ass fit in my palms.

She was so small and tender.

She was so strong and alive.

"Oh my," she said into my chest when we broke the kiss.

"Yeah." A Cable patented witty comeback.

"This is a bad idea, cowboy."

"It feels like a really good idea about now."

"I can feel what it feels like, but you know it's a bad idea." She shook as if freezing water poured through her veins.

I didn't trust myself to speak. Both my hands wrapped around the small of her back. She felt so tiny, yet so alive.

"W-We're involved in an on-going in-investigation," Rita murmured into my chest. "A fucking t-terrorist investigation. We can't be fooling around." She stepped back and looked at me, grabbing a bunch of my shirt in her hands. "Don't you say nothing, Sam—you hear me? Because I swear all you have to say is 'come in,' and I'm done. I'm hangin' on to my willpower by a fingernail here. I'm gonna walk away and get in my car and pretend this didn't happen."

She was right. Getting involved was wrong on so many levels.

I cupped her face, her hair spilling through my fingers. I didn't say anything at all. I should have. I should have said the words that would crack her resolve and keep her with me. I didn't. The words would not come.

As we parted, her fingers fluttered away from my shirt.

She walked away.

And I let her go.

I listened to my breathing.

Chapter 16

"MOST OF THEM DIED INSTANTLY, but a few had time to go quietly nuts." – James Olson as Dr. Mark Hall, The Andromeda Strain

ROGERS

David Rogers met his lead soldier—code-named Sleepy—in the parking lot of a dead strip mall in an older section of Irving. Vacant storefronts, their windows covered in brown paper, overlooked a cracked and pitted asphalt lot. Heavy clouds spat rain in reluctant drops, one or two at a time. Rogers positioned his driver's door next to Sleepy's and rolled down the window.

"Report," he said.

Hooded eyes wrinkled at the corners in something close to a smile. "Success, praise be to Allah."

"Praise Allah." A knot in Rogers's gut loosened. "Tell me."

Sleepy turned his drooping eyes upward, repeating from memory. "Terminal A, near Gate 17. Terminal B, Gate 10. Terminal D, restaurant. Terminal C, American Airlines Admirals Club." Sleepy paused and grinned. "Happy bought a one-day pass to the lounge. He said the target-rich environment was full of rich targets."

"Heh," Rogers grunted in amusement. "Continue."

"Terminal C, again, Gate 33. Terminal E, near the United check-in area. Six devices placed, all set for fifteen-minute intervals."

At that rate, the canisters would remain deadly for at least two days, perhaps longer. The airborne medium carrying the virus would infect passengers and employees in the immediate area, then drift on air currents or be transported by contact to other parts of the busy airport. Travelers would disperse across the country and the world, carrying the infection in their blood and on their luggage, skin, and clothes. Within hours, a day at most, victims would become symptomatic. Perhaps as early as Tuesday night, maybe Wednesday morning, America would begin to feel the pain of Allah's vengeful sword.

During the planning phase, his uncle had asked, "How many will become infected?"

"I don't know," David had replied. "Over one hundred and sixty thousand people use DFW Airport every day. Over two days, if only one percent of those travelers come into contact with Siren's Tears, that would be a victory greater than the Twin Towers. You asked for a big splash, Uncle. I believe this one will be huge."

"A very big splash," his uncle had grudgingly allowed.

"You saw what happened to the economy when the coronavirus raged through America, and the world. The impact far, far outweighed the death toll. Liberties were curtailed. People huddled like sheep in their homes."

"Yes, yes, all good things."

"They will feel this in their bones, the Americans."

That was weeks ago. Today, Rogers nodded to Sleepy. "You have done well. The panic that ensues will shock these fat, lazy dogs to their core. Again, they will cower in fear of a bug too small to measure without a microscope."

Rogers thought use of the word "dogs" was rather clever in relation to the rabies component of Siren's Tears. Sleepy failed to react to the irony. All the man said was "Praise Allah. God is great."

"Yes," Rogers agreed. "He is."

DANNY SINGLETARY

Danny Singletary rubbed his hot, tired eyes and pulled his roller bag across the Dayton airport parking lot. The travel gods had not been kind to him this trip. Delta Flight 1716 had landed in Dayton at ten minutes to midnight, twelve hours later than scheduled. Mechanical problems, weather delays, air traffic snafus—the usual litany of modern air travel excuses had piled up with stunning vengeance and unrelenting malice. Thanks to the delays, he was down to crunch time: one shopping day left to buy an anniversary present. And to top it off, he was coming down with the flu.

Sweaty, clammy, bone-deep aches and pains... Yeah, the symptoms were all there. After six months of quarantine and mask wearing during COVID, he hadn't caught as much as a sniffle. Now look at him. Priscilla would give him that look, the one that said, "If you'd only gotten your flu shot like I told you to, this wouldn't be happening." After twenty-six years of marriage, he could read her looks the way a weatherman could read the clouds. Danny suspected he would be celebrating their anniversary in bed, but not the way he'd hoped. A bowl of chicken soup was a poor substitute for Priscilla in a negligee, giving him that *other* look, the one that still got his motor running, despite a quarter of a century together.

Danny found his car in the long-term lot, covered in dust after a week of neglect. Bleary-eyed, wiping chilly sweat off his forehead, he started up and pulled out of the lot a daze. Thank God traffic was light, because about halfway home, a sensation that something wasn't right squeezed his chest. Danny started pushing past the speed limit, jumping red lights, and swearing when the rare car blocked his path. *Shit, has COVID come back?* There were still lingering cases out there, despite everyone's precautions. *Could this be it?*

Danny keyed his phone and called the house, but Priscilla didn't answer. In itself, that wasn't unusual. His wife hated to be woken by a ringing phone and turned the handset volume down when going to bed.

But still...

His heart was pounding, and he couldn't shake the feeling that something terrible had happened. Vivid images of Priscilla lying dead in a pool of blood or the house burned down to blackened studs cycled through his mind. Anxiety crawled the length of his backbone and squeezed his throat. Confusing random images and thoughts bubbled up from his subconscious, derailing his focus. If he had COVID, then he'd gotten the psychedelic, LSD version of the disease.

His headlights swept the front yard and lit the undersides of their sycamores when Danny pulled into the drive. The neighbor's cat, frozen by the lights, glared from the end of the drive. Maggots dripped from its mouth. Danny blinked, and the cat shot away.

He stumbled getting out of the car and would have fallen had he not been holding the door. Dizziness flushed upward from his gut, and along with it came the airport sandwich he'd eaten at O'Hare. *COVID. Has to be COVID.* Or he'd caught the mother of all flu bugs while squashed into a metal tube with a hundred and twenty germ-ridden fellow travelers.

Danny shivered. He pushed through the front door and into the master bedroom without passing out. The room was dark, and his wife was huddled under a (*blood-drenched*) quilt, her breathing thick with (*punctured lungs, riddled with stab wounds*) sleep. Danny shook off the bizarre images, and when his eyes cleared, she seemed fine. Not dead. No bloody smears on the sheets.

So what was bothering him? Why was he so freaked out?

(*She was in bed with his boss, Jim, legs wrapped around his back.*)

Another wave of nausea clawed its way up his throat. Danny clenched his teeth and managed to hold it down, but he must have made a noise, because Priscilla (*the lying bitch*) stirred and mumbled.

"Priscilla," Danny said, touching her (*rotten, traitorous*) shoulder. "I'm coming down with something."

"Huh? Whah?"

"I've got a bug," (*you cheating whore*) "so I'm going to sleep in the guest bedroom. It may be COVID. I don't know."

"'Kay. Welcome home, Danny-O." Priscilla rolled over, and her breathing smoothed out. She seemed (*well fucked*) so peaceful. And she'd called him Danny-O, a nickname from college based on his name: Daniel Oliver. (*Danny-O, married a ho, whaddya know.*)

Standing over his wife, he shivered and watched drops of sweat plop onto the quilt and soak in. *How could I have been so stupid? Of course it was Jim. Has to be.* The smug bastard was always patting him on the back, telling him what a great guy he was, and all the while, he'd been fucking Danny's wife. His hands trembled. He was too tired and sick to lift a pillow and hold it over her smirking, sexually satisfied face. Priss was strong. She would fight, and he wouldn't be able to hold her down.

"Tomorrow," he whispered, not to be silent, but because his throat was closing up and he found it hard to speak. He couldn't swallow.

Danny shambled to the guest bedroom. Three feet inside the room, Danny's legs petrified, changing from muscle to stone in the space of a heartbeat. He fell on his belly with a thud. Both legs were locked in some kind of spasm, like he'd been... *poisoned. Damn. How did Priscilla slip it to me? When?* She was a cunning bitch, so maybe she'd found a delayed-action poison, some exotic plant or something. She could have done it in the laundry when she washed his clothes. *Put some... some chemical in the fabric.*

He became aware of the rank odor of his body, the vinegary smell of stale sweat mixed with something like pus. The paralysis in his legs eased a bit. He still couldn't move, but maybe the effects of the poison were temporary. Maybe he could beat whatever she'd done to him and come back from the dead. Wouldn't Priss (*dead in a tangle of bloody sheets*) be surprised?

His hope died when the door opened and none other than the traitor herself walked in. She had found the cheerleader outfit she'd worn when they first dated, and she'd had some treatment done on her face and legs, making her looked thirty years younger. Her thick blond hair waved in a breeze, and Danny found his eyes watering.

"Why?" he said—or tried to say. His throat was closed for business. It took everything he had to keep drawing breath.

"Hey-ho, Danny-O," the impossibly young Priscilla Maguffey Singletary chirped. "You're in a fix, ain'tcha? Too bad, so sad, your momma's gonna be mad."

Spiders crawled from Priscilla's hair. First one, then three, then a dozen or more. Small, black, with long legs and sleek bodies, the spiders skittered along her shoulders and down her arms. When they arrived at her fingertips, the arachnids dropped from silken threads to land on the floor with hardly a sound, silent and black and hungry.

"Just so you know, Danny-O," Priscilla was saying, "I'm not only screwing Jim. I'm doing Matt Miscone, that guy from Purchasing you met at my company's Christmas party. He's so hot, I fuck him a lot." The spiders were coming for him, and he couldn't move. She had taken time to change into an evening dress, and her eyes were ringed with purple eye shadow.

Spiders crawled over him, tickling his eyes, exploring his nostrils, getting under his clothes, and biting his belly, his chest, and down between his legs. As they sank their poisonous fangs into his body, Priscilla laughed. "I'll bet that hurt."

He screamed and screamed, but no sound came out. He couldn't swallow. Danny tried to swat at the spiders, but his arms had locked up as tight as his legs in one giant muscle spasm. All he could do was lie on the carpet, as stiff as a board while the spiders ate him and his wife laughed and laughed.

I HUNG MY HEAD AS THE news started coming in. The first reported case came from Tennessee. Chuck Cordero, a battery manufacturer's rep, checked himself into Memphis Methodist with a fever, chills, and "flu-like symptoms." The staff had been forced to restrain Mr. Cordero when he became violent during the intake examination. He died six hours later.

In Sioux Falls, sixty-two members of a high school marching band developed symptoms during third period. The school nurse's office was overwhelmed, and ambulances were dispatched from every available source to start ferrying kids to local hospitals. Parents were notified, and the principal closed the school. Some of the infected students went berserk before the paramedics and the concerned parents arrived. They attacked and subsequently infected a significant number of their classmates and teachers. Eighty-six total fatalities.

A family of six in Modesto—the parents, three kids, and their grandmother—took to their beds after coming down sick. They never got up.

And on it went.

The inevitable comparisons to COVID started, along with the here-we-go-again drama. Voluntary lockdowns were initiated throughout the country as businesses started to close again, mere months after reopening from the previous pandemic.

"We failed," Fiegenbaum told the gathered task force members early Thursday morning. He didn't have to say it; we all knew it was true.

By late Wednesday, 1,627 people had been diagnosed. In twenty-four hours, that number had nearly doubled. It continued to climb. Once diagnosed, very few survived the virus. Anyone who went into the hospital with Siren's Tears had a chance of one in three hundred of emerging.

Goldman created a computer-generated map with a red dot for every known case of Siren's Tears. The dots were so scattered, it looked as though someone had peppered the map with birdshot.

The Department of Homeland Security activated the national Emergency Alert System and advised citizens to stay home and call 9-1-1 if they experienced any symptoms or observed a person acting as though symptomatic. Sixteen states were forced to activate the National Guard when riots broke out at grocery stores, pharmacies, and hospitals. More people died as the panic set in. Toilet paper, disinfectant, and firearms were once again in high demand.

Cases were being reported from outside the United States, as well. Europe, Asia, Africa, Australia... No one was spared. Contract tracing identified the vector as the Dallas-Fort Worth Airport. The entire airport was shut down, and CDC crews in level-A hazmat suits swept the place. They discovered six containers hidden inside time-release atomizers—all empty. The airport was lousy with trace amounts of Doc Hardeston's gift to the world. Aircraft had to be treated as contaminated, as were delivery trucks, trams, buses, cabs, and the cars and homes of the victims and the people with whom they'd come into contact.

Cleanup would take weeks. Maybe months. Maybe years.

"With a major hub shutdown," Fiegenbaum reported, "air travel is a fucking disaster. The stock market has suspended trading. Civilians are scared to leave their homes. Grocery stores have been stripped clean. Fights have broken out over a loaf of bread..."

Why the senior agent felt like he had to recap the list of disasters was beyond me. We could all watch the news. We had seen it all before. Panic in the face of a virus was nothing new. We had lost the battle. People had died. The terrorists had kicked us square in the gut, using only a portion of their virus supply. They had thirty canisters left.

Goldman and I locked eyes across the table for an instant. She looked away, and so did I. Whatever had happened between us Saturday night—or nearly happened—had ripped off the top layer of skin and left exposed a raw bundle of nerves. Our mutual reaction seemed to be: *That hurts, don't touch it!* We had barely spoken beyond "hey" and "how-wah-ya."

Our personal issues seemed trivial in light of the disaster unfolding around the world. Hard to ignore, even so.

"The only bright spot," Fiegenbaum said, "is that most of the infected people are getting to a hospital before they become aggressive or hydrophobic. That's kept down the follow-on infections and limited the damage... Huh." The senior agent huffed a hollow laugh. "Limited. The damage. My God."

In an all-night video-watching session of DFW's security footage, the FBI had found the six perpetrators who had planted the devices. Still photos had been released to the media, and one had been identified—Rashid bin Al Nayan. A Chechen Muslim, Al Nayan was an engineering student at Jefferson Davis College before graduating to terrorism and mass murderer.

Fiegenbaum went around the table with the same basic questions: Any leads?

What came back was "no," "no," and "fuck no, if I did, you think I'd keep it a secret?"

That last one was Goldman's.

After the meeting, I grabbed my hat and coat and stopped by my office to make a call to Bouche at Jefferson Davis College. Now that people were dying, Megan Stewart—Rogers's one-time girlfriend and punching bag—might be more willing to talk about little Davey and his activities. Maybe, just maybe, she would have a clue about where he would hide. Thinner straws had led to breaks before, so it was worth a shot. I missed reaching Bouche but connected with Officer Marta Ruiz and told her what I wanted. She agreed to help, and I left to meet up with her.

I nearly collided with Goldman as she was coming back through the glass entrance doors from the parking lot.

"Oh." She blinked and stepped back. In one hand, she clutched a folder of documents and held a cup of coffee in the other. "I forgot this"—she held up the folder—"in my car. Was just getting it."

"Okay."

"You going somewhere?"

"Yep."

"Need any help?"

"Nope."

"Well," she said with a too-bright smile. "Okay then."

"See you around." I detoured around her and pushed into the bright heat of an early-June day.

Goldman's look of disappointment gnawed at my gut as I crossed to my borrowed DPS brown-wrapper car. Was I being an asshole? Was I blaming her for pulling back from a relationship that was never going to work anyway? She was right to not want to get involved. Forget about being co-workers. Look at the facts: it was as clear as polished glass a relationship would never work. For starters, she was way smarter than me. Not by just a bit, but by a country mile. Two, everything about her upbringing—from religion to culture—were foreign to me. Three, she could bring strong men to their knees with that awful, horrendous Bronx accent. And four, she was a co-worker.

I needed to forget about hormonal urges, pretend that little incident on the porch had never happened, and concentrate on the job at hand. Citizens were dying, and a passel of shitwads were running around with death in a spray can. Here I was, whining about not getting laid.

I settled myself into the seat of the unmarked Crown Vic I had borrowed and turned the key to crank it up. *Time to go see little Miss Megan.*

"Forget about Goldman," I told that little voice inside me that wanted her in my bed. "Move on."

That little voice reserved comment.

Chapter 17

"SOMETIMES, WE HAVE to make deals with lowlifes because we have our sights set on life-forms even somehow lower on the ladder of lowlife than they." – Timothy Oliphant as Raylan Givens, Justified

MEGAN STEWART WAS NOT in her dorm, in class, or anywhere else on campus. Officer Ruiz took me to talk with Megan's roommate in their dormitory room. We had to dodge people wearing surgical masks and carrying suitcases to waiting cars. Ruiz told me that classes had been canceled until further notice, and two-thirds of the student body was headed home for the duration of the Siren's Tears crisis. Parents were in a panic, rushing past us with their arms loaded, dragging their kids behind them.

Room 222 turned out to be smaller than a cheap motel room. A tornado inside a Nordstrom's couldn't have blown more clothing around the tiny space. Books, papers, electronic gear, and empty yogurt cups covered the flat surfaces. I toed aside an unmatched flip-flop and some heart-dotted panties to find a spot for my feet.

"When did you last see Megan?" I asked the young woman seated in one of the room's two chairs. Short and comfortably plump, Kelly Forrester had dark hair cut in a pageboy, creamy-pale skin, and brown eyes. She wore running shorts, flip-flops, and an oversized loose-neck T-shirt bearing a beer company logo.

"Um, last... um, Sunday?"

"Is it unusual? Her being gone this long." I shifted to lean against the ladder to the upper bunk bed. Ruiz stayed in the open doorway since all of us wouldn't fit in the room. Students passing in the hall fell quiet when they saw Ruiz at the door.

"Um... no." Kelly ducked her head. She brushed the hair back over her ear with one hand. Red blotches appeared on her neck. "Megan goes out, you know... a lot."

Is this girl embarrassed? Why is she blushing?

"She date a lot of different guys?"

"No, just one. Like, off and on."

"Who would that be?"

"David." Kelly inspected her toes some more. Her voice dropped low. "David Rogers?"

"Tell me about David," I prodded.

"I don't like him." Kelly fiddled with the string ties on her running shorts. "He's like, you know, like maybe a dealer, I think? Drugs, maybe?"

"And Megan?"

"She, um, uses a little. I think David got her hooked." Kelly winced and peeked from under the canopy of her bangs. "She's not in trouble, is she? About the drugs?"

"No, Ms. Forrester." I squatted to her level. No way did I want to sit on the other chair, upon which rested an open box of feminine hygiene products. I would rather be launched into space on a Russian rocket than handle a tampon. "I just want to find her, make sure she's all right. David's not a nice character, and she could be in danger. Did Megan ever mention anywhere special they'd go? Maybe in Tyler or Dallas?"

Kelly looked up, and her forehead creased in a frown. "Um... no. Not that I can think of. Mainly, she stayed over at his house, you know? The one on Myrtle?"

"Yes, I know the one. Anywhere else?"

I stopped talking and let her think. Ruiz shifted position in the doorway, and her leather gear belt creaked. Kelly rubbed her nose then scratched her thigh.

Her head started a slow side-to-side shake, as if she were about to say no. Her eyes widened, and she said, "David's friend has a ranch. You know, in the country? Megan sometimes went out there with David, and they'd ride horses and stuff."

"Really?" An electric cattle prod to the chest would have been mild compared to the impact of her words. "Tell me about the ranch."

Click.

RITA

Rita Goldman paged through Rashid bin Al Nayan's bank and credit card statements. Then had to go back and do it again when she realized nothing she'd seen had penetrated past her eyes. *Fuck.* She hadn't been this upset since she caught Steven sleeping with his intake nurse, Kimberly Nguyen. *Stupid, stupid, stupid.* How could she have let herself get attracted to someone like Samuel Duncan Cable, with his big hat, his broad shoulders, and Randolph Scott-Gary Cooper jaw?

A cowboy, of all things!

Her phone buzzed, and Rita's pulse jumped when Cable's name popped up on her phone. *Think of the devil...*

She took a deep breath and thumbed it on. "Hey."

"Hey, listen. Write this number down—" Cable read off a ten-digit phone number. "That's Megan Stewart's cell phone. She may be with our boy Rogers. See if you can get your three-letter cloak-and-dagger buddies to locate the phone. That's number one—"

"Wait a sec. Just hold up a minute, Mr. Texas Ranger." Rita's face heated, and a number of swear words bubbled under her tongue. She bit them back and said, "Do I look like your goddamn secretary? Am I your fucking flunky, Cable? Hah? I thought we were partners, here."

"We... We are partners, Goldman. It's just—"

"Just nothin', you bone-headed, dim-witted hick *cowboy*!" Her voice had risen along with the heat in her face. She was aware that conversations around the office had gone quiet—no doubt everyone was listening to her come unglued. She didn't care. "You don't freeze me out, then call me up and tell me to do this and that, jump here, jump there, and get me *caw-fee* while you're at it!"

Silence answered from the other end of the line. *Did he hang up?*

His breath whooshed out, and he sounded sincere when he said, "You're right. I treated you like shit today, and I'm sorry for that. I, uh..." *Ding. Ding. Ding.* The sound of a car's door alert chimed in the background. It cut off when a door thunked shut. "I don't know what to do about... you know... us. About what happened the other night. I'm all screwed up."

The anger drained out of Rita. She took a deep breath and lowered her voice, very conscious of the possible listeners in the other cubes. "I agree. I have the same problem."

"We should maybe, uh, talk about it."

"Not your strongest skill, cowboy."

"No."

Rita drummed her fingernails on the desk and swallowed past a dry throat. "Maybe not mine, either, okay?"

"Okay."

"So," she said. "Bring me up to speed, tell me what you got, and let's see what we can do. We'll deal with that other later."

Cable told her about his conversation with Kelly Forrester, roommate of Megan Stewart. "If we can find Megan, maybe we find Rogers. Also, there's a ranch, supposedly belongs to an acquaintance of Rogers. She didn't know who. It's somewhere on FM 2204, down in the Piney Woods of Gregg County. I'm thinking maybe if you could pull the records of all the homeowners along that road, maybe we find a connection."

"Okay, that actually makes some sense. What are you going to be doing while I'm working my ass off here?"

"FM 2204 is not that long, and it's close to where I'm at. I'm gonna haul ass down that direction, in case you get a hit. I'm also going to hunt for a yellow Corvette, which is what I last saw David Rogers driving... and a big sign out front saying Lair of Evil Chechen Terrorists."

"And if you find either, you're gonna *call me*, correct? You're not doing something stupid like, I don't know, knockin' on the front door and sayin', 'Howdy, motherfuckers'?"

After a long beat, Cable said, "I would never do that. If I see Rogers, I'll shoot him in the face first, then say, 'Howdy, motherfucker.'"

DIRTY-GRAY CLOUDS TRAPPED the heat and blocked the noon sun. The weather idiots had forecasted rain through tomorrow, with some flash flood and tornado watches thrown in to scare the bejeebers out of the old folks. Given the heavy feel of the air, they might have gotten it right this time.

After stopping at a hardware store to replace the field glasses that had burned up in my old vehicle, I pointed the Crown Vic north on US 259. I made a right turn on FM 2204. The Farm-to-Market road ran about ten miles east from Kilgore to the East Texas Regional Airport. It didn't escape my attention that 2204 was in close proximity to the county road where Hardeston's warehouse lab was. *Coincidence or intention? Had Rogers caught a lucky break in having a bolt hole close to Hardeston's lab? Or had he known all along where the professor kept his stuff, and had he planned to be close by, just in case their partnership went to hell?*

I wasn't sure how reliable Kelly Forrester was, either. She might have been way off about the place, or Rogers might have gone somewhere else entirely by now.

I filed my questions in a folder labeled Who the Hell Knows. Answers would come with time and patience. *But how much time do I have?*

The DFW Massacre was a delayed-reaction catastrophe—people had died like dominos falling, and the more folks who fell ill, the greater the panic. Newscasts kept a running tally on the death toll. It crawled across the bottom of everyone's TV screen on every cable news station. A stock ticker of horror. So far, the word "terrorist" hadn't made it into the news cycle, but it would only be a matter of time. Once that happened, Katie bar the door on crazy, because the citizens of the United States would burst a collective blood vessel to nuke those responsible.

Rural scenery appeared almost the second I turned off 259 and headed east. A squat building—JD's Liquor and Gas—flew by on my right, and then it was nothing but trees and single-family homes, which became more widely spaced the farther I traveled from Kilgore.

I drove the length of 2204, all the way to the airport, made a wide U-turn, and headed back. On that first pass, I'd accomplished nothing more than a peaceful drive in the country, double-heaped with bucolic settings and sprinkled with rural simplicity. No wild-eyed terrorists with AK-47s had jumped out of the briars. No yellow Corvettes were hidden in the honeysuckle. Goldman's voice rang in my head: *"Fuck all is whatcha got here."*

On the return, I pulled off to the grassy shoulder at every residence and took a look through my hardware-store binoculars. I jotted notes on a yellow legal pad to keep track of what I saw at each address.

1604. Wht. Ford dbl cab, tx LY7-9942, muddy. Swing set.

1625. Brn Dodge Ram, no lic vsble. Red Honda Accord, no l.v. 1-w/ m, 6-2, 200 on lawn trctr.

And so on.

A couple of places were so deep in the trees, I couldn't see any details. I marked those for later and continued my catalog of the habitations visible from the road. By two in the afternoon, I had a list of every homestead along 2204. Six of the forty-two properties were either too far away or too heavily screened by trees to get an eyeball on the people who lived there. Of the remainder, I ruled out thirty-two based on appearance alone. Some places just looked too... native... to be the home of terrorist plotters. Like the trailer house with a half dozen vehicles in front, each of them sporting bumper stickers declaring Jesus Saves! *Apparently not enough to buy them a bigger house.*

I had not heard from Goldman.

I stopped at a convenience store and bought a bathtub-sized cup of Dr Pepper and a bag of trail mix. The store shelves looked like they had been pillaged by invading Huns, they were so bare. All the bread, milk, and canned goods were gone. The clerk wore a surgical mask and latex gloves.

Dribbling trail mix on my legal pad, I reviewed my notes. Four of the thirty-six properties visible from the road, I couldn't rule out by looks alone. No activity, no cars out front, and nothing that shouted Innocent Civilian Lives Here. I had to keep them on the list for a closer look. The remaining six not visible from the road were set so far back, I would need a covert approach, on foot, to get a closer look.

Not too long ago, sneaking onto a Texan's land was a good way to get a man's hair parted by a .30-30 bullet. Stalking through the woods and scoping out *anybody's* house carried a risk, and when the house in question might be filled with angry zealots sporting superior firepower, the risk flew off the end of the actuarial table.

Shitty jobs, my daddy used to say, *don't smell better with age.*

I looked at my reflection in the rearview, put the car in gear, and rolled out. "Best done before it starts to stink any worse."

OF THE LAST FOUR HOUSES, I had ruled out three. One remained a question mark. The last house on my list was so deep in the woods, I considered putting on a red cape with a hood and carrying a basket of treats in for Grandma. The owner had money. A wrought-iron automatic gate set into brick panels blocked the entrance, and a white three-rail fence disappeared into the woods on either side. A call box on a post stood to the left of the unpaved driveway, set at car-window height. It was not unusual to find a high-end property mixed with the run-down farms in East Texas. Wealthy people retired or built country estates for weekend getaways, and a few local doctors, attorneys, or politicians made enough to afford a mansion away from the city. These properties were sprinkled among the trailer homes and modest farmhouses like diamonds in fields of weeds.

The bold and stupid way to find out if the house was full of terrorists would be to drive up, push the button on the call box, and ask politely, "Is this Mr. Rogers's neighborhood?"

Instead, I eased my Crown Vic onto the soggy shoulder two dozen yards beyond the driveway. I drank the last of my watered-down soda from my Biggest Gulp on the Planet and swallowed a pair of Tylenols. My scalp wound had commenced itching, and salty sweat burned the cut. I couldn't wear any kind of hat, which sucked. After my last two stops for reconnaissance—and related forest stalking—I was soaked with perspiration from eyeball to crotch. Burrs stuck to my jeans.

Goldman still had not called. The phone was nearly dead, gasping on the last bar, so I plugged it into the charger and left it in the seat. I stepped out, eased the car door shut, stretched the kinks out of my back, then resettled the Kimber on my hip.

Thunder rumbled. The sky had grown darker throughout the afternoon, the clouds heavier, but so far, the rain had held off. A semi rig blew past, buffeting me with wind. A discarded hamburger wrapper, trapped in the breeze from the passing truck, swirled and snagged in the knee-high weeds filling the drainage ditch between me and the fence.

I pocketed my keys. "Well, Sam, let's go see if Grandma got eaten by the Big Bad Wolf."

Splashing through an inch-deep puddle of scummy water, I crossed the ditch. Weeds crackled as I pushed through them. I swung a leg over the top rail of the fence and dropped to the other side. After a breath to steady my sore head, I slipped between the trees.

RITA

Rita muttered an inventive string of curses. Nothing appeared when she searched for Megan Stewart's cell signal. Her phone was either turned off or dead. Not much of a surprise there. If the girl was hanging out with David Rogers, he was probably too canny to let her keep a working phone.

So next.

Dumping the property records for the stretch of road Cable identified had proved to be tedious. The county database was organized by zip code, so she downloaded a CSV file of all the records in the target area and sorted it by address. Next, she filtered for FM 2204 and cut that section into a second tab on her spreadsheet. This subset, she organized by name, just to see if anything popped up right away, like "Rogers" or "Tarasov" or "Fucktard Terrorist."

No joy.

Running each name through NCIC and ViCAP took an hour. She followed that by checking the Terrorist Watchlist, the Global Terrorism Database, Rand's Database of Worldwide Terrorism Incidents, and Interpol. Another two hours drained away.

Nothing.

None of the people living along that stretch of rural highway had any obvious connections to David Rogers or Chechnya. She did find eight DWIs, two larcenies, three misdemeanor batteries, and four for possession. Apparently Texans liked to get drunk, get high, and get in fights.

She rolled her eyes and muttered, "Holy no shit, Batman."

Rita toggled her head and popped her neck. She glanced at the clock. *How did it get so late? Ten minutes till five and nothing, nada, zippin-zahooley. Fuck.* She hadn't heard from Cable all afternoon. The schmuck. Probably still pissed about her leaving him hanging—and wasn't that a loaded word!—the other night.

The feel of Sam's body imprinted her skin the way sunburn lingered days after exposure. She recalled his very male scent, the firmness of his very manly muscles, and the very, very male iron bar of heat pressing against her belly. She shivered now, from memory alone. How in the hell had she walked away from *that*?

"Wobbling and wet," she answered herself. "That's how."

Was it the right thing to do? Could she work with him and sleep with him, too? And then there was the inevitable breakup. They were so different, so... alien to each other—how could they not break up? Would her heart survive being ripped apart again, after all the shit Steve had put her through? *Ugh. That way lies madness.*

"Or maybe distemper," Rita said with a grim smile. *And speaking of...*

Rita tried Cable's phone and got voicemail, the generic computer voice greeting. *Of course. New phone.* Sam hadn't recorded a personal message yet. She missed hearing that laconic drawl, which had somehow poisoned her mind with its syrupy twang.

She called again at six, then thirty minutes later. She ran the same location trace she'd used with Megan's phone. Nothing. At seven o'clock, she called his number again. Same result.

"Shit," Rita snapped and banged the phone handset down. Hard.

Detective Winston's voice rolled over the cube walls. "You okay over there, Agent?"

"Why are men such pig-headed bastards?" she groused.

"Ah. What's Cable done now?"

Rita navigated the maze to the detective's desk. Propping a hip against the cube wall, she brought him up to speed on what Cable had learned from Megan Stewart and what they were doing about it. "The numbskull's gone off the grid and won't answer his frickin' phone."

Winston frowned. "You think he found trouble?"

"Hah! Does the Pope shit in a funny hat?"

The detective blinked.

"Of course he's in trouble," Rita growled. "That's how the man lives. I swear, I let him out of my sight for five minutes..."

"You want to go look for him?"

She sighed. "We should, I guess."

"Bring the cavalry?"

Rita puffed the hair off her forehead. "Not... yet."

Winston lifted an eyebrow. His shaved ebony head gleamed under the office fluorescents.

"We don't know where to bring 'em. And if he really has found Rogers," Rita said, "he might be watching, y'know? If we—"

"If we roll up hot, we might spook the bad guys." He tilted his head and squinted one eye. "You sure?"

"No."

"Well. Okay then."

"C'mon. Let's roll." Rita grabbed her bag. "Show me this FM 2204 before I change my mind."

RITA

The rain hit five minutes out of Longview.

Winston drove his unmarked brown Dodge Charger while Rita rode shotgun, both of them squinting through the thumping windshield wipers. The downpour came hard and steady, pounding the car and slashing the road in white sheets. Lightning blossomed high in the black sky, and strong gusts shoved the Dodge in petulant fits. The fifteen-minute drive from Longview had taken thirty due to the thunderstorm.

"Well, that's it," Winston said after they'd run the length of FM 2204 and reached the outskirts of Kilgore. "Nothing."

"Whaddya bet he's home, with his feet up, watching TV?" Rita was fuming. They'd crawled along the length of a two-lane, horror-movie road in the pouring rain, sweeping the Dodge's spotlight from one shoulder to the other, hunched up with their faces near the windshield, trying to spot Cable's borrowed Crown Vic. Well, guess what? Mr. Superhero Texas Ranger had run off somewhere without calling, texting, or sending a freaking smoke signal. "That... *asshole!* When I find him, I'm gonna kick his cowboy nuts so high..."

"How high?"

"I... I can't think of anything high enough."

"Let me put in a call to Longview PD." Winston wheeled in to a convenience store parking lot. "Have them check at his place, see if he's there."

"Good idea." Rita sat back and rubbed her temples. "If he is, let's go kill him."

While Winston made the call, Rita braved the rain and dashed for the store. She used the ladies' room, reluctantly, and bought two coffees. By the time she'd run back through the rain and negotiated the passenger door, she was as soaked as a drowned duck. Water drizzled from her hair, and her toes squished. She didn't even want to know what her Ferragamo flats—the ones she'd practically stolen at a Nordie's clearance sale—looked like.

"Anything?" she asked.

"They're checking." Winston took the Styrofoam cup she offered. "Thanks."

The aroma of steaming coffee and wet special agent filled the car. Winston switched off the engine, and the sound of thrumming rain intensified. Immediately, the windows began to fog over. Rita closed her eyes and willed her leg to cease bouncing in place.

"How long have you known Cable?" she asked to fill the silence.

Winston chuckled in a deep baritone. "We played against each other a time or two. High school football. He was a defensive end, and I was a quarterback. He didn't get to me often—too slow for my fleetness of foot, you see—but I recall a time he came off my blindside and pancaked my ass into the dirt. I lost track of time for two quarters." The detective grinned, teeth gleaming. "He was a big ol' boy, even then."

Boys. Pfft. Rita leaned her head back, kept her eyes closed, and let the coffee—which was surprisingly good—work its magic on her system.

Winston's warm laugh filled the cab. "It do seem to me, the cowboy's more than a mite smitten by you. If I may be so bold as to say."

Her heart twitched a double-beat, and heat flushed Rita's neck. "Why..." She cleared her throat. "I mean, what gives you that idea?"

"Maybe 'cause he follows you around like a calf follows its mama."

The warble of the detective's cell phone saved Rita from having to respond.

"Yeah? This is he... Uh huh... And you knocked on the door, right? Uh huh... Okay, thanks... No, that's all for now. 'Preciate you." Winston thumbed off the phone and looked over at Rita. "He ain't home. Now what?"

She deflated with a sigh. "Shit. Okay. Let's go over the road one more time. Maybe we missed something."

"And if that don't work?"

"I dunno." Rita sipped coffee and listened to the rain pound the roof of the car. "Go door-to-door, I guess. Ask people if they seen a dumbass cowboy wandering around lost."

"In Texas?"

"Oh my God. Okay. Good point."

Chapter 18

"WE'LL PLAY A LITTLE game I invented. One of us opens the atlas at random, sticks a pin in the open page. Wherever it lands, that's where we go." – Rex Harrison as Dr. Doolittle, Doctor Doolittle

STUPID. STUPID, STUPID, stew-PED.

On my knees, hands in plasticuffs, and feet strapped together. Fresh blood on the floor. Mine.

Idiot. Sneaking through the woods like the ghost of a Cherokee scout, I'd slipped from tree to bush then found the nose of a yellow Corvette peeking from inside the garage.

Heavy rain had muted all the sounds around me. I hadn't heard the guy step up behind me. Too late, too slow, too stupid.

They took my gun. Marched me to the house, a big place surrounded by pine trees. Rogers was there. Lurch, too, whom Rogers called Marat. There were a few other guys with beards and Kalashnikovs. Martyrs-R-Us.

"Howdy," Rogers said—or words to that effect. And then he proceeded to beat the stuffing out of me—with a brick, a club, or a bulldozer. Or maybe just his foot. He was too fast to see. Hurt like hell. He laid into me with his kung fu bullshit. I had to say he made it fair, though. He left both my hands free so that I had a "sporting chance." But fight back? Hell, no. All I could do was take a beating.

The guy was fast as fuck. A blur. I couldn't hit him. He laughed at me the third—or maybe fourth—time he knocked me down. "I thought Rangers were tough."

"Tough enough," I told him. Spat blood. Got up.

And got knocked down. Up, down, up, down. Like an elevator.

They tied me up and dumped me in a garage stinking of oil and turpentine. Bare walls. Two cars. Room for me in between. Overhead doors locked. Door to the house locked. Cars locked.

Just had to see, didn't I?

Rain lashed the roof. Cold concrete gritted under my knees. I shifted, tried standing, and fell down. Again.

Oh, my head hurts. Jesus, does it ever. Stitches in my scalp had popped loose. Tacky blood oozed over my ear, coating it. Dust puffed away from my nose. Cheek pressed to the cold floor, I scrunched my eyes shut and held back a sneeze. Sneezing would hurt.

I remembered my phone, turned off, plugged into the charger in my car.

"Ah hell." My raspy voice echoed. "Goldman's gonna kill me."

RITA

Their second slow cruise after getting coffee netted nothing.

Rita and Winston started at the east end of 2204 and headed back toward Kilgore, stopping at every house. They made up a story about a victim infected with the latest virus, running around loose, acting crazy. *White male, six-four, two-twenty, stitches over his right ear. A law enforcement officer, unfortunately. Go figure. Have you seen him?* Rita told the detective to take the lead, figuring it was better a local guy show the badge rather than a fed. Feds brought more attention than they wanted right now.

"Besides," she told Winston, "if we happen to run across Rogers and his bunch, they might not freak out if they think it's only the locals. No offense."

"None taken." The detective gripped the steering wheel, his lips pursed in thought while the car idled on the side of the road. The rain had finally slacked off to a misty drizzle, and Winston had set the wipers to time-delay sweeps. One squeaked at every slow *shwack* across the windshield. "You still think low-key's the way to go? If the Chechens swallowed up Sam Cable, they may be just a tad more'n you and I can handle alone."

"No, I'm not sure." Rita blew damp hair off her forehead with a lungful of air. She winced. Her breath smelled like coffee. "Okay, look-it. We have our phones, right? Cell signal strong? Okay then, we come up on something suspicious, we'll call for backup."

Winston rapped out a two-handed drumbeat on the wheel. He didn't seem convinced, but after a long pause, he shrugged. "Okay, but first we call Reyes, tell him where we are and what we're doing. And we put on vests."

"Have you got a vest that matches my outfit?"

"Better than a bloodstain will."

Rita glowered at the damp material of her CK suit jacket. Wrinkles. Everywhere. "I'm tellin' you, if that jackass is sitting in a bar drinkin' a beer right now, I'm gonna cut the bastard."

Winston grunted a laugh. "I'll hold him."

RITA

The dashboard clock showed straight-up ten o'clock when their Dodge crunched to a stop in the gravel drive of the ninth place they'd tried. The rain had stopped and left behind muggy—and buggy—humidity. Despite the cool air blowing from the vents, Rita sweated under the bulk of her Hi-Lite vest. Even the smallest female size made her look like a kid in an adult life jacket.

Winston buzzed down the window and pushed the button on the call box. He flicked a glance at Rita. "You need to start taking the lead."

"Howzat?"

"It's late. It's dark"—Winston slipped into a cornpone accent—"and folks 'round heah don't be takin' well to a black man calling at they front door."

The call box squawked with a curt male voice. "Yes?"

Winston reeled off their cover story in the dull cadence of Joe-Friday-It's-All-Routine. He finished with "We need to check the property, if that's okay with y'all."

Silence from the speaker was followed by "Wait."

"He don't sound too Texan, you ask me," Winston confided in an aside.

Night breezes, wet and heavy, breathed into the car, overwhelming the air conditioning. Fresh sweat broke out under her collar. She loosened the SIG in her hip holster, the leather creaking with her movement. "You think—?"

Buzzz-click.

The gate unlocked and squealed open, rolling from right to left.

"Come," the speaker croaked.

Winston raised an eyebrow at her. Rita shrugged in return. Without a word, he toggled the window shut, put the car in gear, and rolled through the opening. When she looked over her shoulder, the gate was already crawling closed.

The headlights picked out a graveled tunnel between the trees. Fog covered the ground to knee-height, thicker near the trees, as if the forest had generated the mist and sent it forth to blind travelers to the dangers therein. An ice snake slithered up Rita's spine, and she shifted in the seat.

She reached for her cell phone. "I'm calling Reyes..."

"There it is," Winston said. She twitched at his voice. "Up ahead."

A yellow-haloed dot grew to a glowing security light mounted over the garage of a two-story stone-and-brick house. An arched entrance—was there a modern house without an arched entry?—was flanked by tall, curtain-covered windows. The harsh sodium vapor light pooled in the driveway, leaving the corners of the house in shadow.

The front door opened the second Winston brought the Dodge to a stop in front of the garage. A man stepped out, and for a second, Rita's heart spasmed. Cable. Same height. Same big shoulders. But no. This guy had a hammered face uglier than Freddy Krueger's. A tiny bell went off in the back of her brain. She fumbled with her phone.

"Maybe we should—"

Winston was already out. He palmed his ID and said something Rita didn't catch. The monster said something back—a monosyllable.

Why is this guy familiar? Something Sam said. What was—Oh shit! Lurch!

She scrabbled at the door handle. "Winston! Get back!"

Movement came from the corner of the house. A shadowy figure had soft-footed up behind Winston. The detective must have heard it, or heard her. He pivoted, hand sweeping back to his hip. The newcomer straightened his arm. Fire bloomed, and a shot hammered Winston's head. Gore sprayed in a fan, black in the yellow light.

Rita spilled from the car. Her gun filled her hand. She didn't remember drawing it. She rolled to her feet. More shots banged out from behind her. A mule kicked her in the back, and she skidded across the gravel. She lost her weapon. Her palms burned from scraping the rocks. She couldn't breathe. Rita crab-walked forward, using her momentum to keep heading for the darkness. Under the light, she was exposed, a frizzy-headed target. Cover. She had to get under cover.

A foot appeared in front of her nose.

She looked up. And up. David Rogers smiled at her from a million miles overhead.

"Hello," he said. She heard the swish of sound and recorded the image of his other foot whipping toward her head.

Oh, fuck—

Her brain exploded.

TIRED OF FALLING DOWN, I had stretched out between Rogers's yellow Corvette and a dark-blue Suburban and gone to sleep. I jerked awake at the sound of a gunshot. Yelling. More shots. Then raised voices speaking in a Slavic language. Slavic was not good. Slavic meant the bad guys were still alive. *Who are they shooting at?* They weren't deer hunting off the front porch with automatic weapons.

I tensed when the opener engaged and the overhead door clattered on its track. The smell of fresh rain and wet earth blew in. Would now be when they shot me in the head and dropped me in a shallow hole? Not much I could do about it except bleed on their shoes. The straps around my wrists had not completely cut off my circulation, but my hands tingled on the edge of numbness. I tested the plastic, straining against the restraints until snot blew from my nose and an aneurism threatened my brain.

Lurch walked backward, dragging a body. Loose, black hair. Small body. I froze.

Ah, shit.

I bared my teeth. "What have you done to her?"

Lurch ignored me, dropping Rita by my side. Her eyelids fluttered, and I remembered how to breathe. They had stripped off her jacket and left her in a pair of dark slacks and a cream blouse. She would shit a brick when she saw the blouse was torn at one shoulder. A dark-blue bruise colored her right cheek. Her chest rose and fell.

Lurch spoke with a bearded henchman, having an animated discussion in a foreign language.

"You speaking Chechen?" I grunted. "Sounds like pigs fucking."

They both ignored me. I should have gotten used to that by now, but I had to say it: they were being damned impolite. Bearded Boy produced a roll of duct tape and, with enough hand gestures to conduct a symphony, explained something in full-auto gibberish to Lurch, who fumed and spat back single words that translated to *idiot*, *moron*, and *fuckwad*. I could read body language well enough to figure out they were short on duct tape.

I cackled. "Never a Home Depot open when you need one."

Lurch kicked me.

With a lot of grunting and swearing, the Chechens trussed Goldman to my chest so that her back was against me, with my arms around her. They left the straps around my wrists and ankles. The last of the duct tape went around us, clamping her arms to her sides and squishing us together for... *For what? Easy transport? Reduced shipping costs? One hole in the ground instead of two?*

Kinky hair tickled my nose. Sneezing still hurt, at a level of fifty-two on a scale of ten. I rolled onto my back and focused on breathing. Goldman's weight compressed my fractured ribs, and I struggled to breathe without whimpering. The way my hands were strapped down, I was touching Rita in a very... *sensitive* place. I worked to minimize contact—the last thing I needed was Goldman waking up to find me palming her crotch.

The gritty crunch of concrete underfoot preceded an appearance by the handsome kung fu terrorist himself. Rogers examined us like we were a science experiment gone bad. "You cozy, Ranger?"

"Oh, lookee," I croaked. My dry throat made me sound like a sandpaper frog. I coughed and tried again. "If it ain't the Anti-Chuck Norris."

A thin smile curled one side of his mouth. The Corvette sagged on the driver's side. Lurch had gotten in while Rogers and I stared each other down. The engine cranked and rumbled to life, spewing exhaust fumes over me and Goldman. Bearded Boy jumped in the Suburban and fired it up, dumping more exhaust. Were they trying to gas us to death?

The Vette and the SUV pulled out of the garage and stopped. I craned my neck to see outside. Five more guys appeared in the garage entrance and hung out. The Corvette idled, the red of its brake lights backlighting Rogers as he loomed over me. "I was going to shoot you, but your pals showing up makes me think the police are closer than I hoped. We're moving our timetable forward, and my uncle says we shouldn't waste hostages. This will be more fitting." He leaned over and spritzed a cold, wet mist on my face then on Goldman's. "Have a little Siren's Tears to brighten your day, Ranger."

With that, he pivoted and walked out.

"What?" I yelled. "No evil monologue?"

He slipped into the passenger seat and shut the Vette's door. Four of the Chechens surrounded Goldman and me, shutting off my view of the sports car's vanishing taillights. The fifth Chechen opened the SUV's hatch. Showing the skill of gorillas on a government job, the terrorists gathered us up and tossed us into the rear compartment.

"Hah!" I said. "You guys are all exposed now. Welcome to rabies, bitches."

A Chechen lifted his sleeve and showed me a red dot on his bicep. "Inoculated, bitches." He and his buddies cackled and slapped palms.

It took some shoving, spindling, folding, and mutilating to get us packed and the hatch closed. The gang boarded the vehicle, filling the remaining seats, and we drove away. With my head twisted at a strange angle, all I could make out through the back window was a black sky.

The virus-laden liquid chilled my face and trickled down my cheeks. With every breath, Goldman and I sucked more of the disease into our lungs. I had kept up on my Bayrab shots, which should have inoculated me against the virus. In theory.

But Goldman? Standing orders was for all the task force members to get the treatment, but the last time I'd asked her, she'd told me, "Yeah, yeah, I'll get around to it."

The Suburban thudded over a bump in the road, and we bounced. My head thunked against the interior panel hard enough to make my eyes water and kick off a steel drum banging inside my skull. My right arm was going numb beneath Rita's weight.

Did she get her shots like she was supposed to? Maybe I should ask to see the tag on her collar. Wouldn't that be funny? Headlines would read, "Ranger Found Head-butted to Death, Testicles Ripped Off."

If Rita hadn't gotten her inoculation, she was on the countdown clock to developing a nigh one hundred percent fatal illness. We were trussed together by a couple dozen turns of duct tape, tighter than a rusted head bolt on a '42 Ford. I suspected we would be that way until one of us went rabid or the terrorists shot us.

Did the feds know where we were? I wouldn't know the answer until Rita woke up.

Would they be able to find where the Chechens were taking us? I could answer that one on my own.

"Fuckmuppets," I muttered.

Chapter 19

I KEPT BLACKING OUT, which wreaked havoc with my sense of time. We could have driven for as little as an hour or as many as two. At times, we traveled at freeway speeds, and other times, we slowed or stopped. Reflected lights and small-town buildings appeared in the window glass during the stop-and-go moments, making me think we were on a minor highway, maybe US 259. My best guess put us fifty to a hundred miles away from where we'd started. From the pitch-black sky, I got the feeling we were still deep in the country, which didn't make a lot of sense.

Why not head for Dallas? It was the obvious choice: a big city with lots of places to hide. It was Tarasov's base of operations, and a gang of bearded assholes would blend in better there than in rural Texas.

I asked if we were there yet, but the men up front failed to answer. "I'm giving you a one-star Uber review!" I yelled in complaint.

The SUV slowed then navigated a series of turns. Grit crunched under the tires. In the backwash from the vehicle's taillights, a narrow tunnel of trees glowed red. I gathered we were on a dirt or gravel road somewhere in the boondocks.

Goldman stirred and moaned. I had shifted around the best I could to relieve the pins and needles prickling my arm. Curled sideways in the cargo space, taped up like a redneck's radiator hose, the best I could do wasn't much. The warmth of her body squished against me had generated a patch of damp sweat. Her butt was pressing into my groin, which had the unfortunate side effect of triggering a manly response, despite the predicament.

Women loved spontaneity, but there were limits. Weren't there?

The Suburban's brakes squeaked, and the SUV rocked to a stop on spongy shocks. The Chechens broke their silence with the driver issuing commands that sent his passengers into motion. Doors opened then thunked shut. The hatch lifted, and hands dragged us out like a sack of dog food, dropping us in a heap on soggy grass.

"Oof!" I took the brunt of the fall on my back and side. Knives of pain sliced deep, like a mad butcher, chopping up my lungs for lunch.

Goldman stirred, mumbled, "Wazzit?" and shifted her weight, squishing a broken rib.

I grunted when she dug an elbow into my ribs. *Oh, thanks. Needed that.*

Standing in a circle around us, the Chechens prattled on like a group of guys around a campfire. Women, cars, or sports was my bet. Through their legs, I could see we were in the front yard of a steroidal log cabin. "Log mansion" was probably a better description. Set among heaps of trees, the three-story structure peaked in the center, with glowing wagon-wheel chandeliers lighting the interior. The mother of all front windows dominated the second floor. It was flanked by smaller windows and overlooked a balcony supported by brick columns. Under the balcony, the front porch featured an ornate door with a crystal Texas star flanked by porch rocker chairs under a ceiling fan.

The Vette was parked closer to the house. Lurch stepped outside the mansion's front door and gestured to the Keystone Kreeps to bring us inside.

Hands grabbed us again. They heaved, I grunted in pain, and Goldman said, "What the fuck?"

"You awake?" I asked.

"My head's killing me," she groaned.

"Join the club."

"Why am I—?"

"Shut up!" a Chechen snarled and smacked Rita in the face with his free hand. He was a scrawny, scruffy punk with bulging eyes and a hooked nose. I memorized his face.

"You'll die first," I promised.

Bug Eyes and his pals hauled the Goldman-Cable sandwich into the living room and followed Lurch up an interior staircase. The Gang of Six was sweating and huffing, struggling to manhandle us and not doing a good job of it. We thumped and jostled up the stairs, one cursing step at a time, giving me time to survey the cozy-but-enormous cabin.

The interior décor mixed John Wayne with Cochise in an unsettling way. A Navaho blanket draped the sofa. Steer skulls, deer antlers, and pronghorn antelope heads dotted the walls in between Frederick Remington prints. A Henry Yellow Boy repeating rifle was mounted over a stone fireplace. It was likely unloaded or nonfunctional, but on the plus side, to the left of the fireplace stood a gun cabinet. Full of guns. And there were more weapons laid out on the varnished pine coffee table, arranged like a gun show. Somebody was having a Tupperware party for firearms.

Family photos lined the walls of the stairway. Baby pictures of a little girl. Old black-and-whites of severe people in formal clothes. JC Penney portraits of a family of three: a mom, a dad, and... Megan Stewart. I cunningly deduced we were in a home belonging to Megan's parents.

We turned a corner, and the Chechens carelessly banged my head into a banister, putting an end to my sightseeing. They carried Goldman and me into an upstairs linen closet and dropped us in the middle of the narrow floor. Bearded Boy, Bug Eyes, and the four other stooges stretched their backs, massaged sore muscles, and said something that sounded like, "Whew, that was a hard job well done. Let's go grab a beer!"

They left the room.

"Alone at last," I said.

Rita shifted her ass against me and growled, "That better be a roll of quarters down your pants, cowboy."

"I'm so happy you didn't say dimes."

ROGERS

After his men deposited the police agents in the back bedroom, David Rogers directed his team to split up. Two on perimeter-guard rotation: two on, four off, rotating every two hours. "Get some rest. It will be a long day tomorrow, and you will need to be sharp. Marat"—he looked at his tall lieutenant—"you will stand guard here until relieved."

The ugly giant nodded once and assumed a parade rest position in the middle of the hall. The team scattered into rooms along the hall, and David returned to the master bedroom.

Western paraphernalia decorated the Stewarts' bedroom. Megan remained passed out under an Indian blanket on the king-sized bed. He'd used her earlier and, at the time, regretted the extra dose of Oxy he'd given the girl. It had knocked her out and left her as responsive as a sponge; screwing her had been more work than sex. At the moment, however, her condition relieved him of having to listen to her whiny bitching and vapid questions.

David climbed on top of the bed, fully dressed, and closed his eyes to rest. His uncle was on the way and would arrive sometime in the early hours of the morning. The old man would be a bear to deal with, considering the potential interference by the federal police. How a mobster without much religious zeal had become so involved in jihad had often puzzled David, but one thing was true about his uncle: he hated US federal agents.

The expression on the Ranger's face when David had sprayed them with Siren's Tears had been priceless. Although, now that he thought about it, the Ranger seemed more alarmed about what was happening to the Jew FBI agent. Something going on there? *A relationship, maybe? Something to exploit?* David shook off the thought. In a few hours, it wouldn't matter. He would have no need to exploit anything.

David shifted on the bed and winced at a sharp pain under his ribs. The Ranger had gotten in one good body blow during his beat-down, and it still ached. The tall cowboy would pay for that small inconvenience soon. He was alive now as a potential hostage in case the US forces were closer than David thought. Once the plane arrived, the man wouldn't be needed anymore.

David smirked and closed his eyes.

Soon, Ranger. Soon.

"YOU KNOW, IT'S VERY flattering and all," Goldman told me, "but now is so not the time."

"Well, stop wiggling your butt against me."

"How'd we get here? And where is here?"

I brought her up to speed on what I knew, starting with me getting bagged and tagged by the Chechens. "I didn't see any sign of Megan or her parents. Rogers is around somewhere. His car's parked out front."

A male voice filtered in from the hall. It sounded like Rogers. Feet thumped, doors opened, doors shut, and a man laughed. Rita and I breathed together and listened until it turned quiet.

Her voice came out of the dark. "Winston's dead."

"Ah, hell." The headache settled between my eyes and clamped down with a promise of long-term agony. "Did you get your shots?"

"My—" Rita stiffened against me. "What shots?"

"Rabies vaccine."

"Oh no. Don't tell me."

"He squirted us both with the virus."

"Shit. Goddammit."

"You didn't go, did you?"

She sagged and murmured, "I hate needles."

"Dammit, Goldman!"

"I know, I know. Don't nag."

We were quiet for a time, lying on our left sides and facing the door. I put my lips close to her ear and whispered, "We'll get out of here. Get to a hospital in time."

"I know." She didn't sound like she believed it.

ROGERS

Clomping feet on the stairs jarred David awake. Sergei Tarasov's driver and bodyguard, Nidal, knocked on the bedroom door and called out, "Your uncle is downstairs." Left unspoken was the command: Attend to him now.

David stood and stretched stiff muscles. He jogged downstairs and found Tarasov in the Stewarts' kitchen, poking at the single-cup coffee brewing system as if it were a Christian conspiracy. The old man's sour expression would curdle milk by staring at the cow. Looking as if made from poorly hewn bricks, Tarasov resembled a mechanic more than he did the head of an organized crime syndicate, and even less so a holy warrior.

Sometimes, though, it was hard to know how much warrior and how much crime boss Tarasov was at any given moment. His uncle insisted all his activities—from drug-running and prostitution to deploying Siren's Tears—struck at the heart and soul of the crusaders and capitalists. Undermined their society. Sapped their will to fight. That it made the crusty bastard rich was immaterial.

Conversely, David's commitment stemmed from his deeply held beliefs. He despised that his uncle had played the stock market like a capitalist. He had gone long on several pharmaceutical companies with viable rabies treatments, while simultaneously shorting airline and insurance stocks. He had earned $16.2 million as a direct result of their first strike in Dallas.

David kept his sneer private. "Would you like a cup of coffee, Uncle?"

"Pah!" Tarasov waved away the coffee maker and settled with the finality of an avalanche into a chair at the kitchen table. Smaller and cozier than the one in the grand dining room, this table was made of pine, polished to a glow, and was littered with the debris of everyday life, such as condiments, napkins, mail, and a cordless phone. "Where are the owners of this house?"

"Megan Stewart's parents are behind the barn." David couldn't help but add, "In the compost heap, becoming one with the earth."

Tarasov's eyes glistened. Small and set in deep folds of skin, the old man's eyes were perpetually wet, as if always on the verge of tears. "And the girl?"

"Upstairs. High as a kite."

"She knows of her parents?"

"She doesn't even know her own name at this point."

"And the plane?" his uncle demanded. "Where is it?"

David checked his watch. "Should be on the way from New Orleans, where it was diverted by the storms. Since the arrival of the FBI on our doorstep forced us to relocate here, we must wait for dawn. The Stewarts' private airfield has no lighting." David leaned against the doorframe and crossed his arms. He shrugged. "Men plan; Allah laughs."

"Indeed. It is fortunate you knew of this place."

David acknowledged his uncle's words with a tilt of his head. "Mr. Stewart took me for a ride in his airplane once."

Elbows on the table, Tarasov tented his fingers and tapped his yellowed front teeth. His wet eyes were fixed on a middle distance. A toilet flushed upstairs, and a door thumped shut. David sauntered to the spinning rack of K-cups and checked the available selection of coffees. *No tea, of course. Barbaric Texans.*

"How did they find us?" Tarasov rumbled.

"Excuse me?"

"How did the FBI find us so quickly?"

David frowned. "I honestly don't know. The black man was a detective from the county, not the FBI. I believe they were looking for the Ranger, who has been sniffing around for a while now. Oh, wait. Something I think you'll appreciate... The woman was wearing this." He dug in his pocket and pulled out a thin gold chain. A six-pointed Star of David pendant dangled from the end.

"A Jew," Tarasov grunted. He tapped the pendant, sending it swinging. "Bring her to me."

RITA'S BODY HAD RELAXED against me, and during short moments when I could ignore the pins and needles in my extremities, I almost imagined us spooned together in a romantic huddle. I dozed in fits and starts, listening to her breathe and feeling her body's rhythms. In other circumstances, I could get used to the feeling.

I lost track of time, falling into a semi-stupor during the early-morning hours, until the sounds of footsteps, voices, and movement brought me out of it. Hall light washed into my eyes when the door swung open. I flinched and squinted as a backlit giant tromped into the room—Lurch, followed by Rogers. Without a word, Lurch flicked open the blade of a lockback knife and sliced into the duct tape holding us together.

I glared at Rogers. "What game are we playing now?"

"You're not part of the game at the moment, Mr. Ranger." He put his hands on his hips. With his face shadowed, I couldn't read his expression, but his tone suggested cocky smugness. "My uncle wants to see the Jew bitch. Maybe cut off her tiny tits unless she tells us how you found us. Or maybe share her with the men, just for fun."

Lurch dragged Rita upright. Her weight leaving me felt like a part of my body being torn away.

"No!" I twisted with a grunt of effort, struggling to get upright. Lurch kicked me in the solar plexus, driving the wind out of me in one gust. I hit the floor and gasped.

Rita returned the favor, snap-kicking the tall man's shin. Without apparent pain or effort, Lurch wrapped his arms around her. The tiny woman looked like a child in the grip of a monstrous troll.

They were gone before I could draw breath. The door clicked shut, cutting the light to a thin strip at the base. I banged my aching head against the floor again and again. When I could breathe again, I kicked the door open. It thudded into the back of the man standing guard, who glared at me and slammed it shut again, shutting out the light.

Chapter 20

"SILENCE! I KILL YOU!" —*Jeff Dunham as Achmed the Dead Terrorist*

RITA COULDN'T STOP shivering. Tremors pulsed through her, and she clenched her teeth to keep them from chattering. Was it fear or fever? Was she about to start foaming at the mouth from rabies, or was she just more scared than she'd ever been in her life? The virus had been in her system for several hours, and Tancredi had posited a twelve-hour incubation period, at minimum.

Has it been twelve hours? She didn't think so, but then again, maybe the virus worked differently than the CDC had theorized.

The ugly giant carried her downstairs like a rug, gripped tightly around the arms and legs, immobilizing and intimidating her at the same time. Rogers bounced ahead of them, whistling a bad rendition of "Camptown Races." From her skewed view of the front windows, the darkness outside seemed thinner than the pitch-black of deep night. Dawn wasn't far off.

The monster carrying her followed his master through the living room and into the Ponderosa's kitchen. Her first impression was of red-brick walls, pine cabinets, and enough copper-bottomed pots to cook a mile of spaghetti. Her second impression was of the thug seated at the table in the center of the room.

Bulky and square built with a Lego-block head and a brush of gray hair, Sergei Tarasov had the appeal of a cockroach on a wedding cake.

Rogers indicated a chair opposite Tarasov. "Put her there, Marat."

Marat, aka Lurch, dropped her into the seat like a sack of grain. She saved herself from falling off the seat by grabbing the table. Her stomach clenched at her first up-close look at Sergei Tarasov.

The mob boss-turned-terrorist regarded her the way a man might study dog vomit on the carpet. "You are a Jew."

"Incorrect. I'm a federal fucking agent," she shot back then added after a pause, "Dipshit."

The old man lifted a bushy eyebrow. "The government of the United States must be cutting back on expenses." He pinched his fingers almost together. "You are very small."

"I'm big enough to put a nine-mil between your eyes, you fat fuck."

Marat slapped her from behind, spilling Rita to the floor. The room spun, and her ears rang. With one hand clamped around her bicep, the giant lifted and manhandled her back into the chair.

Tarasov said something she couldn't hear. She shook off Marat's paw and snarled, "What?"

"I said, how did you find our safe house?"

"You *dragged* me here, you dumb fuck."

"No." Tarasov waved a hand. "The first safe house. Where you were caught."

"Oh, that was easy." Rita smirked. "We just followed the stench."

Whap!

Even though she was prepared for it, Marat's open-handed slap hurt like a bitch. Rita followed the momentum, allowing it to carry her to the floor. She let herself go limp as Marat dragged her back into her seat. The gun poking out of his waistband—a SIG, similar to the one she used—was only inches away from her right hand. After one or two more slaps to the head, they would relax, thinking they had her cowed. The next time she went down—

Rogers's cell phone twittered a happy tune. He answered, listened, and ended the call in less than ten seconds. "The plane is thirty minutes out," he told Tarasov. "They will land at first light."

"All right." Tarasov blotted his damp eyes with a paper napkin and grimaced. "Okay, then. We will go. Get the men, then come to the car. You will show us the way to this airstrip, David." He turned to Marat. "Bring her with us. We will make a movie of her turning rabid, for the propaganda. It will make a good show, a Jewish FBI cunt like her."

"Kiss my Bronx ass, pinhead."

Marat hauled her out of the chair and shoved her in the back, toward the living room. Rita used the momentum of the push and crumpled to the floor. She made sure to land on her right side so Marat would have to take her left arm to pull her up, occupying at least one hand. It would only take a second to release her, but a second was all she needed to snag the weapon from his pants. Marat stood between her and Rogers, and the table blocked Tarasov, so both of them would be out of play.

Go straight for the gun, or punch him in the nuts first? Is a round chambered, or did diddlywits leave the pipe empty?

Rita could not see the thumb safety, but she assumed it was engaged. Even somebody as dumb as this tree stump appeared wouldn't stuff an unsafe weapon down the front of his pants. She rehearsed the steps in her mind as the big man stepped closer. *Drag the weapon free, disengage the safety, stuff the muzzle into his guts, angle it up toward the chest cavity, and pull the trigger.*

Except she never got the chance to do any of that.

Marat thumped her ribs with a solid kick. "Get. Up."

"Fuck. You."

This kick launched her an inch off the floor. She felt and heard the snick of a short rib cracking, and a wicked knife of pain stabbed through her side. Rita gasped and curled up in a ball, eyes watering. She sipped air through her clenched teeth. When Marat set up for another kick, Rita stopped him with a raised hand.

Tarasov stood next to Marat. "I have no patience left. If she gives you any more trouble, shoot her and come on. Meet us at the car, David."

The big man tugged the pistol from his waistband and grinned, flashing a picket fence of bad teeth. "Get up."

"Okay, okay," she wheezed. "Getting right on up, ya fuck."

Rita sighed. *Next time, Lurch.*

ROGERS

After Marat and his uncle left with the FBI agent, Rogers woke his team and ordered them to meet in the front room, including the man standing by the closet door. For the moment, the captive was going nowhere, so Rogers felt it worth the risk of leaving the closet door un-guarded. The first hint of a gray, sodden sunrise lit the eastern windows, so when the men were gathered, Rogers led them in the *Fajr* prayer, despite his impatient uncle waiting outside. The old man had no time for prayers, so for added rebellion, David added two *sunna raka 'āt*, and followed those with two *fard raka 'āt.*

As a child, Rogers had recited prayers by rote, receiving little emotional benefit from the act. In his teens, the nature of the struggle of Islam—to defeat the enemies of the true faith who wanted to destroy it—were revealed by his imam. Once this enlightenment came to him, the movements and words of prayer brought an enveloping peace, a calmness, and a sense of... destiny. Today's prayers were especially cleansing, infusing Rogers with energy and power.

Today will be a great day.

Rogers took a deep, cleansing breath and faced his assembled team. The leader—whom he had named Sleepy because of the man's protruding eyeballs—had been born in Grozny, to Syrian immigrant parents, and was probably the most devout of all his people. "Rashid bin Al Nayan, have your men load the Suburban with the material and follow us to the airstrip." Taking Al-Nayan by the elbow, Rogers led the man away from the group. He stopped in front of a display of classic Bowie knives pegged to a wall near the gun cabinet and selected a wicked-sharp blade of polished steel. Rogers placed the bone handle in Al-Nayan's palm. "I have chosen you to carry out Allah's will. There is not room in the aircraft for all of us, so someone must remain behind. It is a difficult thing I ask, but of all the men, I know you will do your duty and remain true to the cause. Yours will be the hardest burden to bear, though there are compensations. Am I right about this? I can trust you to remain steadfast?"

"Yes. Yes, of course."

"As your reward for this sacrifice, you may use the woman upstairs—Megan, she is called—for your pleasure, then kill her. Also, get rid of the infidel policeman. Cut off his head."

Al-Nayan's bulging eyes glittered. "It will be done. *Insha'Allah.*"

"Stay here twenty-four hours, minimum, to avoid attracting attention. By then, we will have achieved either our goal or martyrdom, and there will be no need for the authorities to torture you for information. If the police show up before the strikes have been completed..." Rogers laid a hand on the man's shoulder and cocked an eyebrow. "Rashid, you cannot allow the authorities to question you. Understood?"

Al-Nayan bobbed his head and swallowed hard. "It shall be as you say."

"Good," Rogers said. "Now. I've kept my uncle waiting long enough."

"*As-salāmu alayka.*"

"*Allah u Akbar.*" Rogers patted Al-Nayan on the shoulder. "We will meet again in heaven, my friend."

A BRUSQUE, QUIET ORDER sounded from farther down the hall, followed by footsteps thudding away from the door. The guard had left his post. Wiggling and twisting like a gangster on cross-examination, I fought my way upright and pressed my ear against the door. I heard Rogers gather his troops and hold a prayer meeting. A few minutes later, there was some thumping and clattering downstairs. Voices raised in farewell were followed by the whump of the front door shutting. Soon afterward, footsteps pounded the stairs—one person, moving fast. I bunny-hopped to the hinge-side of the door, preparing to jump the first person through it.

Instead, another door in the upstairs hall opened and closed. There came a low-pitched male voice, sounding demanding and harsh. I couldn't hear the response. Whatever it was pissed the man off, because next came the crack of a slap followed by a cry of pain in a woman's voice. It wasn't Rita. The pitch and tone of her squawky voice would have been recognizable from a mile away. *Who then? Megan?*

Things went quiet after that. Sounds came, but they were so faint that even pressing my cheek hard against the door resulted in nothing more than a sore ear. Had everybody bailed out except a rear guard? Were there more guys hanging out downstairs, keeping quiet?

"Only one way to find out," I told myself.

My hands were crossed in an X and strapped with a zip tie, and my ankles were zipped together, as well. I could move in tiny little tip-toe hops that made a wounded buffalo sound quiet by comparison, or I could make giant boot heel thunder hops that shook the earth and challenged Thor to a fistfight. A deaf man in Tupelo could hear me coming.

The water in the deep end of the self-pity pool had gotten cold. It was time to move. A clock ticked in my head, measuring the hours, minutes, and seconds of Rita Goldman's infection. Rogers had sprayed her between eight and ten o'clock last night, so at best, she had three hours to make it to a hospital before becoming symptomatic. If she didn't get treatment before the onset of rabies symptoms, she would be dead within twenty-four hours.

I'd already searched the linen closet and found nothing sharp enough to cut the zip ties. There was a trick to breaking zip ties, but I had never learned it. Experimentation did me no good. I would have to pogo around the second floor and check the other rooms for a cutting tool. Or I could scoot along on my butt, which didn't appeal at all. I would be better off on my feet than on my ass if someone showed up to investigate the noise.

Hopping it will have to—

Inspiration struck. The Chechens had zip-tied my ankles together over my pants, which covered the tops of my boots. That put two layers between my skin and the plastic tie. I plopped on my butt and wiggled around until I had some room to move. The effort of getting situated left me panting from pain and stress.

Working carefully, I tugged the cuffs of my pants, pulling them up in small hitches through the encircling zips. My right cuff popped free like a dream, loosening the tie by millimeters. The left cuff fought me. The material bunched up, and despite the extra room I'd gained, it knotted up and steadfastly refused to budge. I started again, straightening the cloth and pinching up smaller bites. I pushed the roll of the hem through the zip tie from the bottom with my fingers. With both pants legs out of the way, I had a good quarter-inch of play in the restraint. *Not enough to remove it, but if I could get my boots off...*

After ten minutes—or ten hours—of sweaty labor in the cramped room, desperately scrabbling, tugging, and fighting, I was barefoot. Hot, drenched, exhausted. Head pounding and ribs shooting fire into my chest.

But my legs were free.

I twisted the knob and cracked open the door. No one was in sight, so I eased my head out. The staircase split the hall in the middle, creating a north and south wing. We'd been stuck in the last room on the south, at the back. Balancing with spread fingers against the jamb, I noted two closed doors opposite my room, followed by a short balcony just this side of the stairs. The room right next to mine was open, and by the bit of tile visible, I suspected it was a bathroom. In the north wing, beyond the stairs, were four more rooms, but I couldn't tell if they were open or closed, because the angle sucked.

The house was quiet but for muffled sounds coming from behind one of the six closed doors. Someone was on the second floor with me, but I had no idea who or how many.

Sweat burned my eyes and dripped from my chin. Nausea rolled my guts over, and I swayed in place like a loose tent pole. The battering I'd taken had done some real damage to my hard head. Once I caught my breath, I took one short step into the hall.

Then another.

And another.

Jumping Jesus, dead turtles move faster.

Three more steps brought me to the room directly across the hall—a bedroom done in frilly lace and Scarlett O'Hara ruffles. Nothing sharp lay in plain sight. I tried the next room and found things much the same, except the decor was more *Antiques Roadshow* than Southern belle.

The bathroom was my last chance at a jackpot before I had to cross the open space overlooking the living room. Any terrorists down there would spot me in an instant, and I would be a duck in a shooting gallery. The bathroom should at least have a nail file, or scissors.

After six steps to the bathroom door, sweat soaked me from head to toe. My lungs worked overtime as I tried to quietly draw enough air to keep from passing out. Loosening my feet in a closet with my knees and hands tied had proved to be great cardio exercise. *I should make a DVD, market it as the Trussed Ranger Workout.*

It was a guest bathroom. Cute soaps. Towels. Nothing sharp, which left busting a window and using the broken glass—

A woman shrieked from a room at the north end of the hall. "No! Don't!" She sounded hurt, panicked. In trouble.

"Ah, dammit." I ran, heedless of the noise. In sock feet, I still sounded like a war drum.

Thump! Thump! Thump!

The last door on the right was ajar. Sounds of a struggle came from the room: A man's voice, raised in anger, cursing in a foreign language. A woman gasping and pleading.

I had to take a quick second to catch my breath and let the dizziness pass. Just outside the room, I paused with my hand on the doorjamb.

"Who is that?" the man yelled. Apparently, he had finally heard me coming. "Who is there?"

"Texas Rangers, asshole." I slapped open the door and stepped inside. "You're under arrest."

Chapter 21

*"I UNDERSTAND YOU'RE very good with your hands and feet." –
David Carradine as Rawley Wilkes,* Lone Wolf McQuade

WE WERE IN THE MASTER suite. King-sized bed, sitting area, furniture—I took it all in at a glance. A Chechen knelt on the bed with a fistful of Megan Stewart's blond hair in one hand. It was Bug Eyes. The one who'd slapped Goldman earlier. His pants were around his ankles, and the tip of his dick stuck out of a nest of black pubic hair like a blind worm from a steel-wool forest. A long cold-steel Bowie knife protruded from his other hand.

Megan was nude. Her body was flushed, and she was crying. Bloody red streaks crisscrossed her hands and arms. Defensive wounds.

The Chechen sneered at me. "You say I die first? I say *she* die first." He rammed the knife at Megan's throat. She held him at bay with an effort. The knifepoint quivered an inch from her flesh.

"No!" I bounded forward. I was too far away. Too slow.

The blade touched her throat. Megan gurgled and thrashed. Her eyes took on a panicked look.

I screamed and lunged for the bed, hands outstretched. My socks slipped on the hardwood floor. I was going down.

Bug Eyes ripped the knife free of Megan's hands. He whirled off the bed. His wild-eyed look of hatred was the last thing I saw before I fell on my face. I took the impact on my crossed palms and jackknifed into a kneeling position the instant I hit the floor, but it was too little, too late. I was in a classic decapitation pose.

The terrorist lunged toward me but tangled up with Megan and the bedding. Bug Eyes tripped and spilled to the floor with an *oomph!* The knife bounced out of his hand. Eyes like distended cue balls, his mouth opened in a silent scream, he reached for the blade. I clubbed him upside the head with a hammer fist. I didn't get much behind the first punch, but by the third time, I had the rhythm. I hit him like a man chopping wood. I bounced his skull off the floor hard enough to rattle pictures on the wall. The man's bulging eyes rolled back, and he slumped, limp and semi-dazed.

I bucked and contorted in a rodeo cowboy twist that put me on top of the Chechen. I planted both knees into his spine, looped my crossed hands under his chin, and reared back. Hard. Vision tunneling and turning red at the edges, I pulled like I wanted to string an acre of barbed-wire fence in one try.

He squawked and flopped. Something cracked. He died pissing on the floor.

The world turned gray. My brain jumped into a magic car and headed off to a land far away.

RITA

Rita's stomach churned with acid. She sat in the back seat between Tarasov and Rogers. The flat-faced Marat navigated for Tarasov's driver as he splashed the Porsche Cayenne along a soggy, two-rut trail into the woods behind the Stewarts' home. Plans for escape flashed through her mind, one after the other. The latest one she considered and abandoned involved grabbing the driver's blond ponytail and jerking it back so hard, it broke his neck.

Then what? Karate chop everybody else and run away?

They emerged through a gap in the trees. Below them, a glade opened out, a smooth field of emerald grass in a pocket of the surrounding hills. A hardpack landing strip ran from right to left across the open field. The trail they were on arrowed down the hill to a metal hangar on the far left.

Spinning and slipping, Ponytail revved the Porsche downhill. Obviously not accustomed to driving off road, he hunched forward and choked the wheel like a senior citizen on a major expressway. The car jounced hard, eliciting a curse from Tarasov and a chuckle from Rogers. The driver visibly relaxed when they pulled up next to the hangar.

Everyone climbed out. Tarasov walked away, lighting a cigarette. Marat and Ponytail flanked Rita while Rogers opened the back hatch and retrieved weapons. He handed the two henchmen a tactical shotgun apiece and slung an elegant but deadly MPK-5 over his shoulder by its strap.

Fiery anger clamped her jaws tight enough to ache. She was hot and sweaty. Her clothes were a mess. Her head ached from being kicked by the dickhead, Rogers. Her back hurt from taking a burst from a machine gun on the vest. She'd been infected with a fatal disease, and her time to get treatment was running out. She could almost feel the virus running through her system, taking over her vital organs, destroying blood cells, and rotting her brain. *Or whatever super-microscopic bugs do when they get loose inside you.*

And she was alone.

Her emotions boiled and churned, a kettle under high pressure. It was turning out to be a Ben-and-Jerrys-curl-up-on-the-sofa-and-watch-old-movies kind of day. That, or she needed to shoot some people. She was two scoops of bitchy, and having a gun in her hand would feel really good. *Or Sam. Having that big lug here would be* nice, *too.* Last night, taped together by terrorists and facing an unknown fate, she'd felt oddly safe in his arms.

Rita shivered.

Ponytail laughed at her. "No afraid be. We take care of you good."

"Fuck you," Rita snapped.

Ponytail laughed again, and Marat sneered. Rogers sat in the Cayenne's open hatch and whistled *Yankee Doodle* out of tune.

The rain had passed, leaving the earth and grass saturated. Her shoes were getting soaked. Wetness blanketed the trees, and water dripped with audible plops. Sergei Tarasov smoked a cigarette next to the open hangar door, oblivious to the No Smoking sign over his head.

A car engine revved, and a black Suburban crested the hill. Rita's heart jumped. At first, she thought the FBI was riding to the rescue, but it turned out to be the Chechens from the house. She counted noses when the vehicle stopped and the terrorists piled out. Six of them. No prisoners. No Sam Cable.

Shit.

The Chechens milled around, stretching and lighting up cigarettes of their own. They spoke in hushed tones, glancing at Tarasov and keeping their distance. The day brightened in small degrees, and Rita found she could make out the trunks of individual trees a quarter-mile away on the other side of the open field.

The drone of a small plane came from the east, and everybody stiffened and turned toward the sound. The plane, a twin-engine prop, broke the sodden cloud cover at five hundred feet and skimmed over the airstrip, the roar of its engines rattling her teeth. It banked to the left, made a big circle, and lined up for a landing. Moments later, the medium-sized commuter aircraft settled onto the damp runway with a splash, reversed thrust, and whined to a stop, its nose fifty feet from the hangar.

A fine mist churned up by the props sprayed Rita's face, and she averted her eyes until the blades spooled down. Exhaust fumes made her cough.

Tarasov threw away his cigarette and hitched his chin at the plane. "Come. Bring the woman."

I WAS COMING BACK TO my senses when Megan cut me loose.

I felt the tugging at my hands and opened my eyes to find her sawing at the stiff plastic of the zip tie around my wrists. She had wrapped the sheet around her body, crawled off the bed, and found the bowie knife Bug Eyes had threatened her with. *Brave girl.*

I had rolled off the Chechen. Megan knelt on the far side, away from the dead body.

"Thanks," I croaked when my hands came free.

She sniffed and nodded.

"Let me see." I sat up and took her hands in mine. The cuts on her arms were still oozing but looked to be shallow, already clotting. I struggled up and limped to the bathroom attached to the master suite and found some heavy cotton towels. I came back and wrapped Megan's arms.

"We have a problem, Megan."

She glanced up at me and snorted. *You think?* her tone said.

I told her about Rogers and Siren's Tears, the Chechens, and their plan to use the rest of the virus on terrorist attacks. "They've taken off. I don't know where—"

"The airstrip."

"Huh?"

Her voice was so low and faint, I had to lean over to hear her. "My dad's airstrip is out back. I remember David saying something about... about a plane, I think."

"Tell me where we are."

After she told me the address, I looked at the ceiling and pictured it on a map. I took a breath then let it out. "If I go after them, I can't take care of you."

Her eyes fixed on mine for the first time. Something hard and diamond-bright glittered there.

"Go kill that fucker," she hissed.

I nodded. I knew exactly how she felt. I picked up the phone on the bedside table. No dial tone. Big surprise there. "Can I count on you get to the nearest phone? Call the cops and get me some backup?"

"Yes. Yes, I can do that."

"Okay, then." I patted her shoulder. "Okay. I have to get moving. Stay safe." I wobbled back to the closet, put on my boots, then went downstairs.

On the coffee table, I found my Kimber and its two spare magazines. They went back on my belt. I tucked Rita's SIG into my waistband. The gun cabinet was locked. I smashed the glass with a bronze statue of a horse-mounted Comanche, reached in, and removed a Remington 700 BDL with a scope. I found a box of .243 shells to feed it.

A quick search of the house turned up nothing useful. No Rita. Two cars sat in the garage, an Escalade and a loaded Ford F150 pickup. They were locked. *Who locks their car in the garage?* I searched for keys, checking the wheel wells and bumpers for a Hide-a-Key then the garage and pantry walls and kitchen drawers. Nothing. They were hidden or missing. I tried the phone in the kitchen. Dead. *Of course.*

Rogers's yellow Vette sat outside, covered in water droplets. The Suburban was gone. Rita was gone.

I stood in the yard, turning a slow circle. My brain could hold only one thought at a time, and it reviewed each new fact the way a broken robot would. The question running along my rusted logic circuits started looping like a stuck record album. *What now?*

A twin-engine plane roared overhead on descent, its wheels low enough to touch.

The Chechens.

I came unstuck and jogged in the direction the airplane had gone. Then I stopped, turned around, and went back to the Corvette, where I did a little doctoring on the vehicle with the Bowie knife I'd stuck in the back of my belt. None of these bastards were getting away, not if I could help it.

Behind the house, a gravel road split off into a gap through the trees. It led in the right direction, so I took it at a jog. My boots clumped and crunched on the gravel—they weren't made for running. I poured on more speed until I was in a near-sprint, splashing muddy water high in the air when I crashed through puddles.

I topped a rise and found a clearing below. At the bottom, an airstrip was laid out like a child's model. The twin-engine plane drifted to a stop at the parking apron to the left of the runway, its propellers spinning down. Figures moved about, but I couldn't make out faces. However, a small person with a shock of black hair stood out. *Rita.*

To my right, the forest continued downslope for another hundred yards. I could stay under the cover of the trees and cut the distance to the hangar in half. I loped off through the pines, hopping low growth and ducking branches. Glimpses of the airfield came and went. The pine growth had kept the weeds and briars to a minimum, so I covered ground quickly.

I reached a notch in the trees with a good overview of the airstrip. It was close enough that I could make out individuals. Braced against a pine, I sucked in great heaves of air and blew them out slowly. With unsteady hands, I broke open the box of .243 and shook a pile of brass-and-copper cartridges into my palm.

Rita stood between Lurch and a ponytailed guy. Tarasov hung out near the plane's tail with a swarthy man in a uniform. The pilot, I assumed. Rogers lounged close by, listening to their conversation, but not a part of it.

The plane door stood open, and a staircase hung from the side. Men moved back and forth, carrying boxes and suitcases into the plane. Others dragged a hose from a fuel valve and connected it under the far wing. Another uniformed crewman supervised the refueling operation.

I counted the opposition: six Chechen worker bees, two pilots, Rogers, Lurch, Ponytail, and Tarasov. Twelve guys, at least eight of them visibly armed, against one Texas Ranger with a rifle and a Lone Wolf McQuade attitude.

I had them outnumbered.

RITA

Rita sneezed. Her body felt achy and tired, like she had the flu. Was it the stress and the physical abuse, or was the rabies virus taking hold of her system? She shifted her feet, and Marat growled at her to be still. Rita told him to piss off and glanced over her shoulder, toward the house. She measured the distance to the trees and calculated the odds of sprinting away. Ponytail was chunky and overweight. He would never keep up, and Marat didn't look like a speedball, either. Rogers and the rest of the gang were too far away to catch her if she got a good start.

But she couldn't outrun a bullet. They would just shoot her. The shotguns and the MP5K were short-range weapons, but she couldn't run out of range before all three opened up and blew her away.

Where are you, Sam? Don't be dead, cowboy.

The last of the bags went into the plane's cargo compartment. Tarasov waved a hand at Rogers. "Get the Tears."

The younger man tossed his perfect hair back with a jerk of his head and sauntered to the back of the Suburban. He emerged with a loaded backpack.

"What's the plan here?" Rita asked Ponytail. "We gonna fly over New York and spray the stuff out the window?"

"Shut up."

"You're a fucktard, you know that?" Rita tossed a mental coin. Get shot or fly off to paradise with the whack job terrorists?

She filled her lungs with air and tensed her muscles to make a break for the trees.

SAM

I filled the Remington, thumbing in five rounds, and slapped the bolt closed. I had never fired this weapon, so I had no idea if the scope setting was zeroed at a hundred yards or two hundred. My jogging through the woods might have knocked the settings loose, regardless. On the other hand, the range was less than a hundred yards, and it was a Remington 700, a damn fine rifle. I could hit with iron sights at that range, and I would be able to make every shot count, assuming the rifle wasn't completely screwed up.

The scope picture danced and dipped as I settled the crosshairs on Lurch's back. He stood facing away, looking at the plane and the action on the tarmac. With a deep breath, I took a turn of the sling around my wrist to tighten my grip and settle the sight picture. Lurch had a broad back. An inch or two either way wouldn't make a difference.

I let my breath out slowly, and my world tunneled into the crosshairs. I waited until they settled... *Right... there.*

Squeezed.

The .243 shot truer than a lover's heart. Lurch's spine blew out through his shirt pocket. The giant toppled like a sequoia.

One down, eleven to go.

Chapter 22

"THERE'S MORE THAN A hundred terrorists in there!"

"Yeah? Well, they should've brought more men." – Bryan Larkin as SAS Lieutenant and Gerard Butler as Mike Banning, London Has Fallen

RITA

Rita sniffled. A steamy breeze ruffled her hair.

Marat grunted and stumbled. Blood exploded from his chest and sprayed the ground in front of him. Rita didn't wait for him to fall. She didn't wait to figure out the whats, whys, or wherefores of Marat's sudden demise. Before the boom of the shot faded, she sprinted away as if spring-loaded, arms pumping and runner's legs driving her hard across the damp ground. She stayed in the grass to avoid the muddy track—slipping would be... bad. Really bad.

Men yelled. Her guardian angel fired another shot from the trees. Only one shooter had opened up so far, so this was not a rescue by HRT or a SWAT team—they would have dropped down in force from a flight of black helicopters. That left one option. It had to be—

Sam. It had to be Sam.

Boom! The rifle spoke again. She spotted the muzzle flash and angled left to avoid his line of fire.

Weapons opened up behind her, but Rita refused to look. She didn't need to. Sam would keep the enemy suppressed until she reached cover. She knew that like she knew which way the sun rose in the morning.

Bullets snipped the nearby grass, pouring rocket fuel into her legs. In college, she'd been clocked at 13.3 seconds in the one-hundred-meter dash. Rita would have bet good money she beat that time by a full second, even uphill, in muddy Ferragamos. She blew past the first tree at a dead sprint. Bark splattered from its trunk, and she ducked the hail of splinters.

"Cable, you up here?" she yelled.

"Here," Sam called from a deadfall a dozen feet away.

Relief flushed through Rita's system, wiping away the pain and stress. She dodged and weaved through the trees, hardly noticing the bullets singing past and smacking wood. Nothing could hurt her now. Nobody could stand against Ranger Sam Cable and Special Agent Rita Goldman. Not Rogers, not Tarasov, and especially not a bunch of Chechen mutts.

A Sam-phrase came to mind when Rita jumped the deadfall and saw his grinning, blood-streaked face. *It's time to slather on a big dose of whoop-ass.*

"Fuckin-A!" Rita yelled.

BEFORE LURCH HIT THE ground, Rita dropped beside me. I worked the bolt and found Tarasov with his mouth open in an O of surprise. A savage beat of pure joy thumped in my chest. I aimed, fired, and missed. *Too fast.* The big Chechen ran for cover in the hangar. Rogers had pulled a Houdini and disappeared. So had Ponytail.

I fought the impulse to charge downslope and wade into the bastards, using the rifle as a club. Anger beat at my temples and fried my logic circuits. *Slow down and think!*

One of the Chechens stood at the top of the airplane steps, an AK at his hip. He ripped off a long burst in the general direction of Oklahoma and killed some leaves. I snapped a round home, took a breath, and centered the sight picture on his chest. The Remington bucked against my shoulder, and I rode the recoil upward, using the momentum to chamber another round. The terrorist tumbled down the aircraft stairs. Another martyr sent to paradise.

The inside of the hangar faced toward the apron, three-quarters turned away from my position. A bearded goon peeked from the front corner of the building and lit up the woods with his AR-15, firing semi-auto. I suspected he was trying to use suppressing fire to keep me down. Bullets whined and zipped past, angry and blood hungry. I didn't feel like being suppressed right then.

He knelt by the corner. Only a small fraction of his head showed as he blazed away. The Chechen placed too much trust in the flimsy sides of a metal building. I guessed where his body would be, sighted, and fired. He screamed and flew backward. Hurt or dead, I didn't care which.

Another terrorist ran across the tarmac from the hangar to the plane, ripping off a full magazine as he ran. He reached the foot of the stairs and bounded up them to get on board. I held the crosshairs on the door and waited for my sight to fill. The Remington bucked. Bullets zinged and splattered mulch and tree bark in my face. I hit the dirt and rolled right, behind the trunk of a deadfall.

I rattled a handful of shells out of the box and fed the Remington's empty magazine. Occasional raindrops hissed and died when they struck the hot barrel of the rifle. Heat waves shimmered in the damp air above the Remington's barrel.

The Chechens stayed under cover for the moment, probably trying to figure out who and how many people were shooting. Four of them were down, leaving six shooters and...

The airplane's props were spinning up again.

Wait. When did the pilots get back on the plane?

In the excitement, I'd lost sight of the aircrew. They'd managed to get up the stairs and shove the stairs away from the entry. The aircraft door snapped closed as I watched. The fuel hose was also loose, spilling avgas into the turf beside the parking apron. Blue smoke jetted from the engines as they throttled up.

"Don't let 'em get away," Rita urged. "Why didn't you shoot the pilots?"

"That's how it always goes. Too many bad guys, never enough ammo."

I sighted on the set of double tires under one wing and fired. The bullet spalled off the concrete inches away. I missed with the second shot as well, so I took a deep breath, braced my shoulder against the pine, and squeeeezed. "Hah!" I barked a laugh of satisfaction when the left tire popped. But there were two on each undercarriage, and the plane didn't slow. "What the hell?"

"Shoot the engines!" Rita yelled.

Targeting the engine on the port wing, I snapped my last two rounds into it. Within seconds, smoke began pouring out.

"Hah-hah! Fly on that, you Commie prick."

Automatic weapons fire chewed up the ground in front of our position. I ducked and reloaded. "Did you see where that came from?"

"Other side of the hangar, I think." Rita pointed. "Look, the plane's still moving."

I low-crawled several feet to my right and popped up again for another look. The pilots had feathered the port engine and were using the right to taxi to the end of the runway. "Do they think they're *driving* to Chechnya?"

"They're gonna take off on one engine, dummy," Rita snapped.

"Jesus. How hard is it to kill a plane?" I fired four quick rounds at the starboard engine. Nothing happened. "How'd I miss? Oh, wait." A pall of smoke billowed up, and the second engine stuttered for a few seconds before the pilots shut it down.

My box of .243 had started with twenty rounds. I'd used up thirteen, so after I refilled the magazine, I had only two loose cartridges in my hand. Seven shots total. If the pilots stayed to fight, I had eight enemy combatants to bring down. I wasn't likely to get all of them with the Remington, even if I had unlimited ammo. When they'd scattered, at least one had made the trees on the far side. He would flank us sooner rather than later.

The .45 in my belt holster held eight rounds, and I had two magazines of seven each. I couldn't remember exactly, but I thought that Rita's SIG Sauer held fourteen 9mm cartridges. So, add thirty-six rounds of pistol ammo on top of the rifle.

Add to the equation one highly pissed-off federal agent.

I chuckled up at the gray sky, framed by the tops of swaying pines. Who else but Rita Goldman would I rather have by my side while engaged in a desperate firefight in the woods?

"What's so funny?"

"You are." I crawled back to peek around the base of my new friend, Mr. Pine, and eased the Remington forward, panning the airstrip with the scope. "Did you get your shoes muddy?"

A figure moved. A Chechen, concealed in the tree line on the far side of the airstrip, slipped through the woods counterclockwise. The flanking had commenced.

"Oh, I'm so pissed. You know what these cost? And I ripped my new slacks."

"Tragedy."

"Can I have my gun now?"

"Hold on a second. Let me discourage the wildlife."

I panned along with the jogging man, settling my breathing and trying to find the Zen of long-distance shooting. I could hold my own with most shooters at two hundred yards or less, but I'd never learned how to properly calculate bullet drop over longer ranges. I judged this guy at three to three hundred fifty yards and moving—a shot I would never have attempted under ordinary circumstances.

At this range, the Chechen appeared slightly bigger than an ant crawling across a jittering quarter. I tracked him for a long count of ten, let out a half-breath, and triggered a round more by instinct than plan. The terrorist spun to the ground, screaming. He rolled partway out of the tree line, into clear view, clutching his upper thigh. My next shot missed, high and right. I compensated and punched out another round. The target pitched back, blood painting the grass behind him.

"Booyah!" My ears rang from gunfire, and I thumbed my last two rounds into the Remington. The rain picked up, pattering into the pine needles and dripping steadily from the trees. Heavy drops fell from the branches to splatter my already-damp shirt.

"Good shootin', Tex," Rita said. "Please can I have my gun now so I can kill somebody?"

"Yes, dear." I handed across her SIG.

"How'd you get loose?" Rita checked the chamber and flicked off the safety. Her hair looked like a bird's nest of small twigs and pine needles. Sweat and grime smudged her face, and her clothes were a mess. She looked good to me right then, wild-eyed and fierce. I pushed away inappropriate thoughts.

"Couldn't let you have all the fun." I slithered around to face downhill and clamped the scope to my eye, looking for targets. I tracked across the airplane and zeroed in on the cockpit. The pilots must have abandoned ship when the engines went out. Smoke boiled from the starboard engine, and little tongues of fire licked up around the cowling.

My second dead plane in two years.

I spotted movement from below. The Chechens scattered from the hangar, dodging and firing blindly, some charging our position, some angling away. I tracked the closest one with the scope, but he juked around so much that I wasted two shots before I tagged him.

"Damn, Cable, even I could've hit that guy."

"Nag, nag, nag."

"Disable the cars."

"What?"

Rita trained her weapon over the log and pocked away at the other two guys, sending them diving to the ground. "Shoot the tires. Tarasov and Rogers are heading for the cars. If they make it, we're screwed. They'll be in the wind."

She was right. The three—now two—guys running upslope were a distraction. Ponytail, Tarasov, and Rogers. Rogers carried a biker's backpack.

"That backpack has the Siren's Tears," Rita said.

The Cayenne was closest to the gang, so I zeroed the passenger front tire and popped it with my first shot. Ditto for the passenger rear.

I had one .243 cartridge left, so I shifted to the Suburban, sighted, and squeezed. The rifle rocked against my shoulder, and I muscled it back down to see the rear passenger-side tire on the Suburban deflate... except it didn't.

"You missed," Rita said. "I saw it hit, low left."

"Dammit."

"Remind me to take you shooting sometime."

Tarasov and his gang piled into the Suburban. All I could do was watch. A hundred-plus yards with a .45 was a waste of ammo.

"They'll head back for the highway." Rita scrambled to her feet, keeping low. "I'll cut 'em off at the pass. You take out the twerps down below."

"Wait, I—"

But she had already sprinted away. When I started after her, leaves and bark blew up around me as the pair of flankers jumped up and rushed the trees in full spray-and-pray mode. I hunkered down and drew my Kimber. My fallen-tree barricade shivered from the impact of bullets. More rounds cut the underbrush and trimmed overhead pine needles, which sprinkled down on me. I slithered left, to a point where the base of the fallen tree crossed a standing pine.

Their huffing breath and pounding footsteps helped me pinpoint the Chechens at my one- and two-o'clock positions, twenty to thirty yards out. The stutter of each man's Kalashnikov ran down at about the same moment.

I took a breath and swung around the pine, both arms braced, gun extended. I panned right and picked up the first target. A pair of tree trunks framed a light-skinned man in a lime-green polo shirt. He shuffled forward, trying to change magazines and move at the same time. The bright shirt made an excellent picture over the blade of my .45's front sight. I double tapped, and the Chechen flew back as if bitch-slapped by Allah himself. His rifle spiraled up and away, crashing into the trees somewhere.

The other Chechen dodged farther right and disappeared in the brush.

I hesitated. Go after him, or back Rita up? If I helped Rita, the Chechen would be at my back. If I eliminated that threat, I left Rita on her own against Tarasov and Rogers.

Pop-pop-pop-pop! The flat bark of a pistol flared up from Rita's position.

Sweat dripped from my chin, and I waited. Rita could take care of herself.

She had to.

Chapter 23

"I AM WOMAN. HEAR ME roar!" – Helen Reddy

RITA

Trees whipped past Rita in a green blur until she broke cover near the road—if it could be called that. More cart trail than real road, twin ruts cut through the Texas mud. Rita straddled the track in a shooter's stance, SIG locked in front of her. A gust of wind lifted her hair, but that was the only thing that moved. The big SUV bounced over the rise and barreled straight for her. Splashing and dipping, the Suburban roared as the driver—Ponytail—ducked low and gave it the gas.

My turn now, you pricks.

Rita aimed for the vehicle's steering wheel ring, which was just visible through the windshield. The range was about as far as a bank drive-thru lane—maybe fifty yards. She settled the flat line of her sights and squeezed the trigger—pumping out shot after shot, regular as a metronome, tracking the car as it swayed and hopped through the ruts. The first four rounds hit so close together, a spiderweb of cracked glass surrounded a baseball-sized hole in the windscreen.

Twenty yards.

The SUV hit a bump and reared high, front wheels spinning. Mud sprayed, and the engine screamed. She imagined a wild beast, a charging dragon, set to eat her alive. The Suburban hit the ground, bounced high. The occupants popped up in their seats. Rita tracked the movement and took up trigger slack. *Crack-crack-crack-crackcrackcrack!* Rounds pummeled the windshield, starring and shattering the glass.

Ten yards. She could make out bugs smushed into the grill—and tell what they had for dinner.

"Die, dammit!" *Crackcrackcrackcrackackackckkk!*

The slide locked back.

Rita dove. The heat from the Suburban washed over her. She smacked an ankle on the bumper. A fiery stab of pain shot up her shin. Rita plowed up a foot of Texas mud with her shoulder, flipped and tumbled into a tangle of vines.

"Oh, fuck *me!*" Blackberry vines. With lots of thorns. Lots and lots of them.

The Suburban careened high to the left then veered right, out of control. It slewed off the track and beelined for a tree. With a dull crunch of metal, it met bark. Steam rolled from under the hood. The passenger doors popped open, and two men tumbled out—Rogers and Tarasov.

Fuckers.

The older man held a hand to a bloody gash over one eye. He moved like a rusty Tin Man. Rogers appeared uninjured. He glared at Rita with an intensity that hit her like a slap. His MP5 wasn't hanging from his shoulder anymore. Maybe it had fallen under the seat.

Maybe he didn't feel he needed it to end her existence.

Tangled the way she was, Rita tended to agree with him. The blackberry vines held her with a will. Her pistol was empty, and she had no spare magazines.

"I am so screwed," she growled.

The old man growled something to Rogers. The younger man reached back into the car, digging for something. The pair continued arguing, raging in a foreign language. Tarasov was insistent, pointing and grabbing Rogers by the collar.

Rita peeled away sticky, prickly, clinging vines one at a time, working herself loose. A dozen scratches burned with sweat, and her hair hung over her face, held there by a thorn. The thud of a distant pistol firing in the forest told her Sam was still in the fight. She grumbled under her breath, "How long does it take to kill two bad guys, Sam? Holy shit, I could use a hand about now."

Rogers pulled out the backpack of Tears and threw it over his shoulder by the strap. He spared one look at Rita and sprinted away, headed for the house. Tarasov clomped around the back of the car. His hand dipped into his coat. He appeared as mad as a high school principal who'd been hit by an errant brick thrown by an unruly student—one he wanted to punish with a thousand years of detention in hell.

Tarasov produced a flat black automatic.

A SIG.

Go figure.

Every time she pulled one vine loose, another snagged her. Heedless of scratches, she jerked. Cloth ripped. *This outfit is ruined.* As if it mattered. Tarasov was ten steps away. He couldn't miss even if he tried.

"Hey, Tarasov," she said. "You wouldn't do me a solid, would ya? Help me get outta here so we can fight all fair and square?"

"No." He raised the pistol one-handed. Blood ran into his eye. He cocked his head to get a better view through the other one. His finger tightened on the trigger—

Sam Cable stepped from the trees and shot Tarasov through his block head. The hollow-point mushroomed on impact and blew out a teacup-sized hole upon exiting the Chechen mobster's skull. Gore sprayed like water from Bailey Fountain in Grand Army Plaza. Tarasov dropped straight down, as if slapped in the head with a bat. Tarasov's dying reflex jerked the SIG's trigger. The heat of a supersonic 9mm bullet slapped the side of her face. The slug came close enough that she could swear it flicked her earring.

"Anyone else?" Sam panned the area with the muzzle of his pistol, not looking at her. "Did you get the other two?"

"Rogers got away." She ripped free of the last vine and scrambled through the damp weeds beside the trail. She sat on the edge of the track, barely flinching when monstrous grasshoppers fizzed away, disturbed by her presence. She shivered. "I so hate the fucking country."

"Say what?" He was looking at her. "You okay?"

"Dandy. Just fucking dandy."

"What was that about Rogers?"

"He got away with the Tears." She pointed toward the house. "He went thataway, Kemo Sabe. I imagine he's made it to his pretty car by now. We need to find a phone, get the choppers up, yada yada yada." Rita yawned and shivered. Right at that moment, she couldn't work up a single fuck to give about Rogers. She was tired and wanted to sleep. *And why* was *it so cold out here?* The temperature was approaching ninety, and she still felt chilled.

Sam was kneeling in front of her. His lips moved.

Rita squinted and shook her head. "What?"

"Rogers isn't going anywhere in the Vette," he repeated, as if to a slow child. "I punched a hole in the fuel tank. That baby ain't going nowhere." He looked around. His frown was cute, the way his lower lip stuck out.

If only...

"But I outsmarted myself. Both the other vehicles are toast." Sam looked to the east. "It has to be nearly seven. You have about another hour to get to a hospital. Wait here a sec.'"

"'Kay. Sure."

Sam jogged to the Suburban and peeked in the driver's window through his cupped hands. He jerked the door open, reached in, and flung Ponytail's loose body to the ground with a wet plop. Sam's head disappeared inside the vehicle, and... Rita didn't care anymore. She curled up in the grass and closed her eyes. Her body felt so heavy...

I SHOOK RITA AWAKE. "Come on, girl, stay with me here."

"Huh? Wuzzat?" She yawned and rubbed her bloodshot eyes.

"We've got some walking to do, but help is close by." I took a knee beside her and held her chin, forcing her to meet my eyes. She was lethargic and blinked to focus. "Listen, the GPS in the Suburban showed me where we are. The way the roads lay out, if we cut through the woods on the other side of the airstrip, we'll hit US 84 a lot faster than if we go back to the house and follow the county road back to the highway. There's a fair-sized town a couple of miles away. Bound to have a hospital."

"Phone?"

"Ponytail's phone is broken. Screen is shattered. I can't find Tarasov's." "But what about R-Rogers?" When Rita started shivering, it hit me like a club to the chest. Maybe she didn't have another hour I'd estimated before the virus took hold.

"We'll catch up with him. He can't get far. C'mon, let's get you on your feet." I reached for her arm, but she jerked it back like a grumpy toddler. "I dropped the other two, so we're clear except for the pilots."

"Rogers." She folded her arms and shuddered. "No, Cable. No. You have to go get him."

"No, I *have* to get *you* to a hospital. Now, come on."

"No."

"Yes." I reached for her again, and she slapped me, gently, but it got my attention.

"Listen to me. Carefully." Rita's eyes bored into mine, and she straightened up. "You. Have. To stop. Rogers. If I live and thousands die, I'll... well, fuck, I'll shoot you myself."

I opened my mouth to say something, but she placed a tender hand on the spot she'd slapped earlier. Playing good cop, bad cop, all in one small package.

"Shut up, Sam," she whispered. "You know it's the right thing. Now go put that fucker down." She pulled my head toward hers and kissed me with soft, warm lips. They trembled under mine, either from fever or excitement. I didn't care. I kissed her until she shoved me back.

"Go." She waved and levered herself upright. "I'll start hiking to this highway whatsit, and you come find me when you're done. Preferably in an ambulance. Go!" She shambled a few steps, looked over her shoulder, and saw me waiting. "Don't make me tell you again."

"Don't get your shoes dirty."

Rita paused, lifted a foot, and inspected one mud-caked shoe. She shot me the finger and continued walking.

"Watch out for the pilots."

She waved without looking back.

"The place is called Montclair. Turn left when you hit the highway," I said.

"Left. Got it. Go."

I went.

THE STEWARTS' HOUSE sat atop a small rise, making it a chore to hike up the last bit of trail and sprint across the open yard. My legs were gassed, and the drumline had started inside my skull, pounding with a vengeance. I wiped the sweat out of my eyes with a forearm, and my sleeve came away bloody. I planted a hand against the right rear corner of the log house and leaned on it to catch my breath. Big men didn't run well anyway, but add in getting beat up and tied up, no sleep, and a gun fight...

"Dear God, get me out of this," I muttered, "and I'll go to church every week. I promise. At least every other week. Please help me find Rogers and send him to meet you. And get Rita to a hospital in time. Amen."

When I stopped panting, I resumed my climb around the right side of the house. Since no one had shot at me from the back window, I had to assume Rogers hadn't seen me or was already gone. I'd punched eight widely spaced holes in the Vette's gas tank, so he wouldn't be driving. He would be running down the road or calling a friend on his cell. Or maybe he'd found the keys to the Stewarts' cars and was long gone.

I peeked around the front corner and found I was wrong on all counts. The yellow car faced away from me, about as far as home plate to first base. Call it a round hundred feet away. I had a great view of Rogers pouring a red plastic can of gas into the sports car's fuel intake, on the driver's side. And nothing dribbled out from the tank. *How in the hell?*

I spotted a roll of silver duct tape on the trunk lid.

Seriously? He duct-taped *the holes in his gas tank.* No way that would hold for long. But... he didn't have to get very far, did he? Montclair wasn't far by paved road. From there, he could steal a vehicle and be gone. Maybe his patch job would hold all the way to town, or at least get him close.

Who cares? I was fixin' to take him into custody or shoot him, so he wasn't going for a ride in his pretty little zoom car.

Rogers tossed the can aside and jogged around the back of the car to the right side, where he picked up a backpack which, I assumed, was full of deadly bioweapon canisters. He dug into his pocket, produced a black key fob, and started back to the driver's door.

Thoughts trudged in single file through my cotton-stuffed head. I had trouble focusing. *What was I supposed to do here? Oh, yeah, arrest this guy.*

My anger whispered words of sudden violence in my ear. *Shoot him in the back and be done with him. Kill this bastard and go take care of Rita. You shot the other fuckers from long range. Just do this guy and let's go.* I had the gun half-raised before my good angel said, *You're a lawman, not a killer. This is murder.*

"He deserves it, though," I said to myself. It sounded like whining. *Shoot him, and let's be done.*

I took a breath. Let it out. Then I stepped out, my gun held loose by my leg. Rogers spotted me the instant I broke cover. He froze, and his eyes narrowed. With a purposeful stride, I closed the distance in big chunks. "David Rogers, you are under arrest. If you take one more step, I'll shoot you dead and leave you for the varmints."

"If it is not Ranger Rick himself." Rogers smirked. For a supposedly unarmed man, he seemed very confident. He held the key fob in his right hand, and his left arm was occupied with the backpack. If he blinked wrong, I could kill him before his eyelids closed.

"Yes," I said, covering the distance, "Ranger Rick wants to feed you to the pigs right now, so let me see those hands."

Rogers dangled the backpack, holding it by the strap, and spread his arms, as if offering me a hug.

I stopped just out of range of his deadly hands and feet. I held my pistol low and tight to my side, where no sweep kick could knock it out of my hand, pointed at his belly. "Set that pack on the ground."

"Of course." He flashed that movie-star smile. "No reason for shooting. You got me."

"I—"

He threw the pack at me.

When I drop a knife in the kitchen, my first instinct would be to try to catch it. My rational brain has to kick in and apply the brakes. When Rogers threw the pack, my rational brain said: *Ignore it; let it fall.* My instinct said: *Bioweapon! Catch it!*

Instinct and reason clashed, and I tried to both let it drop and catch it at the same time. My gun hand was way out of position when Rogers hit me with the force of a hurricane. The pack hit the ground with a metallic tinkle. Too late, I remembered the virus was in cans. Knocked clean out of my hand, my Kimber skipped across the yard. He punched me a half-dozen times, all solid blows to the head and body.

I danced back to gain some time, trying to shake off the ringing in my ears. Rogers came straight on, hands up in the same kung fu pose I'd seen the last time he'd beaten the shit out of me. He drove a snap kick at my groin. I twisted and took the hit on my thigh. Jackhammer punches slugged my blocking forearms, driving me back farther. I never saw the side kick into my gut.

"Oompfh." I dropped to one knee, vision swimming. I couldn't breathe.

A blur of motion came from my right. Rogers's heel hit me over the right eye, delivered by a spinning back kick. Lightning flared in my skull, and blood rained into my eyes. I was blind. I staggered up, feeling like Rocky in his first fight with Apollo Creed. Rogers hit me in the gut then the face and kicked me again. I didn't see any of them.

Lights sparkled, and the world lost focus. Sounds traveled across galaxies. Drawing breath was like sucking a flamethrower.

I was on my knees again, but I didn't remember going down.

Rogers materialized in front of me. His perfect, magazine-cover face was twisted into an ugly mask. "Well, Ranger. Not such a tough man after all, are you?"

"Whah?" I spat a wad of blood and mucus, not able to speak clearly.

He stepped closer and snarled, "I said—"

I jammed six inches of Bowie knife into his gut.

And twisted.

I grinned at the look of hurt surprise on his face. "Take that, you fuckmuppet."

Chapter 24

ROGERS'S CELL PHONE was locked, but I could still make an emergency call. While the dispatcher connected me with Ferdinand Reyes, I put the phone on speaker, found Rogers's keys in the grass, and picked up the backpack of Tears. I squeezed into the Corvette with the bag, which I dumped on the floor, and laid the phone on the passenger seat.

Gas would soon be leaking from Rogers's hasty patch job, and the car wasn't designed for off-roading, but it beat jogging back to the airstrip. The engine fired on the first twist of the key.

Swelling closed one of my eyes, and the other wouldn't focus.

"Cable," Reyes squawked from the phone. "Where'n hell are you? We found Winston, shot dead, and a bunch of evidence and shit at this place off 2204. Goldman's missing. We can't find her—"

"Shut up a second!" I dropped the car in gear and slewed a big circle in the yard. Pointing the nose mostly toward the track, I touched the gas pedal, and the Corvette shot away, fishtailing across the yard. "I have the Tears. Repeat, I have the Tears. All the tangos are down." Except for the pilots, but I didn't want to confuse things. "Rogers is down, Tarasov is down. Do you copy?"

"I, uh..."

"Do you fucking copy?"

"Yeah, I copy. You have the Tears, all the tangos are down."

"Now listen up—" I hit a dip, and the Corvette's nose plowed the ground. The undercarriage screeched in protest when I punched the gas and powered through the low spot. I grunted, and everything bounced when we hopped out of the dip. The cans of Siren's Tears clanked together, and my testicles shriveled up. "*Ugh*. Listen, this next part's important."

"And the other part wasn't?"

"FBI Agent Goldman has been infected. She's currently in the woods, south of US 84, east of Montclair. I am going to get her and bring her out to the highway. US Highway 84. Copy?" Mud splashed over the windshield, and I fiddled with levers until the wipers came on. I passed the wrecked Suburban and ran over Tarasov's body.

Oops.

"US 84, copy."

"*East* of Montclair!"

"East of Montclair, copy."

"Send Careflight to that area. Make *sure*—make *damn sure*—they have anti-rabies vaccine on board. She has been exposed for"—I glanced at the dashboard clock—"ahhh... eleven hours." The pounding in my head chose that moment to reach a crescendo. My vision tunneled and darkened. The world fizzed away for a long second.

"What happened, Sam? You there?" Reyes asked.

"Noth... Nothing. Happened." I blinked my good eye until it cleared, letting off the gas, which nearly put an end to my joyride. My brief pause let the rear tires settle in some mushy ground. I hit the pedal, and they spun. Gunk sprayed in a rooster tail, and for a long moment, I thought I was done driving for the day. Engine howling, the car slipped sideways, caught, then bounded off. "I'm fucking up Rogers's car."

"Acceptable. How're they gonna find you guys?"

"I'll call 9-1-1. Let you know when I find her." I topped the rise above the airfield, and the Corvette sailed for a brief moment. I gritted my teeth, and my brain nearly exploded when it *whomped* down.

Everything looked the same as when I'd left it. The plane remained parked at the end of the runway. Dead bodies littered the field. No sign of the pilots. No sign of Goldman.

The car took the hill reasonably well, seemingly happy to be off the sloppy trail. I gunned it past the hangar and on to where the forest picked up again. End of the line. Not even a Corvette could squeeze between trees. I switched off the engine and thanked General Motors and the makers of duct tape.

I looked for Rita's trail by pacing the tree line in slow motion. Truthfully, I couldn't have moved much faster anyway. If a single part of my body wasn't sore, I couldn't find it, and the catalog of physical ailments tormenting me would take up a medical textbook. Blinking hurt.

A small footprint impressed in the soft ground showed me where to go. Rita had cut through the trees in a northerly direction, just like she was supposed to. I stepped into the forest, moving faster despite the screaming protests from damaged and abused muscles.

"Hang on, girl. I'm coming for you."

I FOUND HER NEXT TO a creek within sight of the highway. She'd passed out while walking and had dropped with her hair nearly touching the water. I checked her pulse—fast and thready—and felt her forehead—hot and damp.

Arranging my arms under her back and knees, I lifted with my legs. "Always got to be a drama queen, don't you, Goldman? Okay, one foot in front of the other. Let's go. *Hhnh!*" I stumbled, almost dumping both of us in the creek.

The forest didn't want to let us go, acting as if it had been enchanted by an evil witch. I ducked low branches, but they raked my back or snagged my shirt. I stepped over vines that reached up, tried to trip me. I slipped in mud or stumbled over pebbles. The last line of brush between us and the road appeared nigh impenetrable, thick with intertwined brush. The clear area around the highway beckoned like heaven. I turned my back and shoved through it. Rita's hair got hung on something, and I just pulled without thinking, leaving a hank of black fuzzy stuff behind.

She moaned and stirred.

"Sorry about that," I said. "It'll grow back."

We popped out of the forest and into a drainage ditch next to the highway. I laid her on the shoulder next to a green exit ramp sign and dug out Rogers's cell phone. When the dispatcher came on, I said, "We're on Highway 84. At County Road 6885. Come find us."

I dropped the phone and curled up next to Rita. I smelled oily asphalt and a wisp of something long dead. Roadkill, probably. Tiny pebbles crunched under me when I moved. I listened to Rita breathe and watched her chest rise and fall.

She breathed in.

She breathed out.

I PROCESSED THE UNMISTAKABLE smells and sounds of a hospital—alcohol and disinfectant, beeps of machines and the squeak of shoes passing in the hall—as they seeped into my dreams and pushed me to consciousness. Another scent hit me like a dose of smelling salts—the odor of tobacco, coffee, and gun leather. When I opened my eyes, I flinched back. Captain Les Marshall's craggy face loomed over me.

He grinned when he saw my reaction. "Well, at least you ain't dead, boy."

"Then how come I'm in hell?" I croaked.

Marshall straightened and laughed. "You ain't in hell, son. Damn, you ain't even made it to Oklahoma. You still in Texas." His face turned serious, and he laid a hand on my shoulder. "How you feelin'?"

The drugs they were feeding me kept a nice, fuzzy edge on the pain, but it lurked in the corners, ready to pounce. "Like shit stomped into a messy puddle."

"Good." He nodded gravely. "That's how you look, too. You been under for two days with a major concussion. Your skull, believe it or not, was actually cracked. I said that was bullshit, but they showed me the x-rays."

I found a blue plastic water bottle with a sippy straw on the tray and sucked it half down. When I spoke again, it no longer felt like gargling with rusty knives. "What happened?" I wanted to ask about Rita, but I hesitated. If I'd been out for two days, her fate was already sealed. As long as I didn't know, it could still be good news. I did the same thing with lottery tickets, waiting a few days to check the numbers—every day I didn't know meant it was still possible I'd won.

Marshall frowned. "Look, your mom and them is down in the cafeteria getting some lunch. They'll be back up here any minute. When they see you're awake, they'll be on you like Mexicans at a garage sale." He glanced at his watch. "And I got to get movin'. I can give you the highlights, but they can fill in the dots."

"Okay."

He took a deep breath and looked up as if trying to get his facts in line. "One, you and the she-wolf wiped out a fuck-ton of bad guys, makin' you a pair of honest-to-God heroic sumbitches, as ever I saw. Two, we recovered the little rabies shitcans." He paused to fix me with a look. "Next time, don't go running off and leave a bioweapon in the seat of an unlocked Corvette, y'hear?"

"No, sir."

"Awright, where was I? Oh, and three, we caught the two skinny-ass pilots. They bumbled out of the trees and into the lap of a sheriff's deputy. Four, we got media hyenas jacking each other off all over East Texas. They keep gettin' lost in the woods, fuckin' up the story, blamin' us for the terrorism, sayin' you shouldna kilt 'em all, misquotin' shit, and generally bein' a goddamn nuisance."

"We need a media liaison," I said, thinking of Fiegenbaum.

"We need a goddamn forest fire, clear 'em all out." Marshall wandered around the room as he spoke, fingering bits of equipment, opening drawers, and inspecting the contents. He paused at the end of the bed and ran his fingers over the rail there, as if it fascinated him.

My heart started hammering. "What else?"

"We lost some people, Sam."

"Who?" I managed to get the word out past the blockage in my throat.

"The death toll from the DFW attack stands at six-thousand-some-odd." He sighed and shook his head. "On our team, Darren Winston was shot in the head. He died instantly, they say." Marshall checked his watch again and looked out the door at some activity I couldn't see. "Looks like your momma and brothers are headed back this way. You prepared for the onslaught of the Cable clan?"

"Megan?"

"She jogged all the way from her place into town. By the she got there, the shit was truly spraying through the fan. She's okay, last I heard."

"Captain?"

Marshall cocked an eyebrow.

"Agent Goldman. Did she make it?"

"The devil in high heels? Hell, napalm couldn't kill her." Marshall shrugged. "She's hanging on by her painted fingernails, Sammy. They think they got the nockalation in her in time to stop the procession."

"Progression?"

"Yeah. That. Well, here comes the family." He patted my foot. "I better scoot. Get yer ass outta bed and get back to work soon, y'hear?"

"Yes, sir." I swallowed more water. "I'll be up in no time."

I PLAYED THE HERO CARD on the nurses, and they let me get up
to go see Rita in ICU. They plonked me in a wheelchair, and I sat with
her among the machines and pumps that beeped and whirred while she
slept. The intensive care staff gave me the impression she was getting
stronger every day.

Could've fooled me.

She was drawn, and her complexion was sallow. Between the oxygen tubes, the IV, and the heart monitor on her finger, she looked more
like a refugee than the vibrant young woman I knew. I'd seen better-
looking cadavers.

They let me hang out with her for an hour, and she never moved.
She breathed in. Breathed out. It was enough for now.

SHE OPENED HER EYES for the first time three days later. Twin
brown lasers focused on me. With her voice barely above a whisper, she
said, "Hey, cowboy."

"Hey, yourself."

"You look like shit," she murmured.

I had to agree. Concussion, broken ribs, bruised spleen, fractured
orbital, and a general stomping by a herd of angry buffalo had left me
a poster boy for how *not* to fight a gang of terrorists. The hospital had
cut me loose after charging my insurance company as much as the law
allowed and not one cent less. I had come back to sit with Rita. She had
federal insurance coverage and could stay longer.

"You ain't no prize heifer, neither."

An approximation of a smile tweaked her lips. "I don't know what
that is, but it sounds bad."

"The witch doctors around here seem to think you'll pull through." I patted her arm under the sheet.

"That's nice." Rita's eyes closed, and her voice trailed off. "Too bad you didn't make it."

"A double dose of concussion can't put me down. They'd have to break something vital."

Her lips tweaked again, and she drifted back to sleep.

Epilogue

"YOU DO THE BEST YOU can, and you deal with the consequences. It's all there is."

— Robert B. Parker, A Catskill Eagle

Two weeks after the hospital cut me loose, I was in my office revising—again—my report of the events at the Stewarts' home. My addled brain played hide-and-seek with memories, like skips in a garbled audio-visual transmission. Things would come back to me at odd times, bits that I would have to add in.

Rita had been discharged six days ago, after a full recovery. She had not come by to see me, nor had she returned my phone calls, texts, or emails. I didn't know what to make of that, so I tried to ignore it. I blocked out everything about Rita from my conscious brain, to the point that when heels clicked in the hallway outside my office door, I didn't look up.

"Somebody said they saw Gary Cooper here," Rita's scratchy voice announced. "I told 'em no fucking way. Cooper's got nothing on Ranger Sam Cable."

I stood up and started around my desk. Rita stuck out a hand for a shake, aborting my hug before it was born. She sat in my guest chair with a sigh. Lines had sprung up around her sunken and tired eyes. Her skin, still looking pale and waxy, had yet to regain its olive tone. She might not have met the Reaper, but she had come close enough to spit in his eye. I sat back in my chair and watched her compose her features into a businesslike mask.

"Sam." Her eyes darted away and studied my desktop.

After a long moment, I said, "I'm up here."

"Sam," she repeated without looking up. "I'm being called back to New York."

A fist clenched in my chest. "I see."

"Yeah, I was only on temporary assignment down here, ya know? My boss called last week and said to grab the first thing smoking back to the city. We've got a line on some Saudis who're moving cash for ISIL. He needs me to get on the money trail... and..."

"And you're going."

"I have to, Sam. It's important work, catching these guys. Stopping terrorists and all." Rita's eyes flicked up and away. They were watery and pinched, like she wanted to cry.

Probably the medication.

A couple of guys walked by in the hall, laughing. They glanced in my door and nodded as they passed. Their footsteps faded.

"I see," I said again.

She drew a breath and met my eyes for the first time. "You know it wouldn't work, right?" she pleaded. "You know that. I mean, shit, look at me. I'm a Jew from New York. I'm small and dark and fuzzy, while you're... well, fuck, you're a goddamn giant cowboy with a square jaw and lumberjack shoulders! What would your folks say, you bringing home a runt like me? Huh? Would I have to convert to being a Methodist? How does that even work?"

"My folks?"

"No, Sam, it's better this way." She popped up from her chair. Her voice quavered. "You and I both know that."

"I—"

"G-Goodbye, Sam. I'll—I'll see you around." And she left.

I sat at my desk, frozen in place. My skin had gone cold and numb. Her heels clicked down the hall, the sound growing fainter until... it was gone. The computer on my desk hummed. Air blew from the overhead vent. A phone rang in a distant office, then it stopped.

I breathed in. I breathed out.

For now, that was all I could do.
It would have to be enough.

Author's Note

JUNE BUG is my first novel. I say this with a straight face as I have blocked out all memory of the first version of *Yeager's Law*, which I wrote in 1995. That document has remained locked in the closet, where it will forever remain. In polite company, we will then refer to *June Bug* as the "first attempt" of my modern writing incarnation. In 2011, I said the famous words, "Writing is easy. Anybody can do it," and jumped in headfirst. I started a thing called *Siren's Tears,* and thus Sam Cable and Rita Goldman came to life in my head.

The first draft of *Siren's Tears* was almost farcical, with heavy emphasis on low humor (my favorite kind) and completely goofy behavior from my two main characters. I pictured it as a comedy more than a mystery. Many, many revisions and rewrites later, I decided *June Bug* needed two preceding novels to move Sam and Rita to the place they find themselves in now.

I drafted and revised and drafted and revised several different works before I felt I was prepared for publication. Thirty years after my dot-matrix-printed version of *Yeager's Law* was hidden away, I published it as a standalone novel, no sequel ever intended. Of course, *Yeager's Mission* and *Yeager's Getaway* followed.

All that to say, the (nearly) final draft of *June Bug* was written between 2011 and 2014, before *April's Fool* and before *May Day*. I first published *April's Fool* with a publisher other than Red Adept Publishing. After many months of struggling to get on the same page with that publisher, we agreed to part ways, and I sweet-talked Lynn McNamee into accepting *April's Fool* into the Red Adept family. She took on *May Day* and *June Bug* at the same time, though there was the inevitable delay of editing, proofing, and publishing involved with getting the first two books out the door. All this meant that poor *June Bug* languished in unpublished limbo for many, many years. I have been waiting a *long* time for *June Bug* to see publication, and I was very happy that it was finally getting there.

And then...

The world experienced COVID-19. As a result, once this manuscript was lined up for editing in mid-2020, I realized the material was out-of-date and needed a refresh. I undertook to add some references to our collective experience related to COVID. We have all seen first-hand what happens during a pandemic, so failing to mention it left jarring holes in the world of Sam and Rita, though you will note that in this manuscript, I pretended like everything was "back to normal." This is the magic of fiction.

With that preamble out of the way, I am thrilled that *June Bug* has been released. As Rita might say, "'Bout friggin' time."

In the novel, astute readers will notice I added a college to the small town of Kilgore, Texas. This was done for artistic purposes—read "lying for money"—and this college bears no resemblance to any institution of higher learning in Texas or the world.

Thank you for picking up *June Bug*. I fully expect to see Sam and Rita back in July. I just hope it won't take nearly as long from draft to completed publication. Hang on to your hat!

Acknowledgements

MY THANKS TO THE INCOMPARABLE editor Stephanie Spangler Buswell, who has put in a ton of hours on Sam and Rita's journey. Stephanie makes me look much smarter than I am, fixes my arbitrary comma placement, and otherwise puts up with my whiny needs.

It's well past time for me to give Lynn McNamee a belated and heartfelt THANK YOU. Lynn runs a tight ship at Red Adept Publishing, and she is always looking for ways to help a new author realize their dreams. Whatever little bit of success I have achieved, I owe in large part to her efforts.

No acknowledgement is complete unless I mention the work put in by my wife of thirty years, Margaret Ann Bell. She edits, advises, and cradles my tender ego to prevent bruising from rough handling.

About the Author

Scott Bell has over 25 years of experience protecting the assets of retail companies. He holds a degree in Criminal Justice from North Texas State University.

With the kids grown and time on his hands, Scott turned back to his first love—writing. His short stories have been published in *The Western Online*, *Cast of Wonders*, and in the anthology, *Desolation*.

When he's not writing, Scott is on the eternal quest to answer the question: What would John Wayne do?

Read more at snapshooter4hire.com.

About the Publisher

Dear Reader,

We hope you enjoyed this book. Please consider leaving a review on your favorite book site.

Visit https://RedAdeptPublishing.com to see our entire catalogue.

Don't forget to subscribe to our monthly newsletter to be notified of future releases and special sales.